I0713849

MEMORIES OF MAY

JULIET MADISON

BLOODHOUND BOOKS

Copyright © 2024 Juliet Madison

The right of Juliet Madison to be identified as the Author of the Work has been asserted by her in accordance with the Copyright, Designs and Patents Act 1988.

Re-published in 2024 by Bloodhound Books.

Apart from any use permitted under UK copyright law, this publication may only be reproduced, stored, or transmitted, in any form, or by any means, with prior permission in writing of the publisher or, in the case of reprographic production, in accordance with the terms of licences issued by the Copyright Licensing Agency.
All characters in this publication are fictitious and any resemblance to real persons, living or dead, is purely coincidental.

www.bloodhoundbooks.com

Print ISBN: 978-1-916978-88-1

*To Nanna and Bunny, the two best grandmothers anyone could
have asked for.
Thanks for the memories.*

I f Olivia Chevalier's head hadn't been stuck in a book, she would have noticed a lookalike of the gorgeous fictional man she was reading about entering her bookstore. She also would have noticed him do a double take on spotting her seated behind the counter, and his hesitation as he picked up a random book from the display table then put it back down again. But the first she saw of him was his hand, on her counter, a pile of brochures grasped between rugged, masculine fingers. Her line of sight trailed up the mountainous curvature of his loose-shirt-enclosed arm and shoulder, his thick, tanned neck, and to his face; peppered with stubble and sporting a casual, curious smile. Her eyebrows sprung up and she closed her book with a snap. 'Hi. How can I help you?'

'Hi.' He scratched his chin. 'I was wondering if I could leave these here?' He gestured to the brochures. 'Sorry, I should introduce myself first. I'm Joel Foster.' His hand released the brochures and invited her hand as a replacement. As she moved her hand towards his, her casual assistant, Marcus, dropped a pile of books, then his head poked out from behind the end of the cooking section, his eyebrows arched high.

'All good!' Marcus gave a thumbs-up sign then disappeared behind the wooden shelves.

Olivia accepted Joel's firm handshake and met his ocean-blue eyes with her rainforest-green ones. 'Olivia Chevalier.' She looked down at the offering, noticing his photo on the brochure; a natural-looking headshot with an outdoor, rocky background.

'That's a lot of syllables,' he said.

She looked up with her brow furrowed. 'Sorry?'

'Your name,' he elaborated. 'Ol-iv-i-a Chev-al-i-er. Eight syllables.' He smiled. 'Compared to my pathetic total of three.'

She tilted her head and smiled with curiosity at the intriguing man. 'I wasn't aware that the number of syllables in one's name equated to their level of...' She glanced to the side as though the elusive adjective would appear. *Non-patheticness?* 'Level of...'

'Awesomeness?'

Her smile tickled her lips and became a chuckle. 'Well if you say so, I'm happy to accept that.'

His grin widened. 'You know, I didn't even know what a syllable was until...' He glanced upward. 'I don't know exactly, but sometime far later than someone should learn such a term.'

She glanced at the brochure and scanned the words. *Tell your own story ... turn your memories to memoir ... learn from bestselling author Joel Foster...*

'But you're an author.'

'Apparently,' he replied with a bashful smile. 'But really I just relayed my story of what happened to me, and a wonderful creature known as an editor helped make it understandable and readable.' He drummed his fingers on the counter. 'Dyslexia was my companion all through school, and there was a lot I missed, with that and the sporting priorities I had. It's better than before, but I'm still not the best with words.' He held out his hands to the side and shrugged.

'You're doing pretty well right now though,' she said, amused by his chattering.

'Speaking words, yes, no prob. Reading and writing the words? Not as good.'

Olivia nodded. 'My daughter had some trouble learning to read, but now she can't stop. Once she got the hang of it, she couldn't get enough. Makes my nights easier now that she wants to read by herself.'

Why am I telling him this?

'I bet she likes having a mum who works in a bookstore then.' He smiled. 'Or... runs a bookstore? Owns a bookstore?' He eyed her with a subtle tilt of his head.

'I'm the manager, and part owner. I share ownership with my mother and grandmother.'

'Ah,' he said, 'family business huh? Nice.'

'It is. My grandma did a wonderful job setting up the store when she was young, despite her hardships.'

'How long has the store been running?'

'Around sixty years.'

'Wow.'

'Yep. And if my daughter maintains her love of books, maybe she'll take over one day and keep it running another sixty years!'

'What a great piece of history to have as a family legacy.' He held her gaze with genuine admiration. 'I've never been able to stick with anything for sixty days, let alone the idea of sixty years.'

Olivia glanced back at the brochure, which she had yet to peruse properly. *Ahh...* now she realised who he was. The author of *One More Breath*, bestselling memoir about a wilderness survival experience.

'You stuck with writing a book. *Apparently,*' she said with a corner of a smile. 'I'd say that takes a lot of...' The elusiveness of words affected her again. 'A lot of...' *Stickability?*

'Commitment?' he suggested.

She held up her finger. 'Yes, was on the tip of my tongue!'

'So, so far we've established that I have demonstrated commitment for one thing and you have overall awesomeness, on account of your...' He rotated his hand in circles.

'My eight-syllable name.'

'Yes.' He pointed towards her. 'Was on the tip of my tongue.' He winked.

They both smiled at the same time. 'I need to order more copies of your book, by the way; it's sold out. Otherwise I'd get you to sign them.'

'No problem, let me know when you have stock and I'll pop back in.' He tapped on the brochures. 'Anyway, I won't keep you, and I have a meeting to get to. I'm visiting town to teach a course for the next six weeks. If I can write a book, anyone can. So I'll be teaching what I've learned about the process. There are a few places left. I thought you might know some people who might be interested, possibly some of your customers?'

She fanned the brochures out on the glossy wooden countertop. 'Sure. I mean, I'll ask around. No problem with leaving these here.'

'Thank you, I really appreciate it. And I'll be sure to recommend your store to my students for any books they may need for research.'

'That would be great.'

Ideas swirled in Olivia's mind. Long forgotten ideas and memories, and hopes and plans that had been buried beneath the weight of responsibilities and day-to-day living. As Joel turned to exit the store, she opened her mouth. 'A quick question.'

He turned back as he ran a hand through his sandy hair.

'Is the course only for people writing their *own* real-life stories?'

'Generally speaking. But it could also help people wanting to record memories or stories from their family history, for example. Why do you ask?' He approached her again.

'My grandma. She has some great stories from her life, and how she built this business from the ground up. I've always told her that one day I would have to put them all in a book.'

Joel smiled and nodded. 'Then maybe I'll see you at the class.'

Olivia flicked her hand. 'Oh, I'm not sure. I don't have much time to write, let alone do a class. Maybe one day.'

'Fair enough. But if you change your mind, let me know before those places all fill up.' He gestured to the brochures on the counter and as his eyebrows rose, the furrows in his forehead deepened into intriguing lines.

'I will. Thanks.'

'Nice to meet you, Olivia the Awesome with eight syllables.'

Her face flushed with warmth. 'You too, Joel with...' She'd forgotten his surname and had to discreetly eye the brochures. *Foster.* 'Three syllables.'

He grinned and turned, giving a wave on his way out the door.

Hmm. Nice guy. There might be some customers who could be interested... Mr Donovan is always spinning a yarn when he comes in once a month to buy a new thriller. And then there's that young bookaholic dude who loves the paranormals who learned to walk again after a shark attack, not to mention April's amazing journey after her car accident, and then there's Sylvia Greene who'd been reunited with her biological daughter eighteen years later. They all had stories to tell. Oh, and what about...

'*One* day?' Marcus shoved his face in front of her at the

counter, snapping her out of her thoughts. 'What's this one day business? You're always saying that, and one day never seems to come.' He scolded her with his disapproving glare. 'And that was Joel Foster! Damn, I should have asked for his autograph.'

'That's because I don't have time for things like that.' Olivia folded her arms across her chest, her usual response when well-meaning people tried to tell her what to do with her life. 'One day means when Mia is older and I have more time.'

'Meanwhile, you miss opportunities to live your own life more fully.'

'Mia needs me, I'm all she has. I mean, as far as parents go. I want to do the best for her.'

'And you already are, but don't forget about yourself.' He picked up one of the brochures and sighed at Joel's picture. 'Plus he's super hot. Looks a bit like Scott Eastwood with that sexy furrowed brow. And I'm pretty sure he's straight, and single, you lucky thing.'

'Marcus!' Olivia whacked her employee with one of the brochures, then glanced at the image of Joel who now had a diagonal paper crease across his face. *Oops.* 'Are you going to appraise every straight and single-looking guy who comes in here for potential date material? I'm not even looking for someone, I'm–'

'Too busy, I know.' He placed the brochure back down. 'Okay, forget about that, but didn't you say you wanted to write a book about Mrs May?'

She shrugged. 'When the time is right.'

Marcus stared unblinking at her. 'Ten years from now? Joel Foster is teaching a course here in Tarrin's Bay, and it's not the right time? Think about it. What a great opportunity.'

'I need to place an order and make some calls to customers,' Olivia said, checking the list of special orders that had come in.

Marcus held his hands up in defeat. 'Back to work I go then.'

Olivia read the words on the computer screen but her brain didn't register them. Instead she thought about all those 'one day' things she hadn't yet done.

Buy a house... *one day*, when she could afford to break free of the rent cycle.

Take Mia on an exciting holiday... *one day*, see aforementioned reason.

Write her grandma's book... *one day*, when she could find time for writing.

Meet a man who wouldn't run off from fear of too much responsibility... *one day*.

Maybe.

She wasn't quite sure if a man like that existed.

I f Olivia hadn't accidentally left her phone in the car when taking Mia into her classroom the next morning, she would have heard the chirping birds ringtone of her mother's phone call. And if she hadn't needed to help her daughter carry the cardboard solar system model she'd been up until 11pm fixing, after Mia's enthusiastic 'ice-skating' in socks on the kitchen floor had knocked over the model and squashed it when she landed on it, she would have heard it ring a second time. Instead, she saw two missed calls and one message on her phone when she finally checked it on arriving at work.

'Mum?' she spoke urgently into the phone after checking voicemail. 'Is Grandma okay?'

'She's stable now, but once her tests are completed and she's okay for transport, they'll move her into the high-dependency facility of the nursing home.'

Olivia's shoulders sunk. 'She's going to hate that. She loved her semi-independent room.'

'I know, but she's not getting any younger, and this stroke was more significant than the minor one she had at Christmas. She'll get round-the-clock care there.'

And it'll be the last place she ever lives...

Mrs May Chevalier was known as Mrs May by the locals and Mia, who'd had trouble saying 'great-grandma' when she was little, so Mrs May had become the easier option. At almost ninety, Mrs May had stubbornly refused to go into the nursing home proper, and was adamant about living the rest of her life in her cute little semi-apartment attached to it.

'When can I see her? Should I get Marcus to watch the store and come now?'

'No, they're busy doing tests and she needs to rest. I'll check in this afternoon and see if we're able to visit with Mia after you've finished work.'

'Okay, let me know.'

'Will do.'

Olivia ended the call and opened up the store, sadness filling her heart as she switched on the lights that somehow weren't as bright without her grandma there. It'd been ages since her grandma had anything to do with running the store, but she'd often come in to hang around and chat to the customers. The little kids loved her. She used to read to them in the back corner of the kids' section in her old-fashioned velvet armchair that still sat tall and proud, as it had for so many years.

Olivia wandered to the back of the store, trying to imagine her grandma seated there; smiling, comfortable, and at home as though the armchair was an extension of her body. Colourful children's books framed the walls, each bursting with delicious adventures for the young and young at heart. The small alcove of the kids' section had a secure, cosy feel, as though the walls and books embraced each person who entered and beckoned them to discover amazing journeys and secrets.

The armchair creaked softly as she sat on the firm velvet padding and slid her hands down the sculpted armrests. Goosebumps prickled her skin as tiny fibres of the velvet fabric that was wrapped around the dark wood tickled her skin and triggered memories of sitting there on her grandma's lap as she read to her. Olivia was glad Mia had been able to experience the same magic of Mrs May's armchair several years ago, before it became difficult for her grandma to come into the store. Mia would climb eagerly onto Mrs May's lap and Olivia had to remind her to be gentle with her great-grandmother's frail bones.

Olivia leant back and closed her eyes, drawing a deep breath and filling her nose with scents of furniture varnish, books, and the faint hint of lilies from the perfume Mrs May always wore that hung about this part of the store like a friendly ghost.

Her eyes opened when a cackle of children bustled in. Olivia rose quickly from the chair to see three boys about four or five years old with a woman about fifty entering the store, the kids rushing to the back. She smiled at the woman whose cheeks were rosy and whose words of 'Careful!' and 'Don't run!' went unacknowledged by the kids. 'Sorry,' she said to Olivia. 'I promised them each a new book if they were well-behaved last night while their parents are away enjoying their anniversary. If I can get through the rest of this week with these triplets, I think I deserve a whole pile of books myself. Or a case of wine.'

Olivia laughed. 'It's okay, I love seeing kids excited by books.'

'I want this one!' one of the boys exclaimed, holding up a copy of a book aimed at ten-year-olds.

'Joshua, that has a scary dragon on the front. Choose another,' said the woman.

'Dragon!' the boy exclaimed even louder, hugging the book to his chest. A second later, he dropped the book and picked up another.

'Joshua, pick the book up and put it back where it came

from, please.' The woman gestured to the shelf. He sighed and did as she said, then all three pulled out various books and discussed the merits of each in the best possible vocabulary that four-year-olds could manage, with words like 'cool!' and 'mine!' and 'look, an elephant!'

Despite their rambunctious nature, Olivia smiled at this simple pleasure. With all the technology around these days, it was refreshing to see. She pulled her phone from her pocket and sidled up to the boys' grandmother. 'Would you mind if I filmed them?' Olivia whispered. 'For my grandma, Mrs May. She's in hospital and I think this might lift her spirits.'

The woman's eyebrows rose. 'Oh, of course. As long as it doesn't end up on Facebook or YouTube then no problem at all!'

'You've got my word.' She smiled, then discreetly held the phone facing the boys as they rummaged through books and continued their exclamations and excitement.

One of the kids pointed at a book cover and erupted in laughter. 'Monkey face!' he said, then tried to copy the expression of the illustrated animal, which caused the other two boys to burst out laughing too.

Olivia held back a chuckle, and their grandmother shook her head with a smile. 'Anything will amuse these boys,' she said.

Olivia ended the video and after as much deliberation as a boardroom strategy meeting, they had decided upon one book each, though Joshua had complained that Jack's book was bigger than his. She processedthe sale and sent the video to her mother, thinking it might lift her spirits as well.

Love it, was her text reply. Followed by, *Call you later.*

When she did call that afternoon, Olivia was anxious to see her grandma, fearful that something might happen and she wouldn't get to say goodbye. She arranged for Marcus to close up on her behalf so she could collect Mia from school and take her to the hospital, where Olivia's mother would meet them.

'Mummy, where's Nanna?' asked Mia, not used to her mother picking her up from school.

'She's with Mrs May, we're going to see them both now.' Olivia smiled softly, but waited until they were in the car to explain. 'Sweetie, Mrs May is very sick, so we have to be quiet and gentle, okay? Doctors and nurses are looking after her, and soon she's going to move into a special new room! I think we should bring her flowers for her new place, don't you?'

'Yes!' Mia exclaimed. 'And a new book. And a teddy bear.'

'And a teddy bear. Okay.' Olivia started the engine.

'Mum?' Olivia asked a few minutes into the drive to Welston Hospital.

'Yes?'

'Is Mrs May going to die?'

Olivia gulped down a lump in her throat that had been growing all day. 'Oh, honey. She's just sick right now, but the doctors will give her some medicine and hopefully that will help.'

'So she won't die?'

Olivia eyed her daughter in the rear-view mirror. Her wide eyes were curious but concerned, her fingers fiddled with her school backpack that sat on her lap. Part of the challenge of parenthood was trying to figure out how to respond to questions with honesty, yet without going into too much detail that might distress them.

Yes, Mrs May, her beloved grandma, would die. At some point. Everyone would, of course, but at nine decades of life on earth, her time was coming to an end sooner rather than later.

'Not right now, sweetie. But she will at some stage. Because she's old, and old people do die when they get too old because the world needs to make room for brand-new babies to grow up into children like you and your friends. And then adults like me. But she'll be okay, because she's had a good long life, so we just have to spend as much time with her as we can while she's still here.'

Mia waited a moment then responded. 'So will she die on her birthday? Is that when people die, so you can count how many years they were alive?'

'No, people can die on any day of the year. I'm sure there are some people who have died on their birthdays, but it's rare.'

'What does rare mean?'

'Doesn't happen often.'

'So she could die today then?'

Olivia took a slow, deep breath. 'She probably won't, honey. She's being looked after at hospital. They said she's feeling a bit better, so she might stay alive for many more weeks or months yet. Or even years. We just have to wait and see.'

'I hope she doesn't die before my tenth birthday. I want her at my party.'

'I know, I know. But let's not think that far ahead yet.'

Five months to go until Mia entered the double digits. Ten years she'd had, raising her daughter alone from day one. Where had the time gone? In another ten years her daughter would probably be ready to move out. Olivia shook her head at how fast life passed by these days.

Diana Chevalier met her daughter and granddaughter at the hospital entrance and led them to a room, explaining on the way that the stroke had affected some of her grandma's short-term memory and her cognitive abilities, with some minor weakness on the left side of her body. Olivia held Mia's soft hand as they entered, and the previously tall, strong, smiling woman she knew as her grandma lay small, weak, and unsmiling in her hospital bed with various tubes and drips around her. Her left wrist was in a cast, as it had broken during the stroke when she'd fallen off her chair.

Olivia had seen her like this before, but this time she looked different. More withered and beaten. Like she'd had enough and was ready to surrender. Her first instinct was to guard Mia against any distress, so she pointed to the tubes and whispered 'See? That's all the good medicine going into Mrs May's body to help her.'

Mia nodded as they approached the bed.

'Mum?' Olivia's mother whispered as she leaned over the bed. 'Two lovely visitors to see you.'

May's eyes flickered open gently and focused on Olivia. She appeared to have difficulty lowering her line of sight, so Olivia helped Mia up onto the side of the bed. 'Oh, my favourite girls. All at once.' Mrs May's mouth smiled weakly to the right.

'Hi, Mrs May, I hope you can come to my birthday party in October.'

Olivia and Diana chuckled.

'You're growing up,' Mrs May said.

'Yep. I'll be ten.'

'Ten?' she asked. 'I thought you were turning thirteen!'

Olivia's shoulders relaxed. Her grandma still had a lot of fight left in her, and the stroke hadn't affected her humour and charm.

'When I was ten, I...' Mrs May tried to scratch her cheek, but weakness caused her arm to flop back down. Diana scratched it for her. 'I used to play in the mud.'

'The mud?' Mia cried. 'Dirty mud?'

'Very dirty mud.'

'Yuck, Mrs May!' Mia giggled like crazy and squirmed on the bed. 'Did you still play in it when you were thirteen?'

'Thirteen? Ah... no, my dear. By then, I wanted to spy on the boys next door.'

'Even more yuck!' Mia giggled again. 'What about when you were... twenty?'

May was quiet for a moment. Her breathing quickened and her hand shook a little. 'No mud and no boys,' she said slowly. 'Only men. I mean man. One man.'

'You spied on one man? Oh!' Mia held up her finger. 'Was it Great-Grandpa?' He had died before Mia was born so hadn't needed an easy to pronounce nickname.

'Yes, Great-Grandpa and Mrs May got married when she was twenty, darling,' said Diana, stroking her mother's forearm.

'No, no.' Mrs May's brow furrowed slightly.

'Yes,' Diana responded. 'You were twenty, remember?'

'Yes, but no.' She clenched the sheet on the bed with her right hand.

Diana eyed Olivia and she wondered whether to call a nurse.

'Not him,' May added. 'William.'

Who was William?

'Mum, Dad's name was Jacques.' Diana perched on the edge of her chair next to the bed.

'I'm not talking about Jacques,' she replied with surprising volume, her eyes clear and open. 'William,' she said with a soft exhalation. Her eyes went distant and she closed them and spoke again. 'William. He was the one I loved.'

* * *

Olivia kissed her daughter's forehead and went to turn out her bedside lamp, but Mia held her mother's arm. 'I'm glad Mrs May didn't die today,' she said.

'I'm glad too.' Olivia sat down again, knowing how Mia's mind sometimes got worked up and caused her trouble sleeping. 'It was nice to talk to her, wasn't it?'

'She's funny.'

'She is. Used to have me in hysterics sometimes when I was little.' Olivia smiled at a memory...

The time her grandmother had made spaghetti and she and Olivia had decided to pretend it was worms, wriggling around on the plate.

'Worms!' she'd cry out, lifting one strand with her finger and jiggling it in the air.

'I have a million of them!' Olivia had said, lifting up a handful and doing the same.

'Let's eat them up!' May said.

'Bye-bye, worms!' Olivia had gobbled them up without a moment's thought.

Her mother wouldn't let her eat with her hands, but her grandmother was known for bending the occasional rule.

'Anyway, darling, we should both get a good night's sleep and be ready for a great day tomorrow. 'Kay?' She gave Mia's shoulder a rub.

''Kay.'

Olivia stood.

'Mum?' she asked. 'What happens when people die?'

From the way the conversation was going, she would have to re-boil the kettle she'd flicked on several minutes ago. 'Well, they get taken to a special place where their bodies are taken care of before they can be buried or cremated, and then their family can say goodbye with a special ceremony – a funeral. You know, like the one we had for Peepee?' Mia had been adamant on calling their ill-fated kitten by the slightly ridiculous name. Sadly, the cat had escaped outside one day and tried to cross a street at peak school-traffic time and been hit.

'No, I mean, what really happens to them? Is there a heaven?'

Olivia breathed out a 'hmmm'. 'Many people like to believe

there is. I guess no one really knows. But I like to believe that somehow a part of the person lives on, like their soul. We just can't see them anymore.'

'So they could see us?'

Olivia shrugged. 'Possibly, I'm not sure. Maybe they become present whenever a loved one thinks of them after they've died.'

Mia nodded slowly. 'I don't think they could see us though.'

'Yeah? Why's that?'

'Because they wouldn't have eyes anymore!'

'Oh, Mia!' Olivia shook her head.

'Because if their bodies are buried then their eyes would be too, so souls must have special vision powers.'

Olivia covered her mouth as she chuckled. 'You have a good imagination.' She kissed her forehead again. 'Nighty-night.'

'Goodnight, Mummy.'

Olivia switched off the light and left the room, wondering if Mia would stop calling her Mummy when she turned ten. She would miss that. Things were changing, Mia was growing up and her grandma was growing... older. Sicker. With Diana having been a single parent like Olivia, Olivia had grown up around her grandparents, who had helped out with raising her after her father had left when she was two. She still communicated with him occasionally, but he lived in New Zealand and they weren't close.

Relationships were strange things.

Olivia made a cup of relaxing herbal tea and sat on the couch. She thought of her father, her grandfather, and Mia's father – who had never met his daughter. And then her mind wandered to what her grandma had said today...

William.

Who was she talking about? Was he just a random name she had mentioned in a moment of confusion? Mrs May had fallen asleep after that, and the Chevalier women had left her in peace and gone home to share dinner at her mother's house, along with Diana's boyfriend, Peter.

What if it wasn't random? She had seemed so clear when she'd said it. What if she *had* loved some man called William and had never told anyone before? Her grandma had a lot of stories about her life, but maybe she had more to tell, another secret or two waiting to be revealed…

She retrieved her tattered notebook from the desk beside the entryway, where months ago – or had it been over a year? – she had taken notes about the book she planned to write for May's memories. She also had a folder on her computer with various photographs, family-tree information, and stories her grandma had told her. Somehow, someway, she had to put it all together, and gather the missing details before it was too late.

Olivia unzipped her handbag and grabbed one of the squashed brochures about the memoir course she had shoved in there in case she came across any interested people while she was out and about. But maybe *she* was the interested person. Maybe she should take the opportunity like Marcus had suggested, or pressured, more like. She didn't have that much spare time, and she was often tired at the end of each day, but she could at least look into it further.

Before changing her mind she keyed in Joel's number on her phone, and when it rang she glanced at the time. 9pm. Oops, was that too late to call with an enquiry? She was about to end the call when a voice said, 'Hello?'

She cleared her throat. 'Oh, hi. Sorry, is it too late?' She paused. 'It's Olivia. Chevalier, from–'

'Mrs May's Bookstore,' he interjected. 'Olivia with eight syllables. Hello there.'

'Hello.'

'I got a booking already from someone who found my brochure in your store.'

'Oh, that's great,' she said. 'And actually, I'm calling because I want to know a bit more about the course. I know you said that it could help people who wanted to write stories from their family history, but I'm still not sure. My grandma is ill, and it's making me think I should ask her for more details on her life before she... before she...'

'Before it's too late.'

'Yes.'

'I'm sorry to hear she's unwell.'

'Thanks. It's okay, she's almost ninety.'

'Well, do you have anything already written?'

'Some notes and a bit of an outline. But I don't really know where to start, like do I write it chronologically, and how do I know what to include and what to leave out, and would some details be too personal?'

'Those are all questions my course will answer.'

'Okay, but also how much time would I need to take out of my life to do this. The course, and the book. How long does a book take to write?'

'Tell you what,' he said, 'let's meet for coffee and I'll answer any questions you have about the course, you can show me some of what you have noted down, and I'll give you an idea of whether it would be a good idea.'

Coffee? Now she had to make time for that too. She usually had a quick coffee or lunch while catching up on emails at the store or Café Lagoon. 'You sure? That would be good actually. And of course my shout, and I can pay you for your time, I wouldn't want to get free advice and then not enrol.'

'No need. I don't know anyone in town, so you can repay me with your company and by telling me all about Tarrin's Bay's history and any fascinating secret spots I should check out.' His voice sounded like he was smiling.

'Oh, sure. If that's okay.'

'Of course. I'll be hiking all day tomorrow, so how is Friday?'

'Sounds good. I can take a break about 1pm for lunch, if that suits?'

'Lunch, even better. Where do you recommend?'

'Café Lagoon, a few shops down from the bookstore.'

'Awesome. See you at one on Friday.'

'Great, see you then. Thanks.' She was about to end the call.

'Oh, Olivia?'

'Yes?'

'Do you have a title for the book? Many writers find it helps to start with a title, even if it gets changed down the track.'

The title had come to her almost as quickly as the book idea. 'Memories of May,' she said.

'Ahh, it has bestseller written all over it,' he replied, and she smiled.

The call ended and her smile grew. It felt good to be doing something for her grandma. It also felt good to be having coffee with an interesting man.

Even if she didn't have time for those things.

CHAPTER THREE

Joel's stomach growled as he trudged up the dry hill. The sticks and leaves crunching underfoot were music to his ears. He loved being outdoors, at one with nature, no distractions, no technology, nothing to do except walk. Breathe. Think.

He glanced around and up, then lodged the toe of his boot onto a protrusion of rock, grabbed the rough texture above and climbed higher. After a few steps up the rock face he reached the top, exhaling deeply as he sat on the flattened surface.

The muted grey-blue sky beyond the trees smoothed out his thoughts, freed his mind, and allowed his chest to expand with fresh air. He took in the peace, calm, and freedom for a few minutes, then lifted his backpack off and unzipped it, a bird flapping away from a nearby tree and into the sky.

His stomach growled again at the sight of his sandwich. He unwrapped it and took a large bite. He finished it in a flash, and ignored the slight ache that had developed in the top of his right calf muscle as he took a few gulps of water. 'Time to keep moving.' He stood and replaced his backpack.

He didn't care if talking to himself was considered crazy.

With many hours spent alone while travelling and hiking, he'd grown used to his own company. And talking to himself had proved invaluable when he'd needed someone but had no one. When his life had been on the line. When all he'd had to rely on was his thoughts, his mind, and a choice.

He chose.

He survived.

And if he could survive that, could save his own life, then he could also handle a simple lunch and coffee with a nice woman tomorrow without getting tempted and distracted while enjoying a temporary stay in Tarrin's Bay. Couldn't he?

Joel wandered down the main street, past shops and cafés and people and found Café Lagoon, its flowing layout and blue-green painted walls like walking into a refreshing watery natural environment, apart from the tables and chairs. He scanned the café... where was the pretty caramel-and-vanilla-haired woman with eight syllables?

'Hey, mate. What can I get for you?'

Joel met the glance of the young dude at the counter. 'G'day. I'm just waiting for someone first.'

'No worries. And just so you know, our organic burgers are on special today for half price when you order two. So if your friend wants a burger, it's a great deal.' He flashed a grin.

'Awesome. I'd love a burger. But I'll wait and see what my charming companion would prefer.'

'Oh, charming, eh? Girlfriend?'

'Nah, a potential student of my writing course.'

'You're the guy who wrote that survival story, right? Except that it was real, not a story.'

'That would be me.'

'So cool,' the dude said. 'I went travelling and did some hiking, but don't know what I would have done in your situation. I'm glad you're here to tell the tale. Good on you, mate.'

He held out his hand and Joel shook it. 'Thanks... Jonah,' he said, eyeing his nametag.

'Does your charming companion have a name?'

'Olivia.'

'Oh really? From Mrs May's?'

Joel nodded.

'Well I don't think she'll have a burger. She'll have the organic chicken salad or the soup of the day.'

'A regular, huh?'

'Like most of the fellow shop-owners in town.'

'So,' said Joel, 'how do all the other cafés survive if you guys are the go-to place?'

'Ah, we all have our specialties and people have different tastes, and there are a lot of hungry people around, I guess.'

Joel nodded again. Another customer came up and Joel gestured for the person to go ahead of him. While he waited for Olivia, he eyed the pictures on the wall around the café, including an autographed poster from Aussie singer Drew Williams. There was also a framed plate with knife and fork, the plate signed in black permanent marker by a television chef. At the back of the café was a slightly raised area that looked like it was set up for live performances, and judging by another poster advertising a local singer and guitarist, his assumption was correct. *Hmm...* Maybe he could enquire about doing a talk here for his book one day. He could ask his publicist about it and see what she thought.

No longer did his life simply revolve around his next adventure, it also revolved around his marketing and public profile, since being interviewed on television had catapulted his book to the bestseller lists and made him an in-demand motivational speaker. The great thing was, it helped fund his adventures. Before, he had had to live as simply as possible to save money, and do whatever odd job he could find to accumulate enough to live on. Nine to five wasn't his thing, even though he'd done it for a while to make ends meet. Not only had his survival experience given him a second chance at life, it had given him a new kind of life, one he hadn't expected and was forever grateful for.

'Hi, sorry I'm late!' Joel turned to see Olivia approach the counter with a flushed pink face as she blew a wisp of hair from across her eye with a puff from between her lips. 'A customer wanted my supposed expert opinion on two different cookbooks even though they were both very similar, and I suggested buying both of course – well, why not! – but she only wanted one, so she had me googling the benefits of low-fat versus low-sugar eating and...' She took a breath.

'No problem.' Joel placed his hand gently on her forearm, at the junction of her sleeve, which was cool and soft, and her skin, which was warm and also soft. 'I'm in no rush.' He smiled.

Olivia smiled and exhaled a breath of apparent relief. She glanced towards Jonah and nodded a smile.

'So let me guess, organic chicken salad or soup of the day?' Joel asked.

Her large greenish-brown eyes widened. 'How did you guess?'

'Psychic.'

'I'm sure.' She chuckled.

'But I'm hoping to convince you to try something new.'

'Something new? Why?'

'When was the last time you tried something new?'

She looked at him like he was asking her when she last went bungee jumping.

'I like chicken salad. I like soup.'

'What about a burger?'

She crinkled her nose a little.

'They're organic too. And half price when you order two, so that makes it buy one get one free, and I'll pay and you can have the free one. But if you have the salad or the soup, I'm not paying.' He grinned.

Her eyes opened wider again and she let out a surprised laugh. 'It's okay, I can pay for my own. I don't expect special treatment, and maybe I should be shouting you since you're going to be listening to my book idea.'

'Not at all. Have the burger and I'll pay for your free one.' He chuckled. 'Maybe even a drink if you're lucky.' He held out his hand. She glanced at it and hesitated. 'It's just one burger. Live dangerously.'

'I take it that's your motto.' She phrased it as a statement, then gently shook his hand. 'Burger it is. But no fries,' she said as she glanced at Jonah, who he hadn't realised was witnessing their exchange.

'Two burgers thanks, mate,' Joel said, adding their drink orders and tapping his card. He took a table number – three, his birthdate and birth month. He glanced around and waited for Olivia to choose a table. She led him to one in the back corner.

'Quieter over here,' she said. He raised his eyebrows suggestively and she added, 'So no one overhears my book plans and I can hear you above the loud hearing-impaired couple, Mr and Mrs Rogers.' She gestured near the front of the café then whispered, 'They speak so loudly I can't hear myself think.'

'If they're hearing impaired then why are you whispering?' he whispered as they took their seats.

Olivia's cheeks went pinker. 'I don't know,' she whispered even more quietly as a smile tried to escape, but it looked like she wouldn't let it fully develop. 'Maybe so other people can't hear me talking about them. It's a small town, people eavesdrop and gossip.'

'I'll put on my indoor voice,' he said.

She laughed; a short and sweet, cute little laugh. 'I always have to tell my daughter to put on her indoor voice, sometimes she gets a little overenthusiastic.'

'That's good.'

'Not when you're tired and want some peace and quiet.' She smiled.

'True, but enthusiasm is a trait to be encouraged. What is life if you can't be enthused about something? What do you get enthused about?' he asked.

She tilted her head slightly and studied his eyes. 'What do you mean?'

'Like, what are you passionate about? What gets you fired up?'

She responded with a blank stare.

'Haven't you ever become so excited about something you can hardly contain yourself?'

She glanced upwards, then said, 'Not really. Oh, but some books are so good that I get quite excited by them. And when my favourite chocolate is on special, I love having a treat at the end of the week.'

She was absolutely adorable, but also a little... plain. He had only spent time with women who shared his passion for excitement and adventure. At least, they were the only ones who took his interest. Olivia was intriguing, but not really his type. Which was good, because he wasn't here to date, he was here to work, then move on. And he wasn't even sure if she had a partner, but from the sounds of things she didn't have time for one.

She straightened up in her chair and tucked some of her wavy hair behind her ear, as though sensing his appraisal of her personality. 'You think I'm boring.'

'Boring? What? No, of course not.'

'Yes you do. I don't hike or travel or have interesting stories to tell like you.'

Joel raised his palms. 'I didn't say anything.'

'But let me tell you, I work damn hard raising my daughter on my own and running the store, I have a lot of responsibility and no time for indulging in... in... experiences that take me away from what I should be doing.'

Okay, so definitely no partner. 'Hey, hey, no judgement here. I can tell you do an amazing job. I was just wondering what else you're passionate about. But while we're on the topic, if you don't have any interesting stories to tell, is that why you want to write your grandma's stories? Because you feel they're more interesting than your own?'

She crossed her arms, and her small silver necklace and pendant shimmered against her porcelain-skin chest. 'No, I'm doing it to preserve our family history and honour my grandma's memory, not because of the idea of living vicariously through someone else's interesting life.'

Joel leaned back and exhaled. 'Okay, okay, let's start again, shall we?'

She sighed and uncrossed her arms. 'Yes, let's.'

'I'm Joel.' He held out his hand and she shook it. 'I tend to say what's on my mind, life is too short not to. But I never said you were boring. In fact, I think you're intriguing. For example, I'd like to know what brand of chocolate is your favourite, and just how much do you eat in one go? Because I can devour a whole block in one hit, easy. And what books do you like reading the most? I never used to read much until I wrote my own, now I like the odd biography or novel.'

Her face softened and she took a sip of water. 'A whole

block in one go too, sometimes. But not always. Only if I really need it.'

'Chocolate is *always* needed,' he said.

She smiled and nodded. 'I like your thinking.' Her face lit up more brightly than before. She leaned in closer to the table. 'You know, sometimes I'm a really bad mother and I hide the chocolate from Mia – she's my daughter – so I can eat it all.'

'Wow, you are so bad. No mother of the year award for you.' He shook his head and narrowed his eyes.

'And if she asks if I have any left, sometimes I...' she glanced around then leaned in closer, 'sometimes I even... *lie.*' She almost choked on the word, and Joel laughed.

'Oh no. What hope is there for the future generation when parents are so negligent? Seriously, I think I should report you to family services.'

She chuckled and took another sip. 'But really, I am a nice mother too, and I do give her my chocolate sometimes, but occasionally if I only have the one and I know I really need it, well, what can I do?' She held out her hands and raised her thinly arched eyebrows.

'A happy mother makes for a happy child,' he said, and she gave a firm nod.

Jonah brought out their burgers and Joel smiled in amusement as Olivia opened her mouth wide to take a bite.

'So undignified,' she said with a chuckle. 'Eating with one's hands.'

'It's how it always used to be done.'

'It's just so...' She swiped a glob of mayonnaise from her bottom lip. 'Messy.'

'Messy food is the best food.' He took a huge bite of his own burger.

She moved her hand around as she chewed, as though preparing to say something. 'So, I haven't read your book yet, sorry. But I will. I only know the basics of what happened to you. Sounds like it was pretty intense.'

He nodded. 'You never know what'll go through your mind when you think you're going to die, until it actually happens.' His mind did that thing where it catapulted back in time to that day, that day he thought would be his last. The thoughts he had to endure, the realisation that this may be all his life had amounted to. It had been hard to revisit those thoughts while writing his memoir, but necessary, and with the help of his psychologist, he'd been able to tap into them again safely without getting too deeply embroiled in a mental place he didn't really want to visit again.

Olivia went quiet, nodding slowly.

'Anyway, not exactly the best lunchtime discussion. Onto *your* book.' He took a sip of coffee. She stayed quiet. 'Olivia?'

'Sorry.' She swatted her hand in front of her. 'It's just I never thought of that, what you said. That you never know what will go through your mind until it happens. Do you think that's the same with elderly people? Even if they're not in any immediate danger, but know their time is coming to an end?'

Ah, her grandma. 'I'm sure thoughts do start to crop up that they don't expect. Maybe they always felt like they'd have longer, like time flies so fast. Or maybe some feel like they've been around forever and are like "hurry up!"' he joked, then lightly touched her hand. 'Oh, sorry, that sounded better in my head. Sorry. Your grandma... how is she?'

'She's stable, but may only last another month or two, they think; six at the most if she's lucky.'

'And you were wondering what thoughts she might be thinking.'

She nodded. 'She's been talking a bit, about the past. Mentioned some guy's name we'd never heard of, so I don't know if she's losing it or there are things playing on her mind that she's never discussed before.'

'Ask her. Don't have any regrets. If she's well enough to talk, then let her talk. Take notes, let her tell her stories while she can. Untold stories shouldn't die with the body.' He was so glad his hadn't.

'That's the plan.' She pressed her lips together into a smile that spoke more of resolve than of happiness.

'So tell me,' Joel said, his burger half gone and his stomach relaxing in satisfaction. 'What is the main hook for your story? I know your grandma built up a successful business and probably started it during a time when there was great struggle for people to get by after the war, so apart from the adversity to success theme, is there anything else that sets your book apart from other similar books?'

She opened her bag and fiddled with a notebook. 'Um, well I'm not really sure yet, but I think it's about not only business success, but also a woman's personal journey to create her own life rather than follow one that was expected of her.'

Joel clasped his hands together for a moment under his chin. 'Hmm. Sounds like you *are* pretty sure. That sounds like an interesting angle.'

'Is it enough though? I mean, it's enough for me, for us as a family, but I don't know if the book would have a market or anything, and I'm not doing it for commercial success, but of course if people would find it interesting then I would definitely try to get it published and share Mrs May's story with a larger audience than just our family and friends.'

'What have you got so far?' He snatched the notebook from her hands and she gasped.

'Hey! I'm not ready to show anyone yet!' She tried and failed to take it back.

He held it up above his meal. 'It's okay, I won't read any

without your permission, I just wanted you to see what it could feel like to have your words read by another person.' He grinned. 'Scary, isn't it?'

She shook her head. 'Oh you, you like to tease, don't you.'

'It's fun.'

'Can I have it back, pretty please?'

He held it towards her and she took it with both hands, holding it to her chest.

'Part of my course is about getting used to other people reading your work. You'd have to share some stuff, would you be okay with that?'

She shrugged. 'I guess, since all the students would be in the same boat.'

'Then I think you should definitely join the class.'

'But you've hardly heard anything about my book yet.'

'Don't need to. I can see it in your eyes: the need, the purpose, the urgency, the desire to do this and do it justice. This, my dear, is what you are *enthused* about. Forget about reading other books and your favourite chocolate on special, this is what you need to do, not only for your grandma, but for yourself.'

'Oh, you're putting on a sales pitch, aren't you?'

'Nope, just being honest.' He leaned back and threaded his hands behind his head. 'And I have a feeling...'

'What sort of feeling?' She eyed him with a curious glance.

'That by writing this book about a woman who created her own life instead of one that was expected of her, you might just do the same for yourself.'

CHAPTER FOUR

Joel was right. How could he tell so much about her without having known her very long? Was she *that* easy to read? *Memories of May* was the only thing that stood out from her day-to-day routine, the only thing that had played on her mind for long enough to take up residence as a niggling idea and goal that for some reason would not go away. She hadn't thought about how it related to her own life, but he was right. She did want something else to be enthused about, something out of the ordinary to put energy into, not just for someone else, but for herself. She had her daughter, her family, her store, her health, and a few close friends, but what else? What did she have that was worth writing about if her future granddaughter was to tell her story? Yes, she'd done well as a single mother for over nine years, but plenty of women did that, it was almost the norm these days. She hadn't known that her out-of-character one-night stand one New Year's Eve would become a lifetime of responsibility. In life, you had to do what needed to be done, and so she'd done it.

But maybe by discovering more about her grandma's life, she could also, in the process, discover more about herself.

Maybe she had more in common with May than she realised. Maybe she could learn a few things that would help her in her own life, to take a few risks and create something of her own.

She'd already decided she would do the course, she just needed to book and pay, and of course make sure that her mother could mind Mia every Tuesday for the next six weeks. And possibly some extra times for when she needed to talk with her grandma and take notes for the book, which could become time consuming depending on her grandma's energy levels and memory. It could be a challenge for her mum, as she already helped out a lot, and she knew her mother needed time for her own life too, especially now she had a new boyfriend. But to entice her even further into becoming a student, Joel had offered some extra mentoring, free of charge, every Friday over lunch, so long as she tried something different from the menu each time.

She'd joked that he should be a salesperson. He'd told her how he used to be one in the past, before he swapped his expensive clothes for expensive camping gear and hiking equipment.

'So I'll travel with her to the nursing home tomorrow,' Diana Chevalier said to Olivia as she opened the car door for Mia after visiting Mrs May. 'Then perhaps you two can come over in the afternoon after she's had a rest, and bring some knick-knacks to help her settle in, and help me make her feel more at home.'

'Sure. Marcus is fine to close up shop, so I'll leave at about two and collect Mia from Hannah's house. I'll need to duck home first to take the washing off the line in case it rains later, according to the forecast.'

Diana nodded. Parenthood was mostly about planning and logistics, Olivia had learned. Spontaneity had disappeared long ago, along with her freedom.

Before they opened their own car doors, Olivia said, 'Mum?'

'Yes?'

'I'd like to do a course on Tuesday nights. To help me write Grandma's life story.'

'Oh?'

'It goes for six weeks, but I'd need you to collect Mia from school and give her dinner and put her to bed, and I'll have to eat too, but you might not have time to do the whole shebang, so I'll probably just grab a takeaway.' A million logistical thoughts ran through her mind. She'd have to finish work on time, hopefully have time for a quick shower, eat, then get to class. Then she'd have to make Mia's school lunch and iron her uniform for the next day, although it was probably time her daughter started doing that for herself; the making lunch part, not the ironing.

'Tuesday?' Diana replied. 'That's one of Peter's rare nights off from the gym, do they have the class on any other night? But not Wednesdays, because that's the only night they do the dance fitness class, and you know I adore that one.'

Olivia tensed at the resistance. She got it every time her mother's carefully planned schedule was tested. 'It's Tuesdays or Wednesdays, but I think the Wednesday is full.'

'Drat,' she said.

'If it's too inconvenient, I could look into a professional babysitter, though you know how Mia would feel about that, with her being almost ten, and—'

'No, no, it's okay. If you need me, I can do it. I guess Peter will just have to get used to the fact that I am also a grandmother and not just a fun-loving health-crazed older woman who's always up for a fun night, in or out of the gym.'

'Mum, too much information, please.' Olivia diverted her gaze from her mother's slim figure encased in body-hugging Lycra, the top half of her butterfly tattoo peeking out from the skin above her left breast; the result of a supposed mid-life crisis

—or celebration—just after Mia had started school and her babysitting duties were no longer as intensive.

'What? I didn't say what type of fun, just fun. Anyway, are you sure you want to do this course? I mean, it would be a lot of work, writing this book, and you could spend the extra time with Grandma rather than at a computer or in a class.'

'But that's the thing, I want to do it while she's still here, there are questions I need to ask her, gaps that need filling in, so I can do her story justice. It's now or never.'

Olivia glanced at Mia who, oblivious to their conversation outside the car, had her EarPods in and was bobbing her head up and down to music from her iPad. Yep, time was flying. Soon, she'd be the one in body-hugging outfits and probably getting piercings and dying her hair and maybe even getting tattoos. Olivia shook the thoughts away. When she glanced back at her mother, she was looking at the ground and fiddling with her necklace.

'Mum?'

Diana glanced up to meet her daughter's gaze, but her eyes were glossy in the moonlight.

'Mum?' Olivia walked around to the other side of the car and placed her hands on her mother's. 'Is Tuesday *really* a problem? I know you want your new relationship to get off to a good start, you deserve some happiness. And it's okay, I'll manage somehow, I'll look up babysitters tomorrow and—'

'No, I'll look after Mia,' she said. Her bottom lip trembled. 'It's just...' She let out a long exhalation and fanned her face with her hands. 'It's your grandma. My mum. And what writing this book means.' She glanced up at the sky. 'I'm not ready to let her go yet.'

Olivia's heart shook, and she felt the same. She had been so focused on her own reaction and Mia's to her grandma's ailing health, she hadn't even realised that for her mother, it would be even harder. 'Oh, Mum. I'm sorry.' She wrapped her arms around her and they shared a sniffle. 'I don't want her to go either.'

Diana pulled back and straightened up, holding her daughter's hands firmly. 'You go ahead and book into that course, young lady. And maybe tomorrow you can see if she's up to answering some questions for your book. And don't forget, I have a few stories of my own I can share from growing up.'

A smile grew to life on Olivia's lips and enthusiasm soared in her heart. 'It'll be exciting,' she said.

'It will. And if anyone can do it justice, you can.'

'Thanks, Mum.'

'Don't thank me, thank Grandma. She's the one who created all these memories that deserve to be told and relived. Maybe we'll even learn a few juicy secrets... who knows?'

Olivia returned to her side of the car. 'I have a feeling we just may,' she said with a smile, then laughed at the accidental use of her grandma's name. They got into the car and drove home, while Mrs May was preparing to move into a new home that would be her last; but maybe they could help her create some new memories there before she turned out the light for the last time.

CHAPTER FIVE

'Oh, crap, crap, crap!' Olivia rushed out into the small backyard but it was too late. She wrenched the laundry off the clothesline and shoved it into the basket, then scurried back inside, her hair now stuck to the sides of her face. She kicked the back door shut and exhaled loudly. 'Five minutes, that's all I needed!' she called out above her head, to Mother Nature or whoever gave permission for clouds to spill their load. 'Five minutes, and I would have had them.' She put them in the clothes dryer and turned it on. They would probably end up with rain smell but she had no clean and dry towels, so as long as she had one that would do for tonight's shower it was no big deal.

She quickly ate a banana then got in the car and headed towards her daughter's friend's house. The rain intensified, and she cursed it again. When she got to the driveway, she rummaged in the back of the car and grabbed the only umbrella she could find – a small plastic one with a pink ballerina on it.

'Hi, I was going to bring Mia out for you when I saw something pink racing towards the house!' Hannah's mother, Rachel, said, as she opened the door with a much larger and much less pink (black) umbrella in her hand, when Olivia arrived.

'Ha, not to worry, here now. Thanks for having her again.'

'No problem, she's such a delight. Although...' Olivia's nerves tightened as Rachel turned to Hannah and said, 'Honey, don't forget to go get Mia some of those cookies we baked so she can take them home.'

The children dashed off around the corner, and Rachel leaned closer and whispered in Olivia's ear. 'She mentioned something to Hannah about people who have died and have special vision powers? Like they might be able to see us even though we can't see them. I think it spooked her a bit.'

Olivia covered her mouth and shook her head. 'Oh no, I'm sorry.' She glanced sideways to check the girls weren't coming back out. 'It's just with her great-grandmother being ill, she's been asking lots of questions. It's always hard to know how to explain these things.'

Rachel chuckled. 'Yeah, I know the feeling. Have you had the birds and the bees talk yet?'

Olivia's eyelids stretched wide. 'No. Not yet. Wait, should I have?' From what she remembered, Mia would probably learn that stuff in school next year, so she had planned to wait till then to add her input to the standard curriculum. But she wasn't sure how to expand on what her daughter already knew about her daddy living somewhere else because he had important stuff to do that he couldn't do in Tarrin's Bay, and how to explain that not all babies were made because a mummy and daddy loved each other. Some were made because of that one or two per cent gap of unreliability of modern contraception, but also because she hadn't been thinking straight that New Year's Eve after her boyfriend had left her, and she'd decided to find a temporary one to fill the gap for that night.

'Well, we have, although I'm not sure how much of it sank in and was comprehended, we might need to do a refresher.'

Olivia shuddered. She had enough to think of right now without adding that to the mix. 'Maybe I'll wait till she asks,' Olivia said. 'Anyway, we must be off, need to make sure Mrs May is all settled into her new room, and Mia wanted to bring her some things.'

'Sure, hope she's doing better. I mean, hope she's...'

Olivia waved her hand. 'It's okay. She's much better, thanks. Just needs lots of monitoring and care.'

The girls came back to the door, Mia with a bag of cookies. 'Can we give one to Mrs May?' Her wide eyes beamed as bright as her smile.

'Maybe,' Olivia replied. 'I'm not sure what she is or isn't able to eat at the moment, we'll have to check with the nurses.'

Rachel put Mia under her black umbrella and walked her out, so that Olivia could use the pink umbrella on her own, and they waved them goodbye and drove off.

'Did you bring the teddy bear for Mrs May?' Mia asked, looking around the car.

'Oops!' Olivia did a U-turn and drove back home, picked up the small teddy bear, got back in the car, then drove towards the nursing home.

When they finally arrived, there was a strange sense of calm inside the building, like everything was moving in slow motion. They found Mrs May's room and stepped tentatively inside. 'Grandma?'

She was lying back in bed, but her head was raised from the pillow and she was trying to find something, lifting the covers as much as she could with her muscle weakness.

'Mum, there's nothing under there. There's no letter,' Diana said.

'But I could have sworn it was here.' Mrs May sighed and rested her head back in apparent exhaustion.

Olivia glanced at her mother who shook her head, her eyes looking weary.

'What letter?'

'Shh,' Diana mouthed discreetly.

'From William. It was just here, I'm sure of it.'

Olivia moved closer. She wanted to ask more about this mystery man but she was here to help settle her in, not probe her for information for her book just yet. 'Mia, do you want to give Mrs May her gift?'

Mia bustled over to the bed with the teddy bear in her hand. 'This is for you.'

Mrs May's eyes brightened. 'For me? To keep?'

Mia nodded and her brown ponytail bobbed up and down.

Mrs May patted the bear's fake fur on top of his head. 'He's lovely. I think I'll call him...'

'Benjamin?' Mia suggested.

Mrs May shook her head.

'Bradley?'

Her head shook again. 'William.'

'Oh dear God,' Diana mumbled as she stood, then cleared her throat. 'Mum, how about a cup of water?' She poured some from the plastic beaker into a cup, but her grandma refused it.

'I think William's a nice name,' said Mia. 'William the teddy bear.'

'It is a very nice name.' Mrs May patted his head again.

'He can keep you company while you rest,' Mia said, and Olivia smiled and gently rubbed her daughter's back.

Her grandma held the bear close to her chest. 'Oh, William.'

Olivia was about to ask once and for all who he was, when Mia got in first and said, 'Mrs May?'

'Yes, dear?'

'Are you afraid?'

'Afraid? Of what?'

Mia looked around as though she was about to do something naughty, then whispered, 'Of dying?'

'Mia!' Olivia blurted, then covered her own mouth when she realised it was probably a bit too reactive.

'Dying?' Mrs May responded. 'I used to be, but not now. Besides, more people are scared of living than they are of dying, they just don't realise it.'

Something twinged in Olivia's chest at the words. She didn't know if it was that her grandma didn't seem afraid, or that she had a niggling feeling that her last sentence made too much sense in her own life.

'How's our newest special guest?' a nurse said as she popped her head around the corner of the doorway.

'This one here?' said Mrs May, gesturing to Mia. 'She is good. Such a great conversationalist.'

Mia giggled. 'I'm not a special guest.'

'Yes you are, my dear.'

Mia grinned and adjusted her position on the bed, fiddling with a blanket.

'Sounds like all is okay at present,' said the nurse with a smile.

'Actually,' said Diana. 'Could I just...' She stood and walked towards the nurse, then turned back to Olivia, her thumb pointed over her shoulder. 'I'll just take a quick break, if you're okay in here for a while?' She raised her eyebrows.

Olivia nodded. 'Sure.'

As her mother exited the room, she heard her say something to the nurse about confusion and disorientation, then her voice trailed off.

'How about the special guest draws a picture for Mrs May?' Olivia sat on the chair that her mother had been on. 'And you could listen to your music while you do it, and your great-grandmother and I can have a boring adult chat.' She winked at her daughter and Mia hopped off the bed and sat in the chair against the wall, placing her EarPods in and extracting some paper and pencils from the bag Olivia had brought in.

Mrs May tried to sit up straighter, looking at Mia. 'Is that the letter?' she asked.

Mia tugged out her EarPods.

'It's okay, sweetie, you can put your music back on. No, Grandma, it's not the letter, Mia is drawing you a picture.' She placed her hand on her forearm. 'But... tell me more about this letter.' Olivia pressed record on her phone's audio recorder in case anything interesting came up. And if there *was* a medical reason for her ramblings, then she would have something to present to the doctor.

Mrs May's head relaxed into the pillow, the creases in the cotton radiating out like spokes on a wheel. 'Such a nice letter.' She smiled.

'I'd love to hear more about it. It was from William, yes?'

'Indeed. But I wasn't aware of that at first. It was a secret letter, until the next one came, and the next, and then my secret admirer was revealed.'

Olivia leaned forward. 'Oh, so William was a secret admirer of yours back in the day?'

'Yes,' she said, then breathed out an exhalation that was more like a satisfied sigh. 'But... he was oh so much more than that.'

This sounded like the beginning of an intriguing romance novel, and Olivia wanted to read it. 'Tell me more,' she said, clasping her hands together in anticipation...

May's Memories of Love Letters

Jacques Chevalier smiled at me for the first time that day, that day when everything seemed to be going wrong... I had tripped on the broken bit of flooring outside my room, bruised my knee and bumped my nose on the floor, then spilled two meals worth of soup on the kitchen floor when the heavy crockpot fell from my grasp. Mother scolded me and said I needed to be more careful, and help out more – get another job besides the sewing work I was doing for the locals. Or marry a decent man and leave the family home. So when I walked to town to buy more food supplies with money we really couldn't spare, his smile was a welcome distraction and a light on my dreary day.

I had smiled back of course, but in the sweet demure way that was expected of me, not the gaping wide grin I had wanted to show. But we didn't speak, our exchange had only been through the glass filter of the window of his father's tailor's shop as he carried folded clothing in his hands towards the back room.

The next day I walked into town again and we smiled at each other a second time. Which was why, the next morning when I collected the mail, I thought the love letter was from him. I continued to think that for another week, until my snooping revealed my true admirer.

I still remember taking the letter to my room and closing the door, wondering who had written 'May' so beautifully in ink across the front of the envelope. When I opened it and began reading, my heart fluttered...

Dear Magnificent May,

I know that's a silly way to start a letter, but it's true. You are magnificent. Especially your smile. It lights up my day, seeing you. There are things I wish I could say, but somehow the words escape me. So I decided to attempt writing you a letter, so I don't stumble over my words. I just have to be careful not to make too many mistakes that need crossing out, so if there are, it is only because I want to make sure the words I use are the best I can think of.

I'm now thinking this is perhaps not the most romantic of love letters. I could scrunch it up and start again, but I won't. It will have to do. And it is only the first letter. I will send another, but for now I just wanted to express how amazing I think you are. I mean magnificent, of course.

When I see you I wonder what you are thinking... it looks like you have a lot of thoughts going on in your head. Am I correct? I would be crazy to think that I could be one of those thoughts, but a man can only dream.

I have a lot of thoughts in my head too. Too many to count. Too many to hold me within the confines of this small town... one day they will take me far and wide, I'm sure. My curiosity will fuel my adventures.

It would be a dream come true, to have an adventure with you.

Bye for now,

Me.

Ahhh... an adventure with Jacques Chevalier? I wondered what such an adventure would entail. His eyes seemed to hold many secrets I wished to uncover. I would not let on that I knew it was him. I would not smile any differently, I would let him continue his letter writing for as long as he wished. There were other eligible men in town, many had moved here after the war with their families to be in a calmer, more peaceful environment near the ocean, as we had. Tarrin's Bay was a good place to start. Someone had commented the other day, due to all the new residents, that it was like the Town of New Beginnings. I liked that. Apparently the region's newspaper had caught on and not long after a headline saying those exact words had graced the front page.

Although it sounded like Jacques didn't wish it to be his new beginning. He wanted to explore far-off places by the sounds of what he'd written in the letter. He didn't catch me for the travelling type.

I placed the letter inside the book I was reading. Every time I would open those tattered pages and breathe in that indescribable yet unmistakable book scent, I'd remember the thrill of receiving my first love letter.

My love affair with books became representative of my love affair with memories...

'It's hard to find the words to do it justice,' May said. 'The memories are so vivid, yet words cannot describe them in their full glory.'

'It's okay, Grandma, what you've told me has given me a great understanding of the day you got the letter.' May yawned. Olivia pressed stop on the recorder. 'Maybe we can chat again tomorrow, if you feel up to it.'

'Oh yes, indeed. I need to tell you about that big wide grin I flashed.'

'To Jacques? Instead of the demure smile?'

May smiled softly, her blue eyes twinkling despite their fatigue. 'A storyteller does not give away all their secrets at once, Miss Olivia. A fellow booklover should know that.' She winked.

Olivia kissed her grandma's forehead, her soft and delicate paper-thin skin a reminder of her fragility. 'You get some rest now.'

Diana tiptoed in. 'She asleep?'

'Almost,' Olivia whispered.

'Okay, might head off now and come back tomorrow.'

'Mum, I can come on my own sometimes if you want to spend some time with Peter. Mia's been great while Grandma and I had a bit of a chat.' She eyed her daughter who was still drawing.

'Maybe we'll do shifts then,' she said. 'And I asked the nurse about doing a more intensive neuro exam on her, to check where her mind is at.'

'Mum.' Olivia grabbed her bag and led her mother away from May's bed. 'I think her mind is fine.'

'But she seems to get confused.'

'She's remembering her past, that's all. They say that can happen when an older person starts to prepare for their impending...'

'Don't say it.' Her mother grasped her arm.

'Anyway, she told me about the time when she first started interacting with Grandpa. It was really sweet. Did you know they used to smile at each other through his father's shop window?'

'Huh? Well no, but that doesn't explain why she keeps yapping on about this imaginary William fellow.'

Olivia smiled. 'Mum, I don't think he is a figment of her

imagination. And there *was* a letter. Maybe she did get a bit confused, thinking it was here, but I think it's just the lines of her past and present becoming blurred.'

'She told you who William was?'

'Not quite, just that he'd written her a letter, and she told me what she remembered of it. We're going to chat again tomorrow, so she can tell me more.'

'As long as you're not indulging her illusions.'

'Mum, you should have seen the way she was smiling as she spoke about the past.' Olivia's eyes glanced to her grandma, her eyes now closed and her chest rising slowly and rhythmically. 'I think, illusion or not, it is good for her. And who knows what new information I'll hear to include in my book.'

Diana rubbed her daughter's arm. 'Yes, you're right. If she's happy, that's the main thing.'

Yes. Her grandmother deserved the happiest of happy endings. Come to think if it, so did she. Somehow, it was time to start hoping for, or creating, a few memories of her own.

CHAPTER SIX

Joel took one more look around the room to check that everything was ready. Tuesday night had arrived so quickly. All places had been booked, and he was glad Olivia had decided to make time to do the course.

He sat on the edge of the desk in the community hall and tapped his feet on the floor, and his fingers either side of his hips on the desk. Quiet. Stillness. Except for the faint hum of the ocean behind the building. The overhead fluorescent lights made him blink a few times, and he wished there was a dimmer switch. Artificial light was always too bright for him. And it reminded him of the sharp intrusion of light waking him up in hospital, when before he'd had only the company of stars and moonlight.

The door creaked open. A well-built man entered, he closed the door behind him and offered a brief smile. 'Hey, how's it goin'?'

'Hey, mate, come on in. I'm Joel.' He met him halfway and held out his hand. 'Welcome to the course.'

'Zac,' he replied, withdrawing his hand after a brief shake then sliding his hands into his pockets.

'So have you started writing a book?'

'Not exactly. Poems, mostly. But they'll be included.'

'Yeah? So what's your book about? What's your story?' Joel caught a glimpse of a tattoo poking out from under the top of his shirt, noticed his cautious stance; a calm yet alert posture. Maybe he was another adventurer, but he didn't have that jumpiness, that fidgety nature that he himself embodied.

'My time in Afghanistan. But mostly the time after that.'

'Oh wow, I bet you have some intense stories to tell.'

'You could say that.'

'And so it focuses on your transition back to...'

'Civilisation? The land of the living?' He chuckled. 'Yeah. But the transition took longer than I thought, I was lost for a long time.' His eyes widened suddenly and he snapped his fingers. 'Oh!' He plucked his phone from his pocket and thumbed in something. '*Lost in Transition.* Another potential title.'

Joel gave a nod. 'Huh. Cool. I like it.'

'Although it may not convey the true theme of the story. Hmm. I'll think on it.'

'We'll be going through the importance of titles during the course.' Joel leant on one of the tables. 'So, what's the true theme of the story? What happened during your transition, can I ask?'

Zac's chest rose high with an intake of breath. On his exhalation, it seemed he was about to speak when the door creaked open again and he turned his head to look.

'Good evening, gentlemen.' A man about mid-sixties tipped and then removed his black velvet beret as he entered. 'Mr Gregory Donovan, here to unveil my masterpiece with the help of one esteemed author.' He held out his hand to Joel, and he shook it firmly.

'Nice to meet you, Mr Donovan,' Joel said with a grin. He

could already tell this man would add some life and colour to the class.

'Call me Gregory. Actually, just Greg will be dandy, thank you.'

'Greg it is.'

Greg turned to Zac and offered his hand also. Joel noticed that Zac had waited for him to initiate an introduction. After they had finished their introductions, Zac took a step back, his hands back in his pockets.

'The lovely young Miss Chevalier recommended your course to me last week,' Greg said. 'Went into Mrs May's to buy a thriller and update her on my latest shenanigans, came out with a brochure and a book idea. Smart girl, that Olivia.'

'Indeed. And she'll be joining us tonight as well.'

'Yes, she mentioned. I think it's great she's honouring her grandmother in this way. May is as much a part of my history as she is hers.'

'Oh?' Joel wondered just how much Mrs May had impacted the lives of other locals.

'When my kids were young they would join her Saturday story time in the store, and they loved it. Still, to this day, they remember how much they enjoyed it and how Mrs May took them to a magical world with their imaginations.'

'She does sound like an amazing person.'

The door opened again. 'Thank you,' said a middle-aged woman, as a teenager or young man, perhaps around nineteen or twenty, held the door open for her, then followed her in, his gait favouring his left side.

'Hello and welcome,' said Joel.

'Awesome to meet you, bro.' The young guy took his hand and gave him one of those special trendy handshakes that were more like a grab. He was surprised he didn't clap a hand on his back. 'Dylan.'

'Hey, Dylan, awesome to meet you too.' He shifted his focus to the woman who was holding on to her bag's shoulder strap for dear life. 'And you must be Maribella?'

She nodded. 'How did you know?'

'You're one of only two women in tonight's class, and I already know what the other one looks like.' He recalled Olivia's cute face and her cautious, almost fearful eyes. 'In stark contrast to my Wednesday night class, which has only three men.'

'Maybe I booked in for the wrong night then, hey?' said Dylan with a laugh. He then turned to Maribella. 'Oh, no offence, I mean I just thought maybe the other class might have some girls my age. Not that you're old or anything. Just. Ah crap, sorry.' He shook his head. Maribella waved away his concerns with her hand. 'See? This is why I need a course. I need to learn how to say things right.'

'Or write things right,' Joel suggested.

'Yeah, that.' He sat on the edge of one of the small desks.

Two more people came in, a thirty-something man in a business suit, and a man about a decade older, in relaxed clothing that suggested he was about ready for bed.

After a few introductions and a bit of small talk, he gave everyone a sticky nametag and got them to write their name on it, and encouraged everyone to grab a desk. Dylan literally grabbed one, his hands gripping the edges. 'Sorry, man, couldn't resist.' He chuckled and so did Joel. Maybe he would add some life and colour to this group too.

Joel made his way to the whiteboard, repositioned it, and switched on his projector, the light shining brighter than the fluorescents.

'Want me to...' Mr Donovan, Greg, said, gesturing to the main light switch.

'That'd be great, mate.'

'I know where everything is in here, been to hundreds of community events over the years, even put on a few myself.'

'Well, if I have any issues I know who to call on for help.'

'Anything you need, buddy, anything at all, I'm happy to help.'

Joel nodded with a smile.

The door creaked. 'Sorry I'm late!' Olivia bustled in with a laptop bag over her shoulder, underneath a handbag, her body tilting to the side. 'Good intentions, but...' She shrugged, then her cheeks went pink as she glanced at all the faces eyeing her. She nodded at Dylan, gave a small wave to Zac, and a big smile to Greg. Small town indeed.

'No problem, we were just about to get started actually. Mr Donovan here, was–'

'Greg,' he corrected.

'Greg was telling us about all the events he's been to in here.'

'Been talking your ear off, has he?' She winked in Greg's direction. 'How are you doing, Mr Donovan?'

'Fine and dandy, my dear. Fine and dandy.'

Joel stepped forward. 'Hang on, let me get this straight... I've just met you and I can call you Greg, but Olivia has to call you Mr Donovan?'

The old man chuckled. 'I've tried, but she refuses to call me anything else.'

Olivia shrugged again. 'He used to teach at my school when I was a teenager. I can't think of him as any other name except Mr Donovan.'

'Ah, gotcha.' Joel angled his head, his gaze still on her. 'Maybe I should have you all call me Mr Foster.'

Dylan laughed, a sharp, short explosion. 'Sure thing, Mr Foster.'

Joel shrugged. 'Sorry, couldn't resist.' They exchanged a

smile. Dylan reminded Joel of himself when he was younger. Loved joking around, milking every class at school for all the fun he could have with it.

'Back in my day–' said Greg.

'Ah, stop right there,' said Olivia, her hand in the air. 'Joel, I mean, Mr Foster,' she said in a fake serious tone, 'sorry to interrupt, but as soon as you hear him say "back in my day", you either have to stop him in his tracks or prepare to settle in for a long conversational adventure.'

'Hmm,' said Joel, rubbing the stubble on his jaw. 'Personally, I'm one for adventure. But we do have to get this class rolling so those who need to leave at the allocated finish time can get home to their families. However, I'd be more than happy for a chinwag after the class if anyone wishes to discuss anything further.'

'If I can stay awake,' said Greg, 'you've got yourself a deal.' He nodded.

Joel logged into his laptop and launched the slideshow. 'Just a few happy snaps from my adventures, to give you some background of where I've been, where I've come from, and what I went through.' The pictures faded in and out, much like his consciousness had done that challenging day, and then the next, until he'd promised himself he'd take one more breath. But that one became another, and another, until every breath was potentially his last. But that single mantra – *one more breath* – was what had kept him going. If he could take one more, then he could take another, and that was how he'd gotten through it. The pictures of him in hospital appeared on screen too, and he spoke a bit about his recovery. 'So in a nutshell, that is how a seemingly ordinary person's life and travels can become a story. Not that you have to go through a life-threatening situation to have a story to tell. I don't recommend that if you can help it.'

Some of the class chuckled.

'So before we get into the nitty-gritty of how to write your story, if you feel comfortable sharing with the group what you will be writing about, that would be great. Nothing detailed, just a few words.' He looked purposefully at Greg.

'Don't you worry, Mr Foster.'

'Joel.'

'Joel, I promise to keep it to three minutes maximum.' He winked.

'Three minutes?'

'Yes, that way we will be done in around twenty-four minutes.'

'Around twenty-four?' asked Olivia. 'I don't recall in our mathematics lessons being allowed to answer questions with the word "around", we had to be exact.'

'Ah yes, you are correct. In that case, we would have...' He appeared to calculate in his head. 'How about you tell me, Olivia? What is the answer?'

Olivia sighed. 'Oops, what did I get myself into?'

'Maths wasn't my forte either,' Joel said.

She widened her eyes. 'I didn't say it wasn't my forte.'

'Neither did I.'

'You said either, meaning that as well as not being yours, it also wasn't the person's you were speaking to.'

'And let me guess, English was one of your best subjects?' he asked.

She sat up straight. 'Of course.' She smiled, then cleared her throat. 'Mr Foster.'

He wanted to continue this banter but needed to get on with the class. He was surprised that her usual slightly shy demeanour had somehow disappeared tonight, and was replaced with an unusual slightly goody-two-shoes confidence.

'I'll start,' Zac spoke. Interesting... Joel hadn't expected him to want to initiate the book summaries. But their chat had been interrupted earlier when Greg had arrived.

He glanced at Olivia. 'Olivia already knows about my book, but if I don't go first and get it over with, I may not get the words out. I'm still getting used to speaking openly about it.'

'Go ahead,' said Joel, sitting on the edge of his desk again.

'Long story short. Ex-soldier, served in Afghanistan. Lost a best mate. Came home and drank too much. Recovering alcoholic now. Also recovering from agoraphobia.'

Wow. That made sense.

'So I hope to be able to help others going through addictions, or mental illness, or those who've served their country.'

Greg clapped, and Dylan joined in, soon others were giving him a round of applause.

Zac lowered his gaze with a bashful smile and held up his hand to halt any further applause.

Joel glanced at Olivia, who hadn't clapped for Zac, but assumed she already knew his story. 'Olivia?'

'Well, some of you probably already know by now that I'm writing about Mrs May – my grandmother who set up the bookstore I now run. So it's a bit different in that I'm writing on behalf of someone else.' She tucked a chunk of caramel-tinted hair behind her hair, and her small earring glimmered.

'That's a great idea,' said Maribella. 'I wish someone would write mine for me, save me some time!'

Olivia smiled. 'Who knows, maybe I'll start a trend.'

'What about your own life?' asked Dylan. 'Do you have any stories to tell of your own?'

Olivia shifted in her seat. 'Um, not really.' She did that hair-tuck thing again. 'I don't have any... book-worthy moments,' she said. 'Unless single parenthood counts, but I don't think anything I have to say on the matter would fill a whole book.'

'Didn't you say your daughter asks a lot of questions?' asked Greg. 'When we were chatting the other day?'

Olivia tapped her chin with a pen. 'Ah yes, I did. When I said she talks almost as much as you.' She winked.

'There you go. Fill a book with her questions.'

'And the answers? I'm still working a lot of them out!' She chuckled. 'Sadly, parenthood doesn't come with instant genius status. Thank goodness for Google is all I can say.'

'Hear, hear,' said Maribella.

The rest of the class spoke about their book ideas and a bit about their life. Dylan had been bitten by a shark (which he'd said wasn't the most awesome thing to have happened) and had shot to instant fame in the local area because of his bravery and amazing recovery (which he'd said was a lot more awesome than the shark attack). Maribella was writing about her experience overcoming illness and depression, Greg's ideas were a bit all over the place but revolved around his life in general as a teacher and then raising a disabled son, and Simon and Gavin (who Greg had decided to nickname Simon and Garfunkel) were joining forces writing about their entrepreneurial experience – the pyjama guy apparently was the internet tech expert who stayed home and the business-suited guy went out into the 'field' as they called it.

'They all sound like great stories,' Joel said, standing from the edge of the desk and switching his PowerPoint presentation back on. 'Now it's time to show you how to get them from your head onto the screen, and eventually into a book.'

'One question,' Greg said after he cleared his throat.

Joel turned to face the old man. 'Sure.'

'Will your book have a sequel?' he asked. 'It's a riveting read, if I may say so. And that ending... sounds like it's not quite the end of your adventures.'

Joel thought back to writing that last line. It was an ending without being an ending. He didn't like endings. They symbolised stopping, and he didn't like to stop for long. 'It's definitely not the end, my friend. Not in the least.' He smiled at the man, then began his introduction on how to hook a reader and draw them in with a great premise, all the while feeling his eyes wandering back to Olivia's glimmering earring and wondering how this ordinary yet somehow extraordinary woman, was hooking *him* and drawing him in.

CHAPTER SEVEN

'I'll unpack that if you like,' said Marcus, as Olivia took the large box of books into the storeroom.

'Thanks but I'm good.' She placed the box down on the floor and ripped off the tape, then turned to see through the doorway that Mr Donovan had entered the store.

'Ah,' she whispered to Marcus. 'You just don't want to get your ears talked off by you know who.' She tilted her head.

Marcus leaned in. 'Seriously, Liv, the man's a walking voice box.' He turned briefly to make sure his words weren't audible. 'Last time, he got talking about how his nephew had contracted some gross infection and that all young men such as myself should get checked out at regular intervals. He even offered to show me some...' he gulped, 'photos. For education's sake.' He feigned throwing up.

Olivia shook her head. 'Well, *have* you been checked?' He feigned puking again, and she winked. 'Go unpack that delivery, I'll be at the counter if you need me.'

He placed his hands together in prayer, mouthed 'thank you', and she went into the store. 'Mr Donovan, how did you enjoy last night's class?'

'Was an absolute delight,' he said. 'I am filled to the brim with inspiration, hence my visit on this fine and dandy day.'

'Yeah? That's great.' She went behind the counter.

He wandered to the memoir section. 'Going to have a look at what's in the market. Joel said to research those "hook" thingamajigs he talked about, so that I can find out what mine could be.'

Olivia nodded. 'Good idea. I'm still trying to clarify mine, though I have a basic idea.' She thought back to her lunch with Joel last Friday and found a little shimmer of anticipation building inside at their next lunch in two days.

'Got some space on these shelves,' Mr Donovan said. 'Making symbolic room for all of our fabulous memoirs to grace the shelves soon, eh?' He chuckled.

'Not yet.' She walked over to meet him there. 'Making room for Joel's book. Just got a delivery of them. We might even do a window display for him while he's visiting town, thank him for being here to help teach us all.'

'Grand idea,' the man said, turning to face the front window. 'I can see a big cardboard mountain – I can paint it if you like, quite handy with a paintbrush, if I do say so myself – and the books hanging from the edge or something.' He held his hands out as though to create the scene better in his mind.

Olivia grinned. 'You looking for a part-time job?'

'You got one?'

'Not really, sorry.' She patted his arm. 'But thank you for the inspiration.' Olivia peered beyond the storeroom door. 'Need a hand with some of those books, Marcus?'

'Um. Nope. All good,' he called out. 'Just um... making sure, um...'

'Just bring some out so we can fill these empty shelves,' she instructed. 'Mr Donovan was just talking about window displays and I know you love window displays, you two could collaborate while I check some things on my computer.' She walked with her chin high and a smug grin on her face, as Marcus emerged with a forced smile on his, a pile of books in his hands. She took one from the top to the counter, and sat on the stool behind the computer. After checking some messages and her Facebook business page, she looked at the tagline on the cover of Joel's book.

When a man's greatest adventure becomes his worst nightmare, he discovers that challenging his mental limits will become his most daring adventure yet...

While Marcus and Mr Donovan continued discussing the merits of various treatments he was trying for indigestion, she read the first page, then flipped to the contents, most chapters named after a song title. Apparently he liked to sing to himself while travelling and hiking, so each had a special meaning and related to various events in each chapter. Clever.

She couldn't help herself, she skipped ahead to the chapter titled *Lost in the Echo* and started reading...

The pain. Oh God, the pain. I'd had pain before, but this was different. I knew I had hurt myself pretty badly, because not only was there pain, but a deep, sharp, icy shiver inside my leg as cold wind whipped at the exposed bone through my torn muscle.

It was all consuming.

I forgot where I was.

I was lost in the echo of my own scream, and no one could hear me.

'Huh?' Olivia looked up, as Mr Donovan placed a book on the counter and said something.

'Good read, isn't it,' he said, gesturing to *One More Breath*.

She gave a slow nod. 'I've only read a small bit so far, but...'

'It has you "hooked", right?'

Olivia smiled. Oh yes. Oh yes, indeed. And now there were two stories she wanted to know more about. The other one would hopefully have its next chapter revealed in about six hours from now when she visited Mrs May, and she couldn't wait.

After Olivia answered Mia's question on the drive to the nursing home about whether animals have thoughts like humans do ('yes I think so, but not as deep'), her mind wandered to Mrs May's words last Sunday...

May's Memories of Fresh Crusty Bread and Gaping Wide Grins

The bell jingled when I entered the general store the next day and Mrs Lambert smiled at me from behind the counter where she was arranging a tray of cookies. 'Fancy one, dear?' she asked.

I shook my head and held up my shopping list, which also included our small family budget noted discreetly at the top to remind me not to go overboard.

Mrs Lambert tipped her head back slightly in apparent understanding. 'No charge,' she said. 'New recipe, I'd love to have some feedback.' She held out her hand and I gratefully accepted the cookie, saying 'thank you' about three or four times. I bit into the chunky, warm, delightful texture of nuts and raisins, chewing and relishing the sweet and savoury combination. 'Delicious,' I said as soon as I swallowed my first bite. 'Thank you again.' She waved her hand like it was no trouble. I would have bought the whole tray-full if we could have afforded it. And I probably would have eaten them all on the way home and never even told mother. I smiled to myself as I turned to face the shelves. But I wouldn't. There was no room for greed in these times.

I picked some cans of beans off the shelf and put them in my basket, followed by spaghetti, potatoes, onions, tomatoes, flour, and butter.

'Some bread, Miss May?'

I turned towards the owner of the warm, masculine voice, who held some fresh loaves in his arms like he was carrying firewood.

'William, it is polite to address a young lady with her surname, not "Miss" followed by her first name.' Mrs Lambert shook her head as she scolded her nephew.

'Sorry, I–'

'It's fine,' I said. 'Miss May is perfectly lovely.' I smiled. Demurely.

William smiled. Non-demurely.

He wasn't traditionally handsome. His sandy hair sat atop his head much like a haystack in a barn, all messy and haphazard, but it suited him. His blue eyes stood out and glimmered like tiny sapphires or diamonds, which was a silly way to describe a young man's eyes, but that's the only way I could think to do so.

'And thank you, but I won't require any bread at the moment. It is more economic to make our own.'

He nodded, and saliva swirled in my mouth at the delicious aroma of the freshly baked bread, wishing I could bite straight into it like I had the cookie.

I took my groceries to the counter and William plonked the bread on the linen tablecloth that hung over one corner. 'I'll handle this, Aunt Anna.'

She gave a nod. 'I'll be out back unpacking those tea chests if you need me,' she said.

William's hair fell over one of his eyes and he pushed it

back, then he glanced behind him towards the storeroom. When his gaze returned to me, he leaned over the counter. 'Here,' he whispered, handing me one of the loaves of bread. 'New recipe. I'd love to have some feedback.' He winked.

My mouth opened in surprise. 'It's okay,' I said. 'You don't have to do that.' I checked my list and the running tally I had jotted down. I had a small amount of money left over, but not enough for the bread.

'Consider it a gift.' He placed it in my shopping basket.

'Your aunt already gave me a gift.' I gestured to the cookie tray.

'This gift is from me. Out of my pocket. Don't worry, you won't be leaving the store short.' He took some coins from his pocket and placed them in the cash register.

I peered towards the storeroom but Mrs Lambert didn't appear to have overheard our conversation. 'Are you sure?' I asked.

He nodded, and started adding up my other items, placing them back in the basket.

'It looks delicious. Lovely and crusty,' I remarked.

And then something rather humorous and somewhat magical happened... We both spoke very similar words at the same time.

'It might make my hair curly,' I said.

'It might give you curly hair,' he said.

And then he stopped what he was doing and looked at me, and I stayed still and looked at him, and then a very un-demure gaping wide grin exploded onto my face, as it did on his. Not only that, but I laughed. An un-demure, un-ladylike, sudden burst of laughter.

I instinctively touched my hair that had been artificially curled with rollers and bobby pins.

'I hope it doesn't give me curly hair,' William said. 'My hair is chaotic enough as it is!'

I laughed again.

'Have a sensational afternoon, Miss May,' William said as I picked up my basket and headed towards the door.

'Likewise.' The bell jingled as I pushed open the door, and so did something inside my belly. At least, it felt like a jingle would feel. Light and fluttery and bubbly and sweet.

But as I walked past the tailor's shop on my way back home, and Jacques smiled at me with a small wave, and I smiled back (demurely), I remembered the letter, and the jingle subsided and my heart swelled.

The next day, my heart swelled even more when I received the second letter, up until that terrible moment when my heart plummeted to the pit of my stomach.

'Okay, Grandma, what happened next? Last time I was here you told me about William and the bread, and you said something about the terrible day that followed. What happened?' Olivia settled in the chair next to Mrs May's bed, her phone recorder at the ready, as Mia had stuck her latest drawing up on the wall with Blu Tack and plugged her EarPods in, ready to draw another.

Mrs May had become tired after reaching that point in the story, and Olivia figured that discussing a 'terrible day' could make her more tired and she didn't want to overwhelm her all at once, so she'd decided to leave it until today.

'Oh yes.' Furrows developed within the permanent furrows in between Mrs May's eyebrows. 'I'll never forget it. How my heart went from elated to devastated in an instant.'

'Tell me.' Olivia lightly stroked her grandmother's hand.

May's Memories of Loss

Mother stood at the stove, steam rising up and fogging her glasses as she tipped the white beans into the potato soup and stirred. She wiped at her brow. 'Are you unwell, Mother?' I asked, noticing the paleness of her complexion despite the steam, yet a light film of sweat dampening her shirt.

'I think I may be coming down with something. I'll get this soup finished and then I'll take some rest.'

'I can finish it, if you like?' I approached the stove.

'No, that's not necessary, darling, it won't take much longer. You go collect the mail and freshen up those plants outside with some water.'

I nodded as she took a cloth and wiped her brow with it, then slung it over her shoulder.

I scurried outside, wondering if it would be too soon to have received another letter. There were three envelopes, and the third was addressed to me. With no one around, I flashed a gaping wide grin for my own pleasure, and didn't even bother going back inside to open it in private, but simply ripped open the envelope, my eyes hungry for the words...

Dear Marvellous May,

So it appears you are magnificent AND marvellous! I hope this letter brings a smile to your face. It brings a smile to mine by simply writing it. I wish I could see you right now, watch your eyes scanning the words on the paper, see your lips curving upwards. But I have a good imagination and I will settle for imagining it. Just as I imagine other things. Other things we could do together. One day, perhaps.

Have you ever watched the sunset over the ocean from way up in the hills? People think it's beautiful to watch it from the beach, or the harbour, but sometimes a sunset is best viewed from far back, because then you get the whole picture. The panoramic artwork that is the sky.

Hmm. Not bad. My letter writing is improving, I think. Do you think?

I've even wondered if I could try my hand at painting the sunset. I believe in giving things a go. Sometimes you never know what could happen until you try.

You seem like such a hard-working young woman, going about your daily chores and helping your family. I admire you. Yes, I think you're beautiful, but even more beautiful is your heart, and your dedication.

Oh, if only I could be so lucky as to have your heart, and your dedication. I would not need to watch the sunset then, because I would see something much more beautiful every day that I look into your eyes.

Until next time,

Me.

My hand trembled as it held the letter and I read it a second time. My heart was no longer swelling, it was pulsing, pounding, urgently wanting to jump out and embrace those *words if it could do such a thing. Oh I wish he would ask me on a date. I would say yes! Perhaps I could write him a letter back, discreetly fold it in a pair of father's trousers that might require some expert tailoring by Jacques' father, instead of my basic sewing skills.*

I pondered what I would say, and as my mind concentrated deeply, I didn't really pay attention to the clash and clang coming from the house. Mother often made a noise while cooking, so it wasn't uncommon. 'Dear Jovial Jacques,' I giggled, imagining my words on paper. 'I know it is you. And I wish to thank you for such kind words and compliments offered. If you do indeed wish to have adventures with me, or perhaps watch a sunset from up in the hills, I would like to enlighten you to my answer in advance of such an... advance. My answer would be yes. I will await your request, and–'

My thoughts dissipated when a loud whoosh sucked my focus from the paper to our house, and sounds of splintering glass prickled my eardrums. And then the flames. Flickering bright orange and red, and black smoke, came from the side of the house where the kitchen was. In an instant they rose up to the second level of the house.

I dropped the letter and mail onto the ground and ran to the porch, threw open the door and blinked rapidly at the stinging heat and smoke invading my eyes. But the only thing I could think about was Mother. No one else was in the house except her. I rushed straight into the kitchen despite the flames, and found her crawling on the floor near the other side where the flames were yet to reach. Oh thank goodness, I thought, as I had feared for a split second I may find her dead near the stove.

I coughed and could hardly see, but crouched down and grabbed hold of my mother, the one who had given me life, so that I could hopefully save hers.

'May! Get out, go!' she yelled. 'I can hardly move! You go, now! I'll try to catch up.'

'No!' I pulled at her. 'I'm not leaving you.' I put all the strength I could muster into draping her over my shoulder and half-dragging half-carrying her out of the burning-hot kitchen, as flames chased and teased around us. Something exploded nearby, and we fell to the floor at the kitchen entrance. I looked behind to see nothing but thick cloudy red and black smoke, and with that dedication Jacques had spoken about in the letter, I grunted and lifted mother, and stumbled closer and closer to the open door that was now fuelling the fire with the rush of air coming in, but was our only escape.

I kept my eye on that light, and didn't blink despite the smoke until we made it out, stumbling further on the porch and then running and stumbling out onto the lawn. I helped Mother further away from the house until we collapsed on the side of the road. As I watched our family home become engulfed in flames, my heart pounding and my eyes in shock, I looked away, to my left side near the letterbox, where a piece of paper wafted up and danced in the turbulent air around us.

'Oh, Grandma.' Olivia reached up and wiped a tear from Mrs May's eye. 'You don't have to tell me any more. I'm sorry I made you bring that up.'

She sniffed. 'It doesn't matter, dear. Memories are memories.'

'I think I remember you talking briefly about the fire, but I didn't realise how traumatic it must have been. And what caused it? Oh, don't worry. You just rest now.' She leaned over the bed and patted her grandmother's cheek.

'Mum's tea towel, we think,' she said. 'She fell due to illness and the pot was knocked over, the tea towel had been over her shoulder and must have brushed past the flame on the stove.'

'She was lucky you were there. You showed such determination.'

'Anyone would have done the same.' Mrs May licked her lips. 'Water, please?'

Olivia filled a glass and brought it to her grandma's mouth. 'There you go.'

She drank it all.

'I don't know what happened to that letter,' she said through tired breath. 'Once they took us to the doctor and I went back to the wreckage afterwards, it was nowhere to be found. Probably got carried away by the wind and either burnt, or made its way to the ocean.'

'But it stayed in your mind, that's the main thing.'

'Yes indeed,' she whispered. 'Memories stay, no matter if they are beautiful or difficult. If only we could choose to keep just the good ones.'

Olivia nodded with a bittersweet smile as she stroked her grandma's hand while she fell asleep, then gathered her daughter's art materials and they made their way back to the car to drive home, knowing how lucky she was to have a home to go to, and a daughter to tuck into her bed.

CHAPTER EIGHT

ater that night, Olivia woke from a nightmare and didn't want to go back to sleep. She picked up Joel's book from her bedside table and read some more, this time from the beginning. Forty-five minutes later she was still reading when a yawn erupted and didn't seem able to stretch wide enough to relieve her tiredness. Without thinking, she got out her phone and texted Joel... he didn't have kids so would probably have his phone turned off each night like her other single and non-parent friends did. She knew she could always text April in the middle of the night and not disturb her, and often, late at night or during the occasional night-waking episodes were the only times she got a chance to be sociable, and it was usually when thoughts of things to say appeared, so she just went with it.

> Hi, really enjoying your book so far. Not that one should enjoy reading about what you went through, but you know what I mean. I hope. It's well written and interesting. Nice work – Olivia.

She placed a bookmark in chapter five and put the book

under her alarm clock, which she groaned at when she saw the time. *So much for a good night's sleep.*

Her phone lit up and vibrated with a low-volume ping.

She squinted at the screen.

> Can't sleep? I had a nap before my Wednesday night class, bad idea. Still awake. Obviously. Extra coffee for me tomorrow. Thanks for your feedback. Glad you are enjoying the book. See you Friday… I'm thinking nachos?

Well, well, well. At least she didn't wake him up. But if she did, served him right for keeping his phone on.

> Nachos? Do you want me to work my way through all the unhealthiest and fattiest things on the menu before I'm allowed to revert to my usual chicken salad or soup?

> Something new each week, remember. Our deal. I also have another idea, a new challenge for you…

> And that would be?

> I'll tell you on Friday.

He replied with a wink emoji.

Olivia hated surprises, and she hated challenges. But for some reason she was looking forward to finding out what this one was.

As she walked along the main street and the crisp ocean breeze cooled her skin, Olivia flicked one end of her scarf around her neck. Winter was coming, and she couldn't be happier. Cosy nights snuggling with a blanket and a good book on the couch after Mia went to bed, a warm cup of tea, and some chocolate – perfect. But nights these days were spent organising her notes for her grandma's book, so she didn't know when she would have much time for relaxing, except in the few minutes before sleep claimed her at bedtime. But she did need to finish reading Joel's book, and wanted to do so as soon as possible so that she could understand more about his experience and why his book was such a hit.

She waved to the short and sweet woman at the chemist as she walked past, who had provided her with much medical advice over the years for Mia. She nodded a hello at the hairy guy who owned the takeaway shop, who had provided occasional emergency meals when she couldn't be bothered cooking after a busy day at work. And she smiled at Jonah when she arrived at Café Lagoon, who despite having provided her with countless coffees, teas, cakes, and delicious healthy meals, was about to provide her with *something new* at Joel's request.

'Burger?' he asked when she approached the counter, noticing that Joel wasn't there yet.

'Not today,' she replied. 'I'll just have the, ah...' She perused the blackboard menu. 'Um... nachos,' she said with a clearing of her throat.

'Say again?' he asked.

'Nachos,' she spoke louder.

'Nachos? Wow, you really are going out of your comfort zone, Olivia.'

Her face warmed, despite the chill in the air. She didn't know why she sometimes got embarrassed or nervous for no reason. Maybe that was why she didn't often stray from her routine or way of doing things. It was safe and comfortable to stay the same, to keep the status quo.

'Make that two nachos, extra sour cream please, mate.'

Olivia turned her head and her gaze crashed into Joel's chest, well-used muscles giving shape to his snug-fitting top. She glanced up and met his ocean-blue eyes, and was reminded of Mrs May's description of William's being like blue diamonds. Joel's weren't as bright as that, they were deeper and darker in parts, a few flecks marking the lighter blue strands, giving a depth to his gaze as he smiled at her.

'Not for me,' Olivia said to Jonah. 'I mean, just the normal amount of sour cream. Not extra. Thanks.' Her scarf end fell across her chest and she flicked it back over her shoulder, accidentally flicking Joel's face on the way. 'Oops, sorry.'

He flinched a little with an amused smile. 'Which table shall we sit at today, somewhere different?' He gestured to one near the front.

'Too cold,' she said.

He shrugged. 'Lucky you have that scarf then.' He accepted the table number from Jonah and took it to the table near the front, which had a nice view of Miracle Park across the road, and the beach and ocean on the horizon. 'Nachos will warm you up.' He pulled back the chair for her.

'You don't have to do that,' she said. 'Pull the chair out, I mean.'

'Too late. Anyway, don't men in books do things like that?'

'Depends what books you're talking about. In many books,' she leaned closer to him, as though about to share a long-held secret, 'women actually pull their *own* chairs out for themselves.' She feigned a gasp.

'Ha, I bet they do.' He pushed her chair back in. 'Go on then.' He waited for her to pull her chair out and sit, then sat down himself. 'Well, my gentlemanly gesture was going to be the segue to my new challenge I have for you, but I'll have to think of something else now...' He tapped at his chin.

'Oh?' she said. 'In that case, my apologies. Please do think of something else.' She twisted her lips into a curious smile.

His eyes went distant for a few moments, and then they brightened, not quite to 'diamond' status but to 'ocean on a sunny day' status. 'Right then,' he said, clearing his throat and pushing his chair back to stand.

Had he had enough and was going to leave her here to eat two plates of nachos on her own?

Was he simply going to order another 'something new' for her?

Was he about to...

Oh. Huh?

Joel crouched down onto one knee. She noticed him wince slightly but then he settled into his rather strange position like he was going to tie his shoelaces, or...

'Olivia Chevalier,' he said, taking her hand in his and looking up into her eyes with sincerity. 'Will you...'

What the hell? Her eyes bulged and she glanced around at the customers in the café, who were smiling and pointing. *What the hell?*

'Will you...'

'Say yes!' someone called out.

Her heart pumped fast and her cheeks flushed.

'Will you... please help me up?' He grasped her hand firmly and made a show of pretending to try to stand.

She released her hand from his and covered her face. 'Oh you, ha-ha, very funny.'

He stood and grinned.

'You said no?' the person called out. 'Why? A perfectly acceptable bloke gets on his knee in public to propose and you don't have the decency to say yes?'

Joel faced the customer. 'Not to worry, she just needs to think about it.'

'No, no, I don't need to think,' she said to the customer. 'I, he was just...'

'Tying my shoelaces,' Joel said.

'That was *so* embarrassing,' she whispered through gritted teeth as he took his seat opposite her again.

He chuckled.

'And what does that have to do with this challenge thing anyway?' she asked, waving her hand about in circles.

'Would you say a proposal like that would be something book-worthy?'

She narrowed her gaze. 'Possibly. I mean, in the right type of book. But it's a bit predictable. And I would have to actually know the person a bit better before accepting their offer to spend the rest of my life with them.'

'But for a brief moment, you felt something... different, right? Something a little exciting?'

'Embarrassing, yes, exciting, no.'

'You know what I mean.'

'Well I didn't expect to sit down for lunch and have a guy get on one knee, that's for sure.'

'Then my work here is done.'

She questioned him with her gaze.

'Consider that an example of a book-worthy moment.'

'And your point is...'

'I was thinking about what you said at class the other night, that you don't think you have any *book-worthy moments* in your life.' He made quotation marks with his fingers. 'Look, I like to teach people to not only write about their lives, but to live them. And whether you like it or not, I am going to help you, my dear, to have a few book-worthy moments of your own.'

Okay, she had to admit, now it was getting interesting, though her cheeks were still hot. 'That does sound rather intriguing, but what do you mean exactly? You're just going to surprise me with random things like fake marriage proposals and whatnot, to add some excitement to my boring, predictable life?'

'No, we're going to make a list. Like a bucket list, but a book-worthy moments list. If you were writing your memoir, what things could you say that you'd done? What adventures would you have had? What new experiences would make for interesting reading, or at least interesting living? What memories do you want to make this May, Olivia?'

She thought about it for a few moments, then Jonah brought their meals over. 'Nachos for the happy couple.' He winked. 'Extra sour cream for the groom.'

'Oh, stop.' Olivia chuckled and gave Jonah a friendly punch on the arm.

She started eating, half because she was hungry and it was lunchtime, and half because she wanted to avoid answering his questions.

'So, anything you haven't done that you would like to?'

She crunched into a corn chip and wiped a bit of sour cream from her lip. 'Nope. Just write my grandma's book and give my daughter a good life.'

'Apart from that.' He held up his hand when she went to speak. 'Wait, I know, you don't have time, right?'

She shrugged. 'Pretty much, but it depends what kind of activities you're talking about. The fake marriage proposal didn't take much time so anything of similar duration should be fine.' She flashed a cheeky smile. 'Oh!' She held up her fork. 'I'm reading your book. Does that count as something new?'

'Hmm, it could. Okay, let's count that as item number one. Purely for research purposes and as an example.'

'Of course. Okay, I will try and finish it over the weekend.' She ate another mouthful. 'And how many items are supposed to be on this list?'

'One for each week of the course? Book makes one, so we need five more.'

'I can't really think of anything, it depends what sort of book, like if it was a crime novel, I don't exactly wish to have the book-worthy moment of finding a dead body.'

He laughed. 'Of course not, but... what makes a crime novel exciting? The mystery, the suspense.'

'So I need to find something to do that is mysterious and suspenseful.'

'Like...' He tapped his fingers on the table. 'Some sort of treasure hunt.'

'And where or how would I find or take part in a treasure hunt?'

Joel rubbed his chin. 'I will just have to make you one.'

Olivia laughed. 'You will *make* me a treasure hunt?'

He held out his hands. 'Why not? It'll be fun.' He grinned. 'Oh, and the treasure hunt can lead to another book-worthy moment, which will have to be a surprise, so you'll have to trust me.'

She shifted in her seat and took a sip of water. This was getting a bit too far out of her comfort zone. 'Um, I would rather know exactly what I am agreeing to before I agree to anything.'

'I understand, but part of having an adventure is not always knowing what's around the corner.'

'How about we think up some things I do know about and will agree to, and then I'll consider letting you do the treasure hunt and surprise.' That was about as much as she could do.

'Fair enough. Do you get out of town much?'

'Only if I have an appointment, or need to do some major shopping, or something for Mia.'

'No holidays?'

She shook her head. 'Not really, we just do various fun things in the school holidays.'

'So you don't ever just grab a tent and camp somewhere nearby under the stars, ponder life, have some nature time?'

She laughed. 'We go to the beach and play in the sand and water, go to the park, but camping? Why sleep on the ground when I can sleep in my bed and have electricity and bathroom facilities?'

'But you've been camping, right? I mean, everyone's been camping at least once.'

Olivia gave a feeble shake of her head.

Joel's eyes bulged. 'Never? Wow.' He got out his phone and tapped something into it.

'What are you doing?' She peered across the table at the notes app on his phone.

'Camping, item number two.'

She stiffened. 'Oh hang on, I have to agree to the things on the list.'

'Yeah, but you've never been camping? It's like a rite of passage for human beings. It's non-negotiable, my dear, you are going camping.'

She wriggled in her chair and adjusted her scarf. 'But Mia, she would have to come, or stay with my mum, and she already looks after her a lot. And I can't go on my own, there could be serial-killer campers around, and also – animals, and creatures, and bugs.'

'So take a friend. Unless you want me to join you?' He smirked.

'Certainly not,' she remarked.

'I've been looking around the nearby areas, and there's a great camping spot up in the hills, there's an area that's targeted at families and they check and scan all campers' IDs before allowing them to set up, so it's safe, and they also have good bathroom facilities so it's not like you're completely on your own there.'

'It's May. It'll be cold.'

'Go in June.' He chuckled.

She shook her head at him. 'It'll be *colder.*'

'Exactly. More adventurous. Bring your onesie or some kind of warm sleepwear.'

'What makes you think I own a onesie?'

'Do you?'

'Definitely not. Oh wait, maybe I could buy one, and that could be something new for my list.'

He shook his head slowly. 'Nice try, book girl.' He dug into more of his nachos.

'Anyway, I can't camp. It would take too much organisation. I don't have time or equipment.'

'I have equipment, you can borrow mine. I'll even come with you to set up the tent, then leave you to enjoy the experience on your own or with Mia or a friend, how about that?'

One night, in nature, secured inside a tent. It couldn't be that bad, could it?

'I'll think about it,' she said.

'How about we make that item number six, so you could do it at the end of the course to celebrate finishing?'

She smiled. 'My idea of celebrating would be having a night off with a friend or two in a cosy restaurant with a nice meal and glass of wine, great conversation, maybe a movie, and then home to snuggle up with a cup of tea and a good book.'

Joel grinned and laughed slowly. 'You are quite the exciting woman, Olivia.'

'Oh, stop. Everyone is different.'

'I know, it's okay. I think it's cute. You're cute.'

Cute? As in charming cute or aesthetically cute? Charming of course, he was talking about behaviour, not appearance. But it made her realise that no guy had ever called her cute before.

She'd been called pretty a few times, and 'nice', but that was about it.

There was a moment of silence when they both chewed on their food and Olivia glanced around the street outside the café. It was fairly quiet with the usual locals wandering about, some children being rushed around by parents, their tiny legs trying to keep up.

'How about we both think of some things you could do, and we can exchange ideas via text later. Then we'll make the list, and it has to be ready by next week's class at the latest.'

'Sounds better, then I can think and not be put on the spot.'

'And also, if you're not keen on doing new and different things, try doing the same things differently.'

She tilted her head. 'How do you mean?'

'Like any of your usual daily tasks, see if you can do anything in a different way than usual.'

'Like with my non-dominant hand or something?' She laughed, then picked up her water glass with her left hand and drank from it, widened her eyes, and gave a smirk of her own.

He gave a little clap. 'Well done. I bet that was hard. But yeah, anything that trains your brain to accept new experiences and new ways of doing things. Give it a try!'

'Okay, mentor. That, I can do.' Now she just had to try to remember and try to be creative in how she did things from now on. Maybe Mia could give her ideas; kids often did things in their own unique way.

After finishing their meal and chatting about the course and her book and what else Tarrin's Bay had to offer, Olivia stood. She went to grab her handbag then paused, a tiny smile forming on her lips. She lifted the bag and hung the strap over her left shoulder, instead of right. It felt weird, like it would fall off. She raised her eyebrows at Joel and flashed an accomplished grin.

'What?' he asked. 'Am I missing something?'

'I just did something *differently*.'

'But what?'

She sauntered past him and smiled. 'See you at class on Tuesday, mentor.'

She left him there at the table with a confused but amused look on his face as he tried to figure out what she'd done. She also realised that she had never really *sauntered* before. So maybe he was right, doing things differently was training her brain to accept new ways of doing things. It was only a small thing, but it was good to saunter instead of scurry. Just what would she do next?

CHAPTER NINE

After a Saturday spent lifting weights at the gym, swimming in the indoor pool outside of town, and catching up with mates online and replying to various messages and emails, Joel grabbed his runners and tied his laces, then locked up the rental caravan where he was staying at the Tarrin's Bay Beachside Cabins and Caravan Park. He attached his phone to the arm strap, put the earphones in, and carried his water bottle towards the beach. Along the way he waved to Emma, who ran the park, as she was exiting the house behind the reception office.

'Nice evening for a run,' she said.

'Perfect,' he replied. The sun was low and bright as it prepared to surrender, the wind cool and crisp.

He walked up to the pathway and followed it towards the end of the park, then lodged his water bottle in a discreet spot near a sand dune. He continued up the path that curved around the headland and along the coastal track that led around the beaches and to the town. He glanced down at the speckled mosaic of sunlight on the ocean surface; his muscles warming up, he broke into a jog, then into a sprint as he went up the hill.

Heat permeated his body and the breeze whooshed past him. He slowed and allowed his heart rate to lower, then sprinted again. After a few rounds of intervals, he changed direction and jogged, walked back to his water bottle, and took several big gulps from it. The sand surrendered beneath him as he sat and rehydrated, the sky turning from shades of blue to a blend of pinks, then deepening to muted reds and orange. He took his phone from his armband and snapped a few photos. He'd seen many sunsets, but they continued to amaze him... how the colours could just appear and mix together so perfectly like an accomplished artist's painting.

He wondered if Olivia took time out of her busy schedule to watch the occasional sunset. He texted and asked her.

Sunsets? Um, not usually on purpose, just if I happen to see one on the way to somewhere or looking out the window.

A sunset is not a backup performance, it's a main act. Come down to the beach and have a look before it disappears.

He remembered the sunset that night he thought it would be his last. It was blurry under his strained vision, but his mind tried to capture it as best as it could, both to distract from the pain and fatigue, but also to have one last good memory.

No time, I'm having a very important discussion with Mia.

Bring her too.

This woman needed to live a life, not a schedule, and kids needed to experience life more organically too.

There was no reply, so he sent her a photo of the sunset.

By the time he'd returned to his caravan, his phone buzzed.

Beautiful, thanks.

He sent a smiley and added:

Important discussion over?

I bloody hope so!

Care to enlighten me?

He waited as the typing bubbles danced on his phone screen.

She asked me how babies are made!

She'd added a shock emoji at the end of the sentence.

He chuckled. And?

I explained it with a computer USB port and a 16-gigabyte memory stick.

He burst out laughing, then replied:

Ha-ha! Hilarious. Cybersex just got a whole lot more technical.

She replied with an emoji in tears of laughter.

Did you make a picture of a baby pop up on the screen when the memory stick was inserted?

No, just a bunch of my book files. But I think
she got the point. At least, she first said 'eww'
then couldn't stop giggling about it. She said
she's not going to do that at all in life and
refuses to have any babies.

This was entertaining. He told her so. And he also mentioned that she had explained the birds and the bees in a very different way than usual, adding to her new experiences list.

After their chat, he opened the internet and looked for options for the next trip he would take after doing his next six-week course further south. *Where to go, where to go?* His foot tapped on the floor in anticipation.

Lead me to a brand new adventure, life, he asked.

And as he knew, when you asked, you very often received.

One more chapter, Olivia said to herself as she read *One More Breath* late that night. And at the end of that one more chapter, she had to read the beginning of the next chapter because there had been a cliffhanger. Not a literal one, though she was sure there would be one at some stage, but an emotional one. The chapter was talking about Joel's earlier life and the impact on his journey as an independent traveller and adventurer.

'Oh God,' she said, her hand covering her mouth. 'Oh, Joel.'

His mother had died when he was seventeen, a victim of domestic violence. His stepfather had been convicted, but it had understandably changed his whole outlook on life, and taught him to grow up more quickly than his mates. Not yet old enough to live out of home, he went to live with an aunt until his eighteenth birthday then got a sales job and lived in a tent until he could afford to move into a share house, beginning his independent life.

She read a bit more...

My mother always stayed. Despite my urging her to move forward, to leave him and go somewhere new, she never listened. She stayed. And staying put was what got her killed.

I knew from that day on that I would never stay anywhere long enough to get hurt by anyone. I would keep moving, for her. A symbolic way of doing what she hadn't had the courage to do. That way, I would always be in control.

I became addicted to starting over in new places, and eventually, to having new adventures and experiences that fuelled my adrenaline. I got used to the excitement and the spontaneity and never feeling bored. It kept me busy and entertained, never allowing any time to stop and think about all that had happened... to stop and feel all that had happened, all over again.

There are always some memories in life we would rather forget.

CHAPTER TEN

W hen Olivia and Mia arrived at the nursing home, they were asked to wait outside with Diana as Mrs May had a procedure done. Olivia told her mother to go and have a break while she spent time with her grandma, and Mia went with her to the nursing home café.

She settled down in the chair. 'How are you doing?'

May nodded and managed a small smile. 'Some days are harder than others, dear.'

'Everything okay?'

She nodded again. 'It's just tiring, being old.' She chuckled a little.

'Are you sure you're okay to talk to me today? Do you want me to leave you to rest?'

'Not at all. I had a nap before the doctor came to do a check-up, while your mother occupied herself with this texting business. I hope that man of hers doesn't let her down. You do know he's younger than her, don't you?'

Olivia nodded. 'Not by much. I think he's been good for her. She's never been fitter anyway!'

'I think she sees how age has taken its toll on me and is trying to resist it as much as possible.'

'Could be true,' she replied.

'And what about you, dear, any younger men in your life?'

Olivia flicked her hand. 'Oh, we don't need to talk about that.'

Mrs May turned her head slightly. 'There is someone, isn't there? You sound different.'

'I do? Do I? I've been doing some things in… different ways, that's all. Trying to get out of the same routine.'

'And what has prompted this change, dear?' Olivia went to speak but her grandma beat her to it. 'A man, correct?'

Olivia's mouth opened in a small gape. 'Well, not really. Sort of. He's not a man in my life, just my writing teacher. For your book.'

'Oh yes, how is that coming along? Did you get all the photos and notes from my old place?'

Olivia nodded. 'I have most of the information, and I'll be speaking with Mum a bit more about those early days, when you were a young mother. So it's just a matter of putting everything in order about your life and business. But what about these new details you've been giving me? Should I include them?'

'The fire, yes, include that. But William? I'm not sure.'

'I won't if you don't want me to. You can just fill me in for your own sake, and mine. It's really very interesting.' She smiled and patted her grandma's hand.

'Then again, Jacques isn't around to read the book, is he? He knew William, of course, it being a small town, but only as an acquaintance. The man who served him sometimes at the general store and did occasional deliveries.'

'And he never knew about the letters?'

'No. I almost asked him outright back then if he was the

writer, but I found out soon enough he wasn't, so I didn't have to. I found a sneakier way to discover the truth.'

'Oh, really? How?' Olivia sat up tall.

Mrs May closed her eyes a few moments. 'Everything started happening so quickly after the fire...'

May's Memories of Surprises

I was filled with loss, but also with relief as Mother received medical care and survived, but her lungs were never the same again. The Chevalier family offered us the downstairs living quarters of their large house to stay in temporarily, until father could find us a new home. That was both wonderful and awkward, as I would sometimes bump into Jacques while in my nightgown when I needed to get a sip of water at night.

William delivered a box of groceries without charge for a few days after the fire to help us all out. If the mail had not yet been brought inside, he would sometimes bring it in too. He was so nice. Though I had heard my mother and Mrs Chevalier discussing how he was one of those 'types' who would probably not amount to anything. I wished they wouldn't speak that way about someone who was being so nice and helpful.

It was on the fourth day after we moved in that Mrs Chevalier handed me the envelope and said, 'Mail for you, love.'

I thought it was sweet that Jacques had written another letter, and had it arrive at his own house with the regular mail, to keep the charade going. He was closing up the tailor's shop at the time the mail was brought in, so I wasn't able to ascertain his reaction to seeing me receive it.

I took it to my room and read...

Dear Miraculous May,

Miraculous, because you survived, and you helped your mother survive. You are an inspiration. Things will get easier, and you will all get back on your feet. Maybe you will end up in an even better house, with fruit trees and chickens and a wide verandah with views to the ocean. Or we could just run off together and live on the road, have great adventures and make our own way.

Oh dear, I appear to be getting ahead of myself. I apologise. Unless... you want that? Of course not, you hardly know me. And you need to be there for your mother. But oh, the visions I can see in my mind as I sit here, a cup of tea in my right hand, the pencil paused above the paper in my left.

You are a strong woman, and I know you are hurting from what happened, but I see how you raise your chin and get on with things. As I said... inspiring. Inspiring, special, unique, and miraculous.

I am going to attempt a poem...

May is sweet.

She's a real treat.

Her eyes are sparkling gems,

She's good at taking up hems.

Sorry! It's not very good. But I know you are clever in all you do, so I am certain if you wrote a poem it would be much better than my offering. And if I am able to come up with something better, I will. Give me time.

That is all for now, just a short note to let you know I still think you're lovely.
Until next time, keep smiling.
Me.

I loved the way he wrote the letter M, with rounded curves at the top instead of the usual slightly pointed tips, the way we had all been taught at school.

I heard the front door open and Jacques' voice as he spoke to his mother. I quickly hid the letter in the drawer housing my underwear and nightgown that had been bought with the donations received from people in the town. I decided I was thirsty and went to the kitchen to make a cup of tea, smiling demurely at him on the way as he sat on the sofa in the living room.

'How is everything?' he asked.

I peered through the kitchen door. 'Very well, thank you. Your mother has been very wonderful, I'm so very grateful.' I turned to face the kettle and cringed at my overuse of the word 'very', and hoped he didn't notice.

Mrs Chevalier re-entered the kitchen and held up a pile of books. 'I've left some in your mother's room, and I'll leave the rest in yours. They are yours to keep. I know you had quite a book collection at home, so I would like to help you restart another.'

My chin quivered then, as I remembered all the books that had burnt. The ones from my childhood, and the one I had hidden that first love letter in. 'Thank you, that's... you're so...' I covered my mouth as I tried to hold back tears I had somehow forgotten to release, in the aftermath of trying to keep my mother well and her spirits up.

Mrs Chevalier approached me and gave my arm a rub. She

wasn't an overly affectionate woman, but was very (there I go again) kind and gentle. I felt like I needed a hug, but the arm rub was enough for now. She left the kitchen with the books and I wiped at my eyes then made my tea, not wanting Jacques to see me like that. I took my tea and was going to take it to my room when he said, 'You are very welcome to take a seat in here to have your tea, if you like.'

I stopped, my hand trembling slightly and rattling the teacup on the saucer. 'Oh, thank you.' And I wondered if his use of the word very was on purpose or if he also suffered the same affliction of overusing the word.

I sat at the chair near the small side table, where I placed my teacup.

'Anything interesting?' I asked, gesturing at the newspaper he was reading.

He flipped a couple of pages then shook his head. 'Not really. I think I may have to find a good book of my own to read instead.' He offered a small smile as he closed the newspaper and wandered to the other side of the room, trailing his hand along the spines of books on the shelves.

'You like reading?'

'Oh yes.'

'What sorts of books?'

'Mysteries, war stories, poetry,' he replied.

My heart shone bright and I bit my bottom lip. Poetry... Should I say something? I wondered.

Mrs Chevalier walked past us. 'I'll be outside bringing in the laundry from the line,' she said.

'Oh, can I be of assistance?" I asked, standing.

'No, you enjoy your tea.' She smiled and exited the house.

I sat and Jacques did too, a book in his hand.

'What do you like to read, May?' he asked me.

'Oh, absolutely anything,' I said with enthusiasm. 'If it's a book, I'll read it.'

'Maybe you should try your hand at writing, yourself?' he suggested.

Oooh! My nerves were bubbling with excitement. He was definitely my secret admirer.

'Maybe,' I said, trying to keep my smile demure. 'Or even own a bookstore one day, that would be wonderful, to be surrounded by such beautiful things as books.' I sipped at my tea but had lost my thirst. Here goes... 'I was actually thinking I might try my hand at poetry. I don't know how clever it will be, but I could try.' I looked him in the eye.

'Oh?' he said. 'Have you always been interested in poetry?'

'Only since about...' I tapped at my chin. 'Today.'

He tilted his head and eyed me curiously. 'Why is that?'

'Oh, I'm not sure. I was just thinking how miraculous it was that Mother survived, and that if I could try something new and be clever at it, it could be miraculous too.'

My words didn't make that much sense, but I hoped by alluding to his choice of words in the letter that I would catch a glimpse of recognition in his eyes, or a flush of his cheeks. But there was nothing. He was very good at keeping a secret.

I glanced sideways towards the kitchen and noticed the shopping list sitting on the side table near the doorway that Mrs Chevalier had placed there earlier, telling me to add anything that Mother or Father or I needed. I stood and went to the list, pretending to add something. 'Do you need to add anything while I'm here?' I asked Jacques.

He shook his head.

Rats. I was hoping to see his handwriting.

I nibbled on my bottom lip and held on to the list, then I took a breath and approached him at the sofa. 'I was wondering if I might ask your opinion?'

'Of course. About what?' He looked up from the book.

'I had to sign some papers recently, but I haven't yet decided on what my official adult signature should be.' I wrote out two options on the back of the list, one with pointy tipped Ms and one with rounded Ms.

'Both look perfectly fine to me,' he replied after taking a look.

I placed the list next to him. 'How would you write my name?' I made my smile a little more flirtatious than demure, to hint that I was just being a bit playful and hoping he would amuse me and participate.

'Why are you interested in how I would write your name?' He smiled back.

'Just curious, that's all.' I handed him the pencil.

He took it and in cursive script he wrote my name, the M with pointed tips.

My smile faded. That was strange. Or perhaps he was writing the letter in a different way so as to keep the secret. Yes, that could be it. My smile returned, until I noticed that he was holding the pencil in his right hand. The letter mentioned he was holding tea in his right hand and the pencil in his left.

My admirer was left-handed. Jacques wasn't.

To be sure, I asked, 'Do you think you'll travel one day, see the world, Jacques?'

He shrugged. 'Maybe, but probably not. I quite like Tarrin's Bay, and I may need to take over the tailor's shop at some point, try to keep it in the family. We have a good life here, it'd be a shame to waste it.'

My shoulders sunk. I took the list back to the table and went back for my teacup and saucer to wash it in the kitchen.

If Jacques wasn't my admirer, who was? Or perhaps it was one of my friends playing a trick on me. I wouldn't put it past Betty. But to continue it after the fire? That didn't seem right.

No, somewhere out there was a left-handed man who wanted to run away with me and have miraculous, marvellous, magnificent adventures. And while I wanted to stay here and look after Mother and help rebuild our lives, part of me loved the idea of starting over, of taking a risk, of having an adventure for myself now that my adult life was only just beginning...

CHAPTER ELEVEN

'M uuummm!' Mia tugged at Olivia's pyjama top. She didn't want to open her eyes, having stayed up way too late working on *Memories of May*, and then reading more of *One More Breath* and learning a whole lot more about Joel.

'Just a few minutes, sweetie,' she mumbled.

'But I'm hunnggrrry!'

'You can get your own cereal sometimes, remember?'

'Yes but I don't *want* cereal,' she whined. 'And it's Sunday, pancake day.'

Oh yes. It had become tradition, except when she had to work the occasional Sunday and didn't have as much time in the morning.

Olivia forced her muscles to co-operate and pushed herself up with her arms, while Mia yanked at her pyjama top, helping her a little.

She met Mia in the kitchen after waking herself up in the bathroom, and made up the batter. She usually made smaller pancakes, like pikelets, as they were handy to freeze and place in Mia's school lunches.

Mia helped her drop spoonfuls into the pan, and when they bubbled Olivia turned them over.

For the second batch, Olivia added the last spoonful that would fit in the pan, but found herself adding a bit extra, making it slightly larger, and then pushing two parts of the edges outward. Her mind was in a daze, but she soon realised that without thinking she had made a different shape.

'Mummy! It's beautiful!' said Mia. 'A heart!'

'Huh,' she said. 'So it is. I don't know where that came from.'

Here she was, doing the same old things differently without it even being on purpose. This was a much better idea than camping.

'It came from your hands, silly. You made it.'

'I did indeed. Would you like to eat the heart pancake?'

Mia nodded rapidly, her hair falling over her cheeks.

'I will put it on a special plate all on its own.'

When all the pancakes were made, she added raspberry jam to the heart and then took a photo of it.

'We should show Mrs May!' she exclaimed.

Olivia nodded and then as Mia gobbled up the pancake, she clicked onto her text messages.

I did something differently, look.

She added the photo of the pancake to her message to Joel.

After she had put jam on the other pancakes and frozen the remaining ones, he replied.

Do you mean you don't normally make heart-shaped pancakes?!

His reply included a shocked emoji.

Never. Circles all the way.

> I challenge you to make a new shape every week. Next week, a butterfly. #PancakeChallenge

> Why a butterfly?

> Why not? Actually, it symbolises transformation.

> Okay. You're on. #PancakeChallengeAccepted

Olivia giggled.

'What's so funny, Mummy?' Mia asked, wiping jam from the corners of her bow-shaped lips.

'Nothing, sweetie.'

'There must be something funny, you're giggling like I did when you told me how babies are made. Are you laughing about that?'

'No.' She chuckled. 'I just feel quite happy right in this moment and felt like giggling. Giggling is fun.' A smile warmed her cheeks and she took her daughter's hands, swinging them up and down in the kitchen.

'Come here,' Mia said, raising her chin and pouting her lips. Olivia bent down and let her daughter kiss her on the cheek. 'I love you, Mummy.'

Olivia's heart swelled, and she kissed Mia back. 'I love you too, my beautiful girl.'

Now *that* was a book-worthy moment.

'Thanks, Peter.' Olivia stepped out of the car with her friend April, and waved at her mother's boyfriend who had dropped them off at the local bar and bistro that overlooked the beach near the entrance to town, with a view of Serendipity Health Retreat in the distance. He would pick them up too, allowing them to have some alcohol with their meal, while he and Diana minded Mia.

'Oh, yum, I haven't had a cocktail in ages!' April sipped through the straw of her margarita, her tattoo ring catching Olivia's eye.

'Me neither.' Olivia sipped from her mojito. 'You don't feel awkward about it?'

'Not if I'm out. I don't keep any alcohol in the house anymore and Zac knows I have the odd one when I'm out, but never when I'm with him.'

'It's great how he's got your support. Sounds like he's going to end up with a great memoir, too, by the sounds of it. I was quite proud of him speaking up at last Tuesday's class.'

'Yeah, he's super keen to do it, and I think he always needs to write stuff down, otherwise I find him pacing the house at night, when his thoughts overwhelm him.'

'Sometimes that happens to me but I'm usually too tired to pace!'

'Ha, I've never been one for pacing, but I'm good at standing with my hands on my hips and glancing around like I don't know what to do next.'

'I can so see you doing that.'

'Hey, wait till the food arrives before you guzzle all that drink, girl!'

Olivia glanced down. 'Oh, I hadn't noticed. Whoops. Don't want to have a hangover at work tomorrow. Not that I've had a hangover in over ten years, I wouldn't remember what they feel like. Have they changed?'

April laughed. 'You know I don't know about that either. I have two alcoholics as loved ones... I've never wanted to take the risk. One cocktail is good enough for me.'

'Me too,' Olivia said. But by the time she was halfway through her meal her drink had run out and she was thirsty. 'Hmm, maybe I could have one more. Do you mind?'

April gestured to the bar. 'Not at all. Enjoy.'

She ordered her drink and this time drank it more slowly, but her head felt slightly woozy. She showed April some of the latest photos in her phone, of Mrs May, of Mia, and...

'What's that? A heart pancake?'

'Umm, yep.'

April narrowed her eyes and tilted her head at Olivia. 'Are you in lurrve or something?'

'No. Just felt like it. And I've been told I need to do different things every once in a while, you know, to start getting out of my comfort zone to have some new experiences.'

'Heart-shape pancakes are getting out of your comfort zone, are they?' April let out a loud laugh. 'We really need to get out together more.'

'Fancy going camping?' Olivia said feebly.

'Camping? No thanks, unless it's glamping? Zac has tried to get me to go, but it's not something I feel the urge to do.'

'Me neither, but I might be.'

'Why? And who told you that you need to do different things?'

Olivia filled her in about Joel and their lunches and his 'challenges'.

'Ohh, I see. I'd like to meet this Joel, might have to come meet Zac at the end of class one night.'

She also filled her in on the handbag strap, and the creative way she explained the birds and the bees to Mia.

'Oh, girl, you do need to get out more. And also, how about for something different you ask a guy out on a date. Maybe Joel, why not?'

'Why not?' Olivia's face warmed and her nerves relaxed.

'Because he's my writing mentor. I'm his student. Forbidden love and all that.'

April laughed again. 'Forbidden schmidden, you're not at high school anymore, he's teaching a six-week informal course in a hall. He's a guy, you're a girl. Just get it on and have a night to remember.' She drank the rest of her cocktail.

Olivia fiddled with her hair. 'I couldn't. And I don't want to. He's leaving at the end of the course and will be off on new adventures, so there's no point.'

'There's every point. Give yourself some time to have fun. And I do recall you and a couple of others encouraging me to have a fling with Mr Neighbour last year. Look how well that turned out.' She grinned.

'I know, but you were neighbours and he wasn't about to leave town. Anyway, just because he's a guy around my age and is decent-looking and nice and friendly and interesting and intelligent and brave and funny and confident and cute and sexy and...' She took a breath. 'Did I just say sexy?'

'Uh-huh. Along with fifty million other complimentary adjectives.'

Olivia let out a burst of laughter. 'What's an adjective again? Is that a doing word or a... no, it's a describing word, isn't it. Forgot.' She whacked herself on the forehead.

'Oh my, you are quite entertaining tonight. And hey, would you like me to take a video of you yapping on with a cocktail in your hand and send it to this Joel guy for you, to show him that you're doing more things out of your comfort zone?'

'No, don't you dare.' Olivia held her phone close to her chest, but it dropped onto the floor. 'Bugger.' She bent down, and had to hold the table to steady herself when she got back up.

'Is there a sex scene in this list of book-worthy moments? Huh? Is there? Is there?' April nudged her with her elbow.

'As if I'd let him write that down on the list!'

'Do you want it on the list?'

'No.'

'Do you want *it*?'

'No.'

'You don't want sex?'

'No, I mean, not as some*thing* to tick off my list, and not with him. I hardly know the guy. And he thinks I'm boring and plain.'

'So get to know him, and show him you're not boring and plain, because you're not. You're sweet and awesome and any guy would be lucky to have you.'

'Aww, well, thank you.' She slipped an arm around April in a hug.

'But seriously, he's only here for a few weeks, we know he's not a serial killer, so why not flirt a bit and see where it leads? If it backfires he'll be out of town and you won't have to worry, if it goes well you'll have a nice memory. How long has it been since you've been with a guy, anyway? I mean, *really* been with a guy?'

Olivia gulped. 'Oh, you know, a while. You still hungry? Perhaps some dessert?' She glanced at the menu.

'Hey.' April leaned in close. 'I know we haven't known each other for that long really, but you can tell me anything. I'm here to chat about anything at anytime, you know.'

Her cheeks flushed and she felt vulnerable, exposed. It shouldn't matter how long it had been, but for some reason it made her feel different, abnormal, compared to other women her age. 'Well, Mia is nine and a half, I've been on a few small dates here and there. Actually, only two. But they didn't lead to anything. Add on nine months for pregnancy, and you have... what... just over ten years?' There. She'd said it out loud. It wasn't like it had been decades, but it was still double figures. And she'd simply grown used to not having anyone in her life.

'So Mia's dad was the last time?'

Olivia nodded, taking a sip of her drink.

April nodded too. 'Huh, well there you go. Decision made. Go get it out of your system. Break the drought.'

'It's not that easy, what do I do, just say, "hey, care to put a girl out of her misery?"'

'I'm sure you'd get a lot of takers. Probably a few in here.' They looked around at the customers, a few middle-aged men drinking beers and eating fries and burgers.

'Oh, please.'

'Exactly, that's what they'd say.' April grinned.

Olivia whacked her on the arm. 'Stop. Anyway, I've just never found the right guy, or any decent guy really, I don't have the lifestyle for it.'

'Then take action. Online dating?'

Olivia shook her head. 'Probably come across too many customers or locals and that would be awkward.'

'Then get to know Joel, see if he has potential.'

'Wouldn't that be like using him? That's a bit cheap. And desperate. And I don't know if I like him in that way.'

'Not if he wanted it too. And he likes adventures. I'm sure he's got a fit bod, am I right?'

An image of Joel popped into her mind, though she'd never seen him without a long-sleeved shirt, in her imagination he was shirtless, and it made her feel things inside she hadn't felt in a while. 'I think those drinks are going to my head.'

'Look, after all those adjectives you used, I'd say you think he's a pretty decent guy. So take advantage of the time he's here and maximise your connection. See where it leads. Ooh, he could go camping with you!'

'What? No! Although he did say he was going to help me set up the tent and then leave me to it.'

'There you go.' April gestured in front of her like the opportunity had been presented on a silver platter in front of them.

'I don't know. I'm not very good at flirting.'

'Um, hello? You sent him a photo of a pancake heart. That's pretty flirty to me. Show me your texts to each other.' April snatched Olivia's phone.

'Hey!'

She peered at the screen. 'You two are so already flirting. Subtle, but it's there. Keep it going!'

'*That* is flirting? Gee, it must have changed in the decade I haven't been on the scene. I thought we were just being friendly.'

'It's all about sexting now, woman. Embrace the technological age.'

'I'm not going to send any of those ridiculous selfies young people take these days.'

'Ha-ha, you don't have to. Be yourself, but extra... sparkly.'

'Sparkly?'

'Like, you know, extra... sparkly. I don't know how else to describe it. Just take a few risks and try to steer the conversation on to more personal matters. And anyway, if he's helping you do some book-worthy moments, maybe they'll naturally lead to something beyond the teacher–student relationship.'

Great. Now, at every class, Olivia wouldn't be able to watch Joel teach the course without imagining him shirtless. And imagining anything beyond that, or anything happening with him in relation to that, that was definitely out of her comfort zone. But her comfort zone was becoming a bit uncomfortable itself.

CHAPTER TWELVE

I would not take one more breath. I would, and will, take many more. And the same goes for adventures, destinations yet to be revealed...

Olivia reread the last line of Joel's book, then closed it with a dull pop, pushing a swish of air up to her face. *Wow. What a story.* It had taught her a lot about him, but instead of satisfying her curiosity, it only made her want to know more about him.

She put the book down under the counter to serve a customer who was buying a copy of the same book, plus a novel. When the customer left, Olivia went to the storeroom to collect something from her bag, then placed it on the counter.

'What's that?' Marcus asked, pointing to the glass jar.

'A memory jar. I'm going to encourage customers to write down one of their favourite memories anonymously on a bit of paper, fold it up and place it in the jar. Then when I eventually finish and publish Mrs May's book, we can have a book launch here and one of the novelty activities could be that we pass the jar around and people read out a random memory.'

Marcus's mouth opened. 'Wow! That is awesome. And wow, you do think and plan far ahead, don't you.'

'The idea came to me in the middle of the night.'

'As all good ideas do,' he said. 'I had a good idea to get up in the middle of the night and have half a tub of ice cream once. Regretted it the next morning, I must say.'

Olivia smiled. 'Anyway, if you like, feel free to add a memory or two of your own. I'm going to add one about Mia telling me she loved me the other day, it was so cute.'

Marcus picked up a pen. 'I could fill the whole jar. But I better let some others get theirs in. And I better only put in the PG rated ones.'

'Yes, I think we'll make that a rule. PG memories only.' She winked.

'How's the book coming along?'

Olivia tidied the counter as she spoke. 'Not bad, putting things in order, writing some of the chapters late at night. Listening to the recordings of my grandma's memories. I'm really enjoying it.'

'Glad to hear.'

She was also enjoying her occasional texts with Joel about random things. He would send her ideas for her list, and crazy pictures of people skydiving and bungee jumping and skinny-dipping. She freaked him out in return by sending him some photos she'd found on the internet of men wearing crochet underwear, adding the text: *These might keep you warm on your adventures.* She also thought that might count as flirting, since it was about underwear. Even if they were God-awful revolting crochet abominations that had compartments for various body parts and could not be unseen.

When he'd replied and said: *Though they are tempting, my Bonds underwear will do me just fine, thank you,* she'd gotten a little flutter in her belly. Was he flirting? Or being funny? Either way, it made her giggle like when she'd made the pancake shape.

And now in tonight's class, she would no doubt either

imagine him in his Bonds underwear, or heaven forbid, the crochet things. And those sorts of things were best left to the private memory jar of one's mind.

'And that, my friends, is what makes a killer opening. Pardon the pun.' Joel turned off the PowerPoint presentation that evening after his second class, which focused on story structure, particularly the importance of those vital opening pages. 'I look forward to reading your opening page or two, send them to me when they're done and we'll workshop them in class.'

'Mine's already done, do you want it now?' asked Dylan. 'And it's definitely a killer opening. An *almost* killer opening. Hence, I'm here to tell the tale.' He patted his right leg. 'I sounded so old then. *Hence,*' he remarked. '*Hence.*' He put on a posh old voice.

'I'm old and I can't remember the last time I said hence,' said Mr Donovan.

'Sure, Dylan,' Joel replied. 'I'll take a look tomorrow.'

Dylan fiddled with his phone then said, 'Sent.'

Joel gave him a thumbs-up.

'Sent mine too,' Zac said. 'Two versions, actually. I'm not sure whether to open with the scene from Afghanistan, or my first day of sobriety.'

'I'll let you know what I think, but trust your instincts. What you feel is the best way to tell your story.' He was fascinated to read about Zac's experiences.

Zac gave a nod.

He glanced at Olivia, whose face was pinker than usual and she was fiddling with her earring. Her eyes often looked like they were distant – seeing things that weren't there, like she was lost in some other world, or her imagination.

'I hope to finalise mine tomorrow night,' she said, and when he caught her eyes she diverted her gaze.

What went on in that woman's mind?

'Oh,' Joel said, raising his finger. 'And don't forget, have a think about what I said before: if you or your life were an object, what would it be? You can bring an object next week, or just tell the class.'

Olivia, she was like a... cardigan. Warm, comfortable, covering up what's underneath. Or a... clock. Ticking away at the same speed, starting all over again the next day.

But after discovering more about her lately via her cute and often funny text messages, which seemed to be the way she communicated the easiest, he was starting to think of her as an alarm clock – ticking away at the same speed, starting all over again the next day, but also surprising him at certain times with sudden bursts that awakened him.

The class shuffled out, except for Olivia who seemed to be taking a long time to pack away her things, and Mr Donovan who was checking some posters on the community noticeboard.

'Can I walk you out, Miss Olivia?' Mr Donovan said when he turned away from the board.

'Oh, no thanks, Mr Donovan, I'd like to have a brief word with Joel,' she said, and he managed to catch her eye for a split second. She probably wanted to tell him that he could take his idea for a book-worthy moments list and shove it where the sun didn't shine, as she had not been too pleased with his suggestions so far via text.

Greg Donovan put his cap on his head and gave a little bow as he exited the hall. Joel switched off the main lights, leaving the one near the entrance on.

He offered her a smile.

'Great class, thanks,' she said. 'And I accept your challenge.'

'The pancake challenge?'

She laughed. 'No. Well, yes, but I mean the other one. The book-worthy moments. I'll do five more over the duration of the course, as long as they don't take up too much time away from my daughter, and I don't have a lot of time off, so they would have to fit in with my schedule and all that.'

He nodded. 'Have you decided what you'd like to do?'

'You can decide. As long as they don't involve life-threatening situations like jumping from a plane, jumping from anything and hanging upside down from a rope, or skinny-dipping. And I'm not getting a tattoo. Or body piercing. Also I'm never wearing crochet underwear, just so you know.'

He raised his eyebrows. 'Skinny-dipping is life threatening, huh?'

She went pinker. 'You know what I mean. Just bring me back home to my daughter safe and sound, and fully clothed.'

'It's a deal.' He held out his hand. She grasped it tentatively at first, her soft skin cool against his, then firmer as she gave it a single shake. 'Send me your schedule with available days and times and I'll send you a schedule back with when I'll pick you up, and what you'll need.'

'So each thing is going to be a surprise, not only the treasure hunt?'

'Yep.' He grinned. 'And I'm surprised, Olivia. I didn't think you would trust me this much.'

'I didn't either. So that counts for something different too.'

He held her gaze for a moment. She adjusted the bag strap on her shoulder, which he'd noticed she often did, and something popped into his mind. 'A-ha! Your bag, you had it on the other shoulder, that day at the café.'

Her eyes widened. 'You noticed?'

'It occurred to me just now.'

'Wow.' She shook her head. 'Even I'd forgotten about that.'

'It's amazing the detail you learn to notice in small things when you're stuck in the wilderness for ages with nothing else to do.'

She nodded. 'Speaking of which, I finished your book.'

'Oh?' He was impressed. And also felt a little bit exposed, knowing she knew so much about him now.

'Amazing, Joel. Really.' Her eyes and smile were genuine. 'You've been through a lot. And you've come out on top, it's inspiring.'

He closed his eyes briefly and nodded a thank you. He'd been told similar things before, but it often felt like unnecessary praise. He had simply done what he had needed to do to survive both his mother's death and his near-death experience. The first event had taught him emotional strength and resilience, the second event had required it. Although sustaining a physical injury when he'd fallen from the cliff face and snagged his leg and calf muscle on a sharp rock protrusion, among other injuries, it had been that mental strength he'd relied on to get him through and take one more breath after the other. When he had run out of food, he'd thought of his mother. When he'd tried to crawl as far as he could and then rest again, before repeating and repeating, he'd thought of his mother. And when he'd resisted screaming after taking that last drop of water, knowing this could be the beginning of the end, he'd thought of his mother and how he couldn't die, he had to live and keep living, for her.

'Thank you for reading it,' he said.

'Challenge number one, complete. And it's selling well at the store so far.'

'Glad to hear.'

He turned off the other light and let her walk outside ahead of him. Before unlocking her car parked nearby, she turned and looked at him with a curious sparkle in her eye. 'You're an arrow,' she said.

'An arrow? Like that dude on that TV series?'

'No, an arrow. That's your object. You launch forward to new places, not knowing exactly where you'll land, but shooting ahead anyway. Then you stop for a while, then launch again. You only pull back long enough to prepare to be launched off into a new place.'

Huh. Cool. 'You know, I think you may be right. Joel the arrow.' He moved his hand forward in a sharp gesture.

'Where will he land next?' She chuckled.

Joel held out his hands wide with an eager smile. 'Life will figure that out for me.'

'So what object am I... I'll have to think,' she said. 'Any ideas?'

Joel held his lips tight, restraining himself from telling her she was a cardigan or an alarm clock. 'Hmm, I'm tossing up some ideas. But I think I may need to find out a bit more about you before I can come to a satisfactory conclusion.' He smiled, and she fiddled with her strap again. 'After all, you don't have a book about yourself for me to read.'

'Not yet.'

'But I hope to help you start writing one. Metaphorically speaking.'

'Chapter two awaits,' she said.

'Chapter two already? What happened in chapter one?'

'Reading your book and beginning my challenge to do the same things differently.'

He nodded. 'Oh yes. But once I organise your schedule, you'll have a new chapter that will be a lot more exciting than wearing your bag strap on a different shoulder.'

'I should hope so.' Her car beeped as she unlocked it. 'Goodnight, Joel.'

''Night, Olivia.' He waited for her to drive away and then stood there in the dim street next to Miracle Park, the terrace shops snug together like a cosy family, the soft streetlamps casting a soothing glow, and for a moment he understood the welcoming appeal of this town. Safe, predictable, and a place many people called home. He had never felt at home anywhere. Movement, adventure, that was his home, if that was even possible.

But for now, he would have to settle for making Tarrin's Bay his temporary home.

CHAPTER THIRTEEN

May Chevalier had always loved books. She'd said that she couldn't imagine a life without them, and that it started around the time of the war when stories were a way to escape. But that was only part of it. What really cemented her love of books was also a simple, honest love letter, tucked inside the pages of a novel, and forever inside her heart...

Olivia typed, backspaced, and typed again, the opening page of *Memories of May*. She wasn't sure at first whether to mention anything about the letters, or William, but that seemed like a way to acknowledge that part of her life without giving away her privacy. Readers need only know that she had a secret admirer once, as many young women could have had, and that the first initial thrill of receiving a declaration of one's affection had made an impact on her in those early days, before she got together with Jacques.

Olivia wrote about the letter, then the fire, and then gave a brief teaser introduction about how this would kickstart Mrs May's first taste of independence and her dreams to capture dreams within a quaint, magical bookstore in small town Tarrin's Bay.

She reread it then emailed it off to Joel for his critique. As the email sent, she wondered what sort of object she was most like. Or what Joel thought she was. Maybe a computer; capable and efficient and helpful, with the occasional crash. Or... she glanced down at her fluffy, plain white slippers. Comfortable, supportive, and warm.

But she didn't want to be those objects. She wanted to be something more memorable, more interesting, like... she glanced to the side of her computer. A pen! Yes, a pen. Able to create her own life by simply writing whatever she wanted. Endless possibilities.

Dull footsteps sounded down the hall and Olivia turned to her door. She stood and walked out quietly, catching a glimpse of Mia's dressing gown flicking around the corner into the kitchen.

'Honey? You okay?' she asked.

'Thirsty.'

Mia had opened the fridge and was about to reach for the juice.

'How about some water, then you don't have to clean your teeth all over again.' Olivia poured some water from the benchtop filter jug into a cup.

'Water's boring,' said Mia.

'Well, that boring water makes up most of our bodies, so I'd say it's very un-boring,' she replied. 'And what are you doing up so late?'

'My brain wants to think.'

Olivia chuckled. She knew all about that, and had probably passed this gene onto her daughter. 'What about?'

Please don't make me repeat the USB memory stick thing again...

'You know how you showed me the USB stick and said

babies are made when people have loving feelings for each other?'

'Yep.'

'Did you stop having loving feelings for my dad?'

Crap. Maybe she should have specified that some babies are made when people have loving feelings for each other and some are made when people have lustful feelings for each other and have also consumed a fair bit of wine. 'Umm.' Olivia sighed. She slid her arm around her daughter's shoulders. 'I guess so, sweetie. Some people aren't meant to be together for a long time, but the purpose of them meeting is to create a brand-new amazing human, and I think that was our purpose. So that you could come into the world.' She bent down and kissed her forehead. 'But I will always have special loving feelings for you that are only between mother and daughter.'

Mia drank the rest of her water then placed the cup in the sink. 'Okay,' she said lightheartedly then scooted out of the kitchen. 'I'm tired, Mummy. You should go to bed too,' she called out from the hall.

'I will! 'Night, my girl.' Olivia laughed. That wasn't too hard. She was expecting Mia to ask more questions, as sometimes giving answers meant more questions were created, and the question-and-answer sessions could go on for ages. But maybe she was embarrassed that her mother had done the USB memory stick thing and didn't want to know any more.

She stood in the kitchen a while longer, her hand resting on the counter, her mind not resting at all. How had so much time passed since that night with Mia's father... had it really been that long? She wanted to have loving feelings for someone, but not if those loving feelings were destined to end. She couldn't cope with the heartbreak, and couldn't put Mia through that. But... lustful feelings? Hmm, maybe she could just have some of those, then there was no risk to Mia if there were no expectations for anything serious from the get-go. But what if she fell more deeply for someone anyway, and they didn't fall for her? Mia might not be exposed, but was it worth risking being disappointed and heartbroken for a time and not being the happy and always caring and available mother that she'd only ever been?

Ugh. Too many thoughts in my head. She took a quick breath and forced herself to stop, moving back into her room.

She jumped when her phone pinged, then she turned the volume off as she saw Joel's message on the screen.

> I'll pick you up Sat 3pm for book-worthy moment #2, text me your address. Wear something comfortable, no skirts.

Olivia's heart beat a little faster. *Oh God, is it something upside down?*

Olivia had checked prior with her mother if Saturday afternoon would be okay to mind Mia, so she replied to Joel and accepted, though tried to get an idea as to what the adventure was.

> Trust me ;)

That was all he said.

Well, she was doing this whether she liked it or not.

'Thanks, darling,' Diana said as she kissed Olivia's cheek at the nursing home the next evening, grabbing her gym bag and walking out in her Lycra gear to make her aerobics class in time with Peter.

Olivia placed her bag down and Mia stuck up her latest drawing for Mrs May on the wall opposite her bed so she could look across and see it; a sky full of cloud-hearts with pink birds flying between them.

'Better than Monet, my dear,' Mrs May said softly.

'Who's that?' asked Mia. 'Is that another man you spied on when you were twenty?'

Mrs May smiled. 'No, dear. He was a famous painter. An artist. Like you.'

'But I'm not famous.'

'Not yet.' Mrs May held up the pointer finger on her good hand.

Olivia helped her grandma take some food, then gave Mia her EarPods and sat on the chair with her recorder at the ready. 'Oh, Grandma, I've been waiting to find out what happened next with the love letter, after you found out Jacques didn't write it.'

'Oh yes, was that where we were up to?' She took a deep breath and adjusted her nasal oxygen tube. 'Did I tell you about the signature? Is that where we left off?'

'Yes, and that Jacques didn't want to travel and that the writer of the letter had to be left-handed.'

'Ahh.' Mrs May went still for a moment, her face softening as though her memories were smoothing out her wrinkles and making her younger again. 'Well the next day, it all became clear...'

May's Memories of Truth

I volunteered to collect some groceries the next day for the household. Staying in the house was making me a little bored, so as Mrs Chevalier was cleaning the bedrooms, I scooted to town with my list and basket, making sure to offer Jacques a wave as I walked past the tailor's shop, but my wave went unnoticed; he did not see me.

The sun speckled the ground as I wandered up the street, and I glanced toward the ocean across from the park and harbour, feeling an impulse to go in for a swim. But there was no time for such luxuries these days, and I needed to be of service as much as possible to the family housing us so kindly.

The bell jingled as I entered the general store.

'May, what are you doing? I could have delivered you groceries this afternoon,' said William, standing by the counter, some papers in his hand.

I swished a hand in the air. 'Nonsense, I am perfectly capable. The fire didn't burn my ability to go shopping.' It was only after I spoke I realised my words may have sounded a bit abrupt. 'Sorry, your help has been wonderful, I'm just needing to get out a bit and be useful.'

'No offence taken, Miss May. You like to keep moving, don't you?'

'Oh yes, I don't like sitting still. Except when I'm sewing, then it's actually necessary, but sometimes I think I'd just like to...' I recalled the secret letter, '...run off into the sunset and have a grand adventure.' I gave a firm nod. I actually hadn't thought about that before, but since reading the letter, something had sparked in me an urge to be ignited.

William's eyes widened. 'You should do it,' he said. 'Everyone should have an adventure.'

'But I have such responsibility. People need me, and we need money.'

'People will get by. Life is for living, is it not?' I exchanged an interesting glance with him then, and he smiled and looked down at his papers. 'I'll let you collect your supplies while I organise this inventory.'

I nodded, and as I weaved between the shelves and gathered items, I kept glancing back at the counter, his ruffled crazy hair falling over his face, his furrowed brow as he concentrated. Something about him was... intriguing. Interesting... appealing. And as I picked up a bottle of maple syrup, William picked up a pencil and wrote something on the inventory, with his left hand. The maple syrup slipped from my grasp, collided with the edge of the basket and was about to topple to the floor when I managed to quickly catch it.

Could it be?

William glanced over, noticing the bottle upside down in my hand. 'You caught it, how very quick your reflexes are! That was lucky, wouldn't want to clean up a ton of maple syrup from the floor.' He winked.

'It was lucky,' I said, after clearing my throat, then curiosity pushed the next words from my mouth. 'It was... miraculous, even.'

William's pencil hung limply from his hand as he went still for a moment.

'I, ah, I think I have everything I need.' I took the basket to the counter and he added up the cost in silence and I paid.

I smiled and thanked him and went to open the door, then turned back. 'William?' I asked. 'Could I ask your opinion on my new signature? I want to make sure I have one I am happy to use throughout my adult life, and I'm so fussy with these things.'

'Of course, show me.'

I placed the shopping list on the counter, pointing out my attempt and Jacques'. 'That one's okay,' he said, pointing to mine, 'but not that one, too boring,' he said, pointing to the other. 'How about something with a bit of a swirl at the start of your name, like this...' He used his pencil and wrote May on the paper, the M with rounded tips and a curly swirl at the start.

Left-handed. Rounded-tip M. His handwriting looked similar to that in the letter.

My heart pounded. How could I not have known?

I stared at the paper for what was probably a bit too long, but long enough for William to realise that he had just provided proof of his identity. His hand went to his mouth.

I didn't know what to say next, so I quickly shoved the list in my basket and scurried to the door, glancing at him briefly before offering a feeble smile and walking outside.

Oh goodness, oh goodness! My feet had a mind of their own, scurrying along the street towards our temporary home, desperate to get away from the heightened emotions of the exchange. What do you say to someone when you've discovered they are your secret admirer? And what does that someone say to you?

I hoped I would not have to visit the store tomorrow for any other urgent supplies.

And it turned out I didn't. The next day I helped sew new curtains for the sitting room with Mrs Chevalier as Mother was able to rest on the chaise longue and observe. But at the end of the day, Jacques brought in the mail and handed me an envelope. 'Something for you,' he said, a curious glimmer in his eye.

This time, the 'May' on the front had the addition of a little swirl at the start of the rounded-tip M, just like the one he had drawn yesterday. My hands quivered. 'Thank you,' I said, tucking the letter in my apron pocket.

'What's that, dear?' asked my mother in her raspy voice.

'Nothing, just a note from a friend. Everyone's being so supportive after the fire, it's nice.' I pushed a few strands of hair off my face, my cheeks warming.

'Are you all right? You seem a bit flustered, perhaps you've been doing a little too much lately after everything that's happened,' said Mrs Chevalier. 'I can finish these on my own, you take some rest, okay?' She ushered me out of the room without any time for me to object.

I went to my room and, with a relieved exhalation, sat on the bed. I took the envelope out and with shaky hands, opened it. I licked my lips as though they were about to devour the most delicious treat, and my eyes moved side to side quickly, as though what I was going to see could disappear at any moment. And I read, this time knowing all too well whose hand had moved the ink across the paper...

Dear Mischievous May,

I believe you know why I am calling you mischievous.

I didn't realise until after I'd written your name that you must have had your suspicions about me and wanted proof. I'm sorry I was speechless, but now that the ink is flowing, so are my words.

I understand if you are too embarrassed to visit the store, so I will gladly deliver groceries anytime they are needed, but if you feel any kind of interest in what I have been writing, and what I have been feeling, even a smidgen of curiosity, please find a way to meet me tonight after supper, around nine, at Lookout Point. I have nothing but the utmost respect for you, and good intentions, but if we could have a chance to meet and be alone, I could talk to you properly, and then if you want me to leave you alone and stop writing these letters I will, but if you don't, then... well, I won't.

I hope to see you, but if not, I understand and I wish you well on your grand life adventures.

From your not-so-secret admirer,

W xx

Even the W had rounded tips, or bottoms, and a little swirl at the start. I didn't know why, but tears welled at the edges of my eyes. Why was this making me emotional? Maybe it was because it felt like a fantasy from one of the novels I loved reading, and I didn't know why or how something beautiful and genuine could happen to me, in this small town, with such a charming, fascinating, and hard-working young man who before now I had not really thought of in that way.

I tucked the letter into my current novel, placed the book under my pillow, then paced the room. I considered telling Mother and Father and the Chevaliers that I was going to visit Betty, but she lived on the other side of town and they wouldn't want me walking late at night that far on my own. So I decided then and there that I would agree with Mrs Chevalier's remark from before and that yes, I was indeed feeling a bit worn out and would have an early night.

But an early night was the last thing on my mind. After supper, I said goodnight to everyone and went to my room, changing into a dress and a woollen cardigan, with flat soft shoes that didn't make a sound yet were slightly too small for me, being one of the donated items I'd received. They pinched but I didn't care. I opened the window slowly, placed a cardboard bookmark on the ledge so that it wouldn't close too tight to ensure I could get back in, and climbed out. The cool *breeze nipped at the skin on my ankles and neck and ruffled my hair around my face.*

I had never been dishonest to my family before. But this was something I wanted to do. Maybe this was my adventure, or the start of one, I wasn't sure. But I would find out very soon...

'And?' Olivia asked. 'Then what? Did you meet him? What did he say? What did he do?'

She sat forward and tensed on her chair as her grandma took a sip of water. 'Oh my,' she said. 'Such a lot to remember. So much excitement, anticipation. My mind is spinning like my stomach was in that moment.'

Olivia was both concerned for her grandma and extremely eager to find out what happened next, but she couldn't rush her. If she got overtired physically or emotionally, she would lay for hours not saying a word until she regained her strength, so she had to space things out. There was no way she could not find out the rest of this untold story. But on looking at Mrs May's weary eyes, she knew it would have to wait till probably Saturday. Except she had her book-worthy moment with Joel, so she would have to go Saturday night, or leave it till Sunday.

'It's okay, you rest now and we'll talk again soon,' she said reluctantly. 'I should get Mia home and start to get ready for bed. Motherhood calls.' She chuckled.

Her grandma nodded. Why did her recollections always end on cliffhangers like in books? Perhaps Mrs May was doing it on purpose to tease her. She wouldn't put it past her cheeky grandmother.

She gathered her things and her daughter's hand in hers, and left Mrs May, smiling at the nursing staff as she left the building.

Then a shiver of apprehension rippled through her when she thought about the coming weekend... She hoped that Joel's plans for her didn't include a cliffhanger of the literal kind. Just like the cliffhangers from her grandma's story, she wouldn't put that past *him* either.

CHAPTER FOURTEEN

After her mother and Peter picked up Mia, Olivia paced the living room impatiently. She wasn't used to not knowing what was about to happen. She was used to being prepared and organised for everything. She adjusted the collar of her canvas utility jacket, and smoothed down the creases of her skinny dark jeans.

A loud and unusual rev sounded outside and she wondered what kind of car Joel drove. She didn't take him for the muscle-car type, probably something more functional and simple. She grabbed her handbag and stepped outside, locking the door, and turned around to face her driveway.

She stood frozen to the spot. 'What on earth is that?'

'It's a Ducati Diavel.' He stepped off the matte-black motorbike that looked large and angry and unwelcoming, like it would growl if she got too close to it.

'Why did you come over on that? Do you need to park it here and we're going to walk somewhere for the book-worthy moment?'

He shook his head. 'I hired it.' He unzipped his backpack

and withdrew a helmet. He held it out. 'Put this on. You'll need protection.'

Olivia crossed her arms and shifted on the spot. 'No, I won't, I'm not getting on a motorbike. Let's walk to wherever we're going. Or I'll drive.'

'But this *is* the book-worthy moment; riding off into the sunset, or at least the glaring afternoon sun, with a dashingly handsome man. It's the journey, not the destination.' He winked, holding the helmet closer towards her.

When she didn't take it, he stepped closer and placed the helmet above her head, and despite her hands instinctively grabbing it, he managed to get it on.

Her lungs craved oxygen but filled with fear. She gulped and he patted her arm. 'You'll be safe with me, trust me. I am fully licensed to ride one of these.'

It's okay, Olivia, it'll be okay, she tried to talk herself around. *It's just like a car, except, it has no roof, and no sides, and... it's like a... a seat! A chair. An armchair, with no arms. It'll be just like sitting down and getting comfortable while someone else does everything for you. I just have to hold on.*

She breathed deeply, and her eyes must have looked terrified beneath the helmet because Joel came even closer and this time held both her arms. 'Seriously, it'll be okay. Fun, even. I won't put you in any danger. And afterwards, I will shout you absolutely anything you want to eat and drink, even if it's not something different.'

'Umm...' She had forgotten how to speak. And couldn't feel her legs. And somehow Joel had managed to walk her to the motorbike. And she was lifting one leg over, and sitting down on the wide seat feeling like she was on a hard horse, and her hands were gripping Joel's waist, and shaking a bit, and then the God-awful sound started up again and she thought she might puke.

Vibrations from the bike radiated throughout her body, making her feel even more unsteady, and after Joel turned his head and said, 'Hold on tight' (like she wasn't already), she gasped as the bike surged forward and off onto the street, then screamed as it tilted sideways around the corner and she thought she might graze her leg on the road.

Oh my God, oh my God! And what if I do need to puke, and Joel can't hear me over the noise of the thing, and I do puke and it goes all inside the helmet and up my nose and down my chin and in my ears and then explodes down and out of the helmet and sprays backwards for miles to the poor buggers behind us on the road!

'Aghhh!' she cried out, as they turned another corner, her body feeling like it was flying, but through intense turbulence. And then, hallelujah, after several turns they made it to the highway and it was straight ahead mostly, and she was able to catch her breath.

'How you doin' back there?' she thought she heard Joel say.

A loud and shaky 'Ahh!' was all she could manage.

Shouldn't they be finishing by now? Shouldn't they pull over and rest for a while? Surely there was no need to keep going, she'd now officially been on a motorbike. Book-worthy moment number two done and dusted. Time to finish, and then she could...

'Eeeeeee!' Some strange sound escaped her lungs as they sped up and the sound and vibrations intensified. Oh dear. She had a feeling they were just getting started. She also had a feeling Joel was grinning widely beneath his helmet. She should have gotten a tattoo instead, at least she could lie down for that.

He veered off the highway and up a hill, eventually reaching a more rural area where their speed slowed down. The terrain became bumpier and she thanked the heavens she was wearing a sports bra, as her boobs wobbled like there was no tomorrow. She was also surprised that Joel could still breathe with how tightly she was holding on to him.

They turned a couple of corners and she tensed again, hoping her legs would not scrape the ground, then they came closer to a small town with only a few shops, a café, and a pub, and he rode into a side street and into a small parking lot where they came to a halt, and for a moment she thought she was going to fall off the bike until Joel put his foot down and held the bike in place.

Her heart pounded, her breathing was fast, and she was still gripping him.

'You can let go now.' He chuckled.

Her fingers appeared glued to his jacket. She peeled her hands off him and tilted to the side to put one shaky foot on the ground, then swung her other over and off the bike.

Joel took off his helmet and then hers. 'Welcome back to the land of the living,' he said.

She took a step forward and almost toppled over, the vibrations still shaking inside of her.

'Awesome, huh?' He secured the bike. He smiled as he looked at her, then his hand came towards her. He tucked some of her hair behind her ear. She peered into the rear-view mirror and adjusted her half-helmet and half-windswept hair.

'What did you think?' he asked with an eager grin, his eyes wide and bright.

'I can't really think straight, I'm not, I'm...' Her heart was still beating fast. But as her brain tried to formulate words, something surprising happened. Her lips arched into a smile. Not a soft, demure smile. But... a big, wide, gaping grin.

She was still smiling the next morning as she made pancakes with Mia, then remembered she was supposed to make a butterfly shape for Joel's pancake challenge. 'Oh!' she said.

'What, Mum?'

'I'm going to try to make a butterfly.'

'Yay!' Mia jiggled next to her. 'With sparkly wings?'

'With jam wings. How about half strawberry and half blueberry?'

'Yes, and I'll eat one wing and you eat the other.'

'Deal, darling daughter.' She held out her hand for a high-five.

Now, how on earth to make a butterfly... She started with the spine, or whatever that middle bit was that butterflies had, but scrunched up her nose. It was a bit fat. She tried to tease the end of it to make it a bit longer, then added two blobs either side to make wings, touching the corners slightly to extend them out a bit before the batter set and bubbled.

She tested the edges to make sure it was set. 'Now to try and turn it over without messing it up!' she said, sliding the spatula carefully underneath. She lifted it slowly then flipped it, the 'butterfly' retaining its shape. 'Yes!'

Except the more she looked at it the more she wasn't sure it looked like a butterfly.

'It's a fat one,' said Mia. 'But that's a bit rude to call something fat, isn't it.'

'Yes, it is.'

'And what's that?' Mia pointed to the elongated middle of the butterfly.

'It's the spine, or middle part of the butterfly. I'll have to google what it's called.'

'But it looks weird,' her daughter said.

'Yes I know.' She held back a giggle. Olivia waited a moment then lifted the pancake again, placing it on a separate plate. She took a photo, then added some small round shapes to the pan, and while they were setting she added jam to the butterfly. She considered trying again, but shrugged. *This will have to do.* She took another photo, finished the remaining pancakes, and sat down to eat with Mia. As she ate, she texted Joel:

> Pancake challenge complete: Butterfly. Except it looks more like a large monster with a giant penis.

She chuckled.

'What's so funny,' Mia asked.

'Just laughing at the giant butterfly.'

'It's like a monster butterfly,' she said. 'Or an alien.'

'I know, exactly what I was thinking!' Though she decided not to mention her extra observation.

Her phone buzzed:

> Bahahahaha! And damn, that was going to be your challenge for next week. Guess I'll have to think of a new shape now. ;)

Olivia smiled. She was going to reply but another text came in from him:

> A caterpillar.

A caterpillar? What would he ask for next, a dragon? She couldn't resist replying:

> With a giant penis?

He replied:

Surprise me.

And she probably would. She was even surprising herself lately.

CHAPTER FIFTEEN

Olivia was anxious to hear more of her grandma's story as soon as possible, so after work on Monday she picked up a takeaway dinner and took Mia with her to the nursing home. Tuesday was her writing class, and Wednesday she had tried to allocate as 'Writing Wednesday', even though she tried to write parts of the book as often as she could, but having a specified day helped to keep her focused. Plus it was Joel's night to teach his other class, so there was no chance of being interrupted by his texts, even though she loved being interrupted by them.

She helped her grandma eat her food first, while Mia munched on her fried rice, and she took mouthfuls here and there of her own. Then Mia's EarPods went on, and so did the recorder.

'Grandma, what happened after you climbed out the window?'

'I didn't climb out any window,' she said. 'I've been in here all day. Silly people don't let me get out enough.'

'No, I mean, back then. In the past.'

'The past?'

Olivia shuffled closer to the bed. Maybe it wasn't a good

time. Maybe it was too much for her grandma, all this talking and reminiscing. But it was now or never, before her health declined further. The nurse had said she'd been more fatigued the last few days.

She held Mrs May's cool, weathered hand. 'Remember when you got the letter from William asking you to meet him at Lookout Point?'

'William? He wants to meet me?'

Uh-oh.

She held a hand to her forehead and was met with a slight warmth, but it could have been from eating her dinner. And the nurse had done her obs beforehand when she'd arrived and hadn't seemed concerned.

'No, but he did want to meet you in secret, back when you were a young lady.'

'Young. Ahh, to be young again.' Her eyes went distant.

'Do you remember that night, when you climbed out the window to meet William?' Olivia probed, as gently as possible.

'Oh yes,' she replied. 'Have you ever climbed out a window before?'

This might take a while... 'No, but tell me what happened when you did, Grandma.'

'For starters, climbing out was the easy bit. Getting back in was harder. And after I climbed out, I tripped on a rock and tumbled to the ground. I thank my lucky stars no one heard me. What I learned is that you need to put something on the ground under the window to help you get a leg up on your way back in, and also, after you've climbed out it's generally a good idea to look where you're going before attempting to run off into the night.'

Olivia smiled and gave an exaggerated sigh at the ramblings. 'Oh, Grandma, if only you'd told me all this when I was a teenager, it would have made sneaking out of home at night so much easier.' She winked. She'd never snuck out. 'Now, *after* you climbed out, and *after* you tripped on the rock, you went to Lookout Point. What happened there?'

'Lookout Point,' she mumbled.

'Yes, where you met William.'

'I thought he was going to do that thing men do in the films, gently stroke the woman's cheek before kissing her. But when his hand came towards me...' She lifted her good hand slowly to her face, as though imagining it was his. 'He took a twig and leaf from my hair and tossed it to the ground.'

Olivia laughed.

'I had no idea it was even there after I fell. Funny thing is, as soon as he did that, for some reason, that's when I knew I loved him.'

A tiny flutter flitted in Olivia's belly. 'You loved William?'

Mrs May's hand rested loosely beside her neck. 'Love is a strange thing, my dear.' She took a slow breath then turned her face slightly and looked Olivia in the eyes. 'You don't choose it. It chooses you.'

May's Memories of William

If I hadn't been so excited, perhaps I would have noticed the graze on my knee and the twig in my hair, but as soon as I landed on the ground, I picked myself up quick smart and scurried off before anyone saw or heard me. My heart felt like a bundle of bees were buzzing around inside my chest, which sounds rather strange, I know; but as I moved as quickly and quietly as I could, nervous but exhilarating vibrations buzzed within like my heart didn't know what it was doing. Later on, it did. It knew. And it did it anyway.

It fell hard and fast for William.

But back to that night. That cool, fluttery, whimsical night that felt like I had climbed out of my window and into the world of a fairy tale...

I came around the bend of the street near the beach and walked quickly up the hill. There was an overgrown tree in the yard of a nearby house blocking my view, but once I got closer to Lookout Point, I saw him; his silhouette, almost blending into the backdrop of the dark blue-grey sky. He wasn't facing my way, I noticed, as I got closer. Perhaps he hadn't wanted to see if I didn't come. But he must have heard my footsteps, though soft, against the pebbled pathway up the hill, because he turned, and as the breeze ruffled his chaotic hair, a huge smile surfaced.

I stole a quick glance around to check that no one else was about, then returned my gaze to meet his. I reached him and stopped, and his hand came towards me. Wow, I thought, he doesn't want to waste any time. But he removed the twig with a small leaf attached to it from my hair and gave it a toss. Maybe if he had stroked my cheek and looked lovingly into my eyes instead, I wouldn't have fallen for him, strangely enough. Maybe that would have been too clichéd, too charming. But the way he tossed the twig and said with a chuckle, 'I see you went to a lot of trouble to look your best,' while gesturing to the twig and my grazed knee, did something to my heart that was different, unique, out of the ordinary. And I think my heart had been craving that for quite a while without me realising.

'Oh,' I said, brushing some dirt from my knee. 'Had a little tumble on my way here.'

William bent down and inspected my knee. I thought for a moment he was going to fuss over it and try to perform some kind of medical treatment or kiss it better, but he said, 'It's nothing. And it kind of suits you.'

'Suits me?'

'Yes. Makes you look like you've been having an adventure. Which perhaps you have.' A glimmer in his eye made my heart buzz even more.

'Perhaps.' I smiled.

'Or perhaps you're ready for one,' he added.

My fingers fidgeted with each other as though the excess nervous energy needed to be moved around in some way, before it burst out of my chest like a million stars exploding in the sky. 'Perhaps,' I said again, this time more softly, my voice unused to my heart's new state of existence.

Then he leaned against the thin railing, only newly erected to guard against sudden gushes of wind as people stood near the rocky ledge. 'I knew you'd come,' he said.

'You did?'

'It's that look in your eye. That curiosity about life and the unknown. I see it.' He crossed one foot over his other ankle. 'Even if you only wanted to come here to tell me to stop writing those ridiculous letters, I knew you'd come.' He grinned.

I leaned my own hand on the railing. 'But they're not ridiculous,' I said. 'They're the highlight of my day.'

His diamond eyes glimmered and twinkled even more, the moonlight above casting small sparkles around us, like those stars that exploded were now falling upon us.

'Then I shall send more.' His hand moved along the railing until it met with mine, ever so slightly. 'Except I only wish to do so if you wish for things to be more than just letters between us. If you wish to see what magic there may be right here, right now.' One of his fingers lifted and rested on top of mine.

My skin tingled. I wanted more than what life seemed to be leading me towards. More excitement, more possibility, more... magic.

I gulped.

'Meet me here, every night before bedtime, if you can. I'll wait. I'll be here. Life is so much more magical at night, don't you agree?'

I nodded. 'And what will we do here, every night, before bedtime?'

'Our hearts will go on an adventure,' he said, more of his fingers now resting atop mine.

My demure ladylike senses would have removed my hand from under his until he had made a proper, more normal attempt at courting me, but it stayed put. Whatever force was responsible for the gaping wide grin I had flashed around William, and my buzzing bee heart, and my tingling skin, was the same force that glued my hand to that railing and let his slide over mine, sandwiched between cool metal and warm flesh.

The cool night air rushed into my lungs, and this person standing before me was no longer just the friendly young man at the general store, but a mystical, intriguing, love-letter writer whose heart sought mine.

I surprised myself then, by entwining my fingers with his, stepping closer, and – our eyes not leaving each other's – asking him to kiss me. If I was going to climb out a window, trip on a rock and graze my knee, potentially disappoint my mother if she were to find out I had snuck out, I might as well get a kiss out of it all.

I must have surprised William, because at first he stepped back a little, as though he didn't want to risk losing his chance by being too forward, but when I stayed put, my chin raised, he smiled softly, and then his hand did come towards my face. For the other reason this time. And as his fingers lightly brushed my tingling cheek, I sighed, and then his lips became one with mine.

From that moment on, my heart was his, and his was mine.
Until they were no more.

'Oh, Grandma,' Olivia said, 'what a magical evening that must have been.'

'Life isn't always magical,' she said, 'but there are magical moments in life, if you let them in.'

I want to let them in, Olivia thought. *I want to feel that magic with someone. I want to climb out a window and step into a fairy tale...* But she knew in this day and age things were different, people were different, and life was different. Those old days seemed more conducive to romance and fairy tales and magic.

Mia approached the bed. 'Look, Mrs May, I wrote you a letter.'

Mrs May's eyes opened a little wider, and despite the grey shadows arching across the lined skin under them, her eyes still held a youthful sparkle, perhaps the faint glimmer of the memories of that night, her mind remembering what her eyes had seen, what her heart had felt.

Olivia peered across the bed where Mia placed the paper.

Dear Mrs May,

You like letters, so here is one.

I hope you have a wonderful day, Mrs May! I like rhyming. Do you?

I also like unicorns. And books about unicorns.

Do you think unicorns are real? Maybe they live in Heaven. If you meet one, can you say hi to it for me? If I meet one in real life, I'll say hi to it for you.

I like writing letters. I will write more letters. They are fun. And you are fun too.

Love, Mia.

Mrs May had to squint, but Olivia got Mia to read it out for her. Her grandmother smiled and held out her hand towards Mia who took it, then cuddled up alongside her.

'It's a wonderful letter, my darling girl,' she said. 'Promise me you'll keep writing them? Not to me, but to anyone, all throughout your life.'

'I will.' Mia nodded. 'Maybe I could even write a letter to a unicorn!' She giggled.

'Will you write one to me?' Olivia asked.

'But I see you every day. We can talk.'

'Ohh.' Olivia pouted and crossed her arms.

'My dear,' said Mrs May. 'Even if you see someone every day, never forget to cherish them. That is how you keep the magic in your life, you always make an effort to love them more than you think is possible. And there is always more. Love grows, if you let it.'

'Does that mean I have to write my mum letters to show her I love her?'

'Sweetie, you don't have to,' Olivia said. 'It's just one way that a person can tell someone how they feel. You being you is always enough for me.' She came around the side of the bed and placed an arm around her daughter.

'But there is something special about a letter,' said Mrs May. 'Especially this one.' She lifted the paper slightly.

Mia looked at Olivia. 'I will write one for you, Mum. I just have to think of something.'

'Then I look forward to it.' Olivia went back around the other side of the bed and turned off the recorder, grasped her handbag and placed it inside. 'Maybe you can hide the letter and I have to find it.'

'Oh!' Mia's finger shot up in the air. 'Like a treasure hunt?'

'Yes!' Which reminded her of Joel's impending treasure hunt he was supposedly going to create for her. What kind of man did things like that anyway? She shook her head in awe. Maybe there was more magic brewing in her life than she realised. And treasure hunt or no treasure hunt, writing this book was becoming one of its own.

They gathered their things and said goodbye, and on the way to the door, Mrs May called out, 'Mia?' Olivia and Mia turned to look towards the bed. Mrs May smiled and waved. '*I believe in unicorns.*'

CHAPTER SIXTEEN

Olivia yawned as she picked up her coffee mug and took a quick gulp. She didn't drink much coffee but needed it today, after staying up way too late the night before listening to May's recollections of her night at Lookout Point, and writing more of *Memories of May*.

'Mum, you have food on your face.'

'Huh, I do?' Olivia scanned her reflection as she peered at the mirror in the hall. 'Oh, so I do.' She wiped it away. 'Anyway, we better get somebody off to school, time is getting away from us!'

She handed Mia her schoolbag, grabbed her handbag, took one last gulp of coffee, and headed out the door.

'Mum,' said Mia, calmly, as though they weren't running late. 'How does time get away from us? Doesn't it just stay the same?'

'No, well, yes. But... Oh, sweetie, not now, Mummy's brain is not working quite well enough to answer tricky questions. Let's talk more after school.'

'But you're going to your class tonight.'

'That's right. You have a good memory. Sometime after my class then.'

'But it'll be my bedtime and I'll be tired and so will you.'

'That is true.' They hopped in the car and Olivia started the engine, almost reversing into the garage door she had forgotten to open. She pressed the button on the key and tapped her fingers impatiently on the steering wheel as it rolled up slowly. 'And that is how time gets away.' Olivia chuckled. 'We get too busy and we think we run out of time, but really we are just silly nincompoops for doing too much and letting ourselves get too busy and making it seem like time is getting away.'

Mia laughed. 'Nincompoops!' She laughed again. 'I'm going to call my friends nincompoops and make them laugh today.'

Olivia reversed out and turned onto the road. 'Maybe you can write your nincompoop friends a letter.' She grinned and shook her head at this silly morning.

'Ha!' Another laugh exploded from Mia's mouth. 'Dear Nincompoop, you're a nincompoop. From your best Nincompoop. Ha-ha-ha!' Olivia glanced in the rear-view mirror at her daughter's rosy-cheeked face in fits of laughter.

They arrived at school and when Olivia handed Mia her schoolbag, she noticed it felt lighter than usual. She zipped it open. 'Ah, crap.' Mia's lunchbox was missing.

'Mum, isn't that a bad word?'

'What? No, not really. But don't say it at school.'

'So it *must* be a bad word, otherwise I could say it. Crap, crap, crap!' Mia giggled, and a mother passing by with a kindergarten child glared at her.

She felt like saying, 'What? At least I didn't say something worse.'

'C'mon, Mia, no time to waste. Let's get you inside. I'll have to drive back home to get your lunchbox, bring it back in for you, okay?'

'What if you don't get back by lunchtime?' Mia looked genuinely worried. 'That would really be crap.'

'Honey, I will be right back, fifteen minutes at the most.' Then she would have to race to the store to open up.

After shuffling her daughter through the small crowd of waist-high little humans through the door to the classrooms, she returned to the car, drove home, grabbed Mia's lunch, then went to go back outside to where she'd parked on the driveway, but something made her stop. Just for a moment, she stopped, breathed and stood still. Would the world fall apart if she took this brief moment? Would time get away from her, as she'd explained to Mia, and everything would be a disaster? Or would it be a disaster anyway and she might as well take this brief moment to have a moment of peace within the disaster? See, even in her brief moment of peace she was overthinking and worrying. She breathed again, wondered what would happen if she simply sat on the couch, put on a movie, and did nothing but veg out all day until school pick-up time. Life would still go on. Maybe it wouldn't be a disaster. But she would lose income from the store. She had to go. And she had to deliver Mia's lunch. Her hand reached for the doorknob but the window at the side of the house caught her eye. Here she was, late-thirties, and she had never once climbed out a window. Wasn't that something that every child or teenager should have done at least once? Or was that only in movies, and her grandma's past?

She could leave now, go to the school, go do another day at work, or she could take an extra minute or two to climb out a window, tick something else off her 'do something differently' list, and then get on with her day.

She laughed that she was even thinking such crazy thoughts, but the side window and the kitchen ones were the only ones without screens on them, each with a knob that wound around in circles to open the glass pane outward. Okay, so she'd have to climb out, come back in the door, then close and lock the window, then go out the door again, but that wasn't the point. And she couldn't do something so silly if Mia was around.

No time like the present.

She shrugged, placed her handbag and Mia's lunch bag on the windowsill, then wound out the window. The question was, could she fit through? She was slim enough, no big boobs to get in the way. It looked wide enough. She sat on the edge, lifted her right leg up and over and through the gap. Easy. She lifted her left leg, the back of her leg muscle stretching as she raised it up to be able to put it on the same side of the winding cable as her other leg. Then pointed her toe to thread it down the gap. Both legs were through. *Now to lift my butt off and slide through...* She wriggled her hips, her hands on the window ledge to steady herself, glad the window wasn't in view of her neighbours. At a slight angle, she lowered herself further, but her left thigh met with the winding cable and snagged on her pants. She yanked at the thread and it came free; still, her thighs and hips were wedged between the windowpane and the wall and the cable. She tried rotating her hips to flatten herself against the wall edge. They wouldn't budge, and she was getting the world's biggest wedgie. *Oh my God, no, no, no!* She glanced around, as though a solution would miraculously appear. She attempted to swivel and twist, and even wondered if anything oily and slippery was in reach so she could somehow slide herself out. Her handbag! Despite needing her hands to hold herself in a more comfortable position, she lifted her left hand to open her bag, and yanked at the zip. It toppled sideways; she grasped it back before it dropped through the gap. Prying the bag open, she hesitated. Hand cream? Was she really going to lather hand cream all over her hips in the hope of slithering through? Then she'd have to come back inside and get changed. But at least she wouldn't be stuck anymore. She found the cream and popped open the lid. *Oh God, am I really doing this?* Apparently so, she thought, as she squirted the cream onto her thigh near the cable, and then onto the other one against the windowpane. She rubbed it around and wriggled her hips again, but they seemed to be swelling either side from the pressure and blood circulation being half cut off. 'Crap, crap, crap!' she echoed Mia's words from before.

Glancing at the time on her watch, her heart beat faster. She had to get back to the school and then to work as soon as possible. She plucked her phone from her bag and pressed contacts. Who was she supposed to call in this situation?

She waited at the sound of the ringtone.

'Hi, you've reached Diana Chevalier, I'm currently–'

Olivia ended the voicemail message. 'Geez, Mum! Answer your phone.' She called again, but still voicemail. She called Marcus's number. When his went to voicemail she remembered he was at a dental appointment in Welston and not due in to work till late morning.

She scrolled her contacts. *A-ha!*

'April's Glow, April speaking.'

'April! Hi, it's me, Olivia!'

'Hey, how's things? Why are you calling the store?'

'Because I needed you to answer.'

'Is everything okay? Mia okay? Your grandma?'

'Yes, yes, but... I kinda need help. Is Belinda there with you?'

'Not yet, she'll be here later, why?'

'I may require some, ah... assistance, from someone. I seem to be stuck in a bit of a jam. Literally.'

'What? Jam? Like, jam you eat? What are you talking about, girl?'

'Not jam, but I'm jammed. Stuck. In my window, at home. I

tried to climb out.' Olivia held the phone slightly away from her ear as April burst out laughing.

'Why on earth are you climbing out your window? Actually, don't answer. Okay, what do you need... fire and rescue, pliers, scissors, forceps?' She spoke and chuckled at the same time.

'Anything, I can't seem to budge no matter how hard I try, and I don't like the idea of slicing my thigh open trying to force myself through.' Olivia grunted with the effort of another failed attempt.

'Okay, well I can come and... hang on. Damn.'

'What is it?'

'I have a sales rep coming in about five or ten minutes for a meeting about her new range of candles.' April hummed. 'It's okay, I can call her and tell her to wait, or reschedule. I'll put the closed sign up and be right over.'

'Oh God, I'm such an idiot. Don't worry, I'll try calling my mum again first. Or Peter.'

'I could ask Zac,' April piped up. 'Oh, but he's on his way to his psychologist appointment, I can't disrupt his routine.'

Was her inner circle really this small that she had only a few local people she could turn to in a situation like this without risking huge embarrassment?

'Hang on,' Olivia said. 'I might know someone who can help. I'll call you back if I can't get anyone.'

'You sure?'

'Yeah, you get on with your day and I'll be back in touch if I'm desperate.'

Like she wasn't already. She didn't like the idea of calling the professionals and being the laughing stock of Tarrin's Bay, perhaps making it into the newspaper. She would be laughed at either way, but better it was only by one or two people. Though she cringed when she called his number.

'Hey there, what's up?' Joel said.

'What's stuck, more like it,' Olivia replied.

'Stuck? Are you still working on that transition point in the book when your grandma takes over the tailor's premises and turns it into the bookstore? Because you should write it the way we discussed, like how–'

'No, nothing about the book! I'm literally stuck. In a window.'

'Whaat?' Joel laughed. 'Whose window?'

'Mine. Can you just come help me, please? I can't find anyone else. And my thighs hurt. And I have a wedgie.'

Did I really just tell him that I had a wedgie?

He laughed again. 'Dare I ask how you got in this literally stuck wedgie-predicament?'

'Just help. Please.'

'Okay, okay. On my way.'

'You'll have to come around the side, on the left. Open the side gate, it has no lock, just a latch if you reach over.'

'Should I hire the motorbike again so I can give you a fast ride to the hospital for emergency wedgie treatment?'

'Oh, stop, you can laugh and make jokes all you want *after* you get me out of here.'

'Awesome. Look forward to it. Already coming up with a few more.'

Olivia shook her head. She should have accepted April's offer to help.

While she waited, she called the chemist near her store and asked if someone could whip up a quick sign to stick on her shop window to say she'd be there to open up ASAP. Thankfully, with their multiple staff and early opening hours, someone was glad to help.

She heard a car's engine abating. Footsteps, the jiggling of the latch on the side gate, then laughter as he came into view.

'Oh, Olivia, look at you. Classic!' He reached into his

pocket.

'Don't you dare take a photo!'

'But don't you want to remember this moment years later when your grandkids want to write your life story? You'll have photographic evidence.'

'Certainly not. Now get me out or I'll boycott your class and tell everyone you're a terrible teacher.' Her thighs were really aching now.

'All right, but first... an explanation?'

She sighed. 'I was just doing something different.'

'That's for sure,' he said. 'From pancake shapes to wedging yourself in a window. Great progress, I'm impressed!'

She turned away from his mocking and sighed again.

'Okay, I'll stop. I can see you're a bit over the whole thing.' He approached and inspected the situation.

'I just wanted to climb out a window. Like my grandma did when she was young, that's all. I've never done it, and when I came back home to get Mia's lunch, I thought what the heck, I'll give it a go. Stupid, huh?'

'Not at all. Actually, I am impressed with how dedicated you're being with this whole *new experience* stuff. And honouring your grandma's life. So you got stuck in a window along the way, big deal. Next week this won't even matter. Life moves on. Even wedgies don't last forever.' He grinned. Then he looked closer at her thighs. 'Is that?'

'Hand cream. My fantastic solution. Great help that load of gunk was.'

'At least your pants will be soft.' He placed two of his fingers onto her thigh near the cable, trying to edge them between it.

'Well this is... awkward,' she said.

'Not for me.'

What did he mean by that?

'If I can just... get... some room between, see if you can

wriggle down further. Otherwise give me your keys and I'll go into the house and help you from there. Or I'll get a screwdriver and undo the screws on the window cable so I can lift the pane out further.' He fiddled a bit and a slight giggle erupted from her mouth.

'Laughing at yourself now?'

'No, I was just thinking... do you think I could write my own survival memoir? Maybe something like... *One More Try*, or *One More Phone Call*, or...' She glanced at his face, trying to read his expression. 'Sorry, that was probably in bad taste. I didn't mean to downplay what you went through, I was just trying to make light of things.'

'Oh, no probs. No offence taken. I was just trying to think of a better title. Like... *One More Squirt of Hand Cream*, or *One More Joke From Joel*.'

This time she laughed properly. 'And I thought this day couldn't get any more weird and ridiculous.'

'Here we go,' he grunted, as he wound the cable to its limit and held it tight. 'When I yank it, see if you can slip through.' He yanked, and she wriggled down further, warmth flooding her skin where her thigh had been jammed. She was still kind of wedged, but her feet touched the ground. 'Almost there. Now, move further through as I...' He pushed the flesh of her thigh against his palm, separating it from the cable as much as possible, while holding the window pane out as much as possible. 'If I get a splinter, you're shouting me a pack of Band-Aids,' he said.

'Of course.' She smiled, wriggling further down, feeling the release as she manoeuvred through the gap, then angled her torso through to slip underneath the pane. 'Oh thank God,' she said.

'You can just call me Joel.'

She whacked him on the arm. 'Very funny. But thank you.'

She adjusted her clothing, and trying to be discreet, her wedgie. 'Oh man, I have to get to the school and work.' She grabbed her bag and Mia's lunch. 'I'm late.'

'Can I help?'

She shook her head, an automatic motherly reaction that made her feel like she could handle everything herself. 'It's okay.'

'You sure? Why don't I go and open your store for you, at least so any customers can wander in and browse. I'll keep them talking and use my old sales powers of persuasion to make them spend a hundred bucks, minimum.' He gave a confident nod.

'You don't have to. I'll just be a bit late. Might not even get any customers until later.'

'Gimme,' he said, his hand out. 'Keys. You go to the school. I'll open the store, turn lights on, and that will save you at least a minute when you do arrive. I promise I won't grab an armful of books and do a runner.' His palm remained open in front of her.

She chuckled and handed him the keys to the store. 'Fair enough, but if you move all your books to the front and block the entrance so people have to see them when they walk in, I'm...'

'Boycotting my class and telling everyone I'm a terrible teacher.'

'I was going to say moving all your books to the clearance bin, but that too.'

'You can trust me,' he said.

'Okay. Off you go. I'll see you there once I've...' She glanced at her pants. 'Changed, and closed the window from the inside, and exited my house in the most normal and boring way possible.'

'Done. See you soon, daredevil.' He winked, walked off and out the gate.

She glanced at her watch. This was going to be one long and interesting day.

CHAPTER SEVENTEEN

Joel was still smiling when he opened up the community hall that night. He'd thought that if he were to get up close and personal with a woman's thighs while in Tarrin's Bay, Olivia's at that, it would be for other reasons than helping to pry her from the grip of an old window.

He set up his projector and laptop, aimed the light at the screen, and prepared the PowerPoint slides for tonight's class, which was all about bringing the past into the present – how to integrate a person's earlier life experiences into the main storyline to show how they had an impact.

Writing this lesson had made Joel think a lot about his own past. Without the challenges he'd been through, he would not have become the person he was, and may possibly never have been in the life-threatening position he'd been in, nor become a bestselling memoir author. It blew his mind how one event triggered another, and then another, and before you knew it life was like a series of falling dominos, the momentum unstoppable until the last one fell.

Olivia was making the Tarrin's Bay domino rather interesting, and fun. He hated to be idle, and helping her with her book-worthy moments was filling his spare time with something different for himself. If he went all out, and if they had more time, her book-worthy moments list and experiences could potentially become a memoir in itself. He mentally reminded himself to put the idea out there to her, if only to give an example of how ideas can be generated, and life can be made the most of. He knew she was busy focusing on her grandma's book, not to mention spending as much time with her as possible before her last domino would fall.

He simply hoped these experiences would add some light-hearted fun to her life while she was under all this extra pressure. He'd be gone in a few weeks, and though he sometimes found himself wanting to create some other experiences with her, he knew it was pointless because he'd be gone soon and she didn't need the distraction. He was inexplicably attracted to her, but she deserved someone better than him. He wouldn't stay, he knew he wouldn't. Life called for him in multiple directions, and he would always follow. He loved the relaxed pace and beautiful landscape here, but staying put in small-town life was not his thing.

When the room was set up, he sat on the edge of the desk and opened the browser on his phone. After his next course further south in a few months, he'd go and explore up north in Queensland, create some new adventures of the tropical kind. Not the touristy things, he'd done all them. He'd started bookmarking websites and making lists of unique experiences he wanted to explore up there. The next phase of his journey was taking shape, and he couldn't wait.

But for now, time to help others with their own journeys.

The door opened and Mr Donovan walked in, gradually followed by the rest of the class. Olivia was last; she entered with a hint of pink on her cheeks and quickly diverted her gaze from his as she took her seat. It was so cute; he couldn't help but smile.

'Why are you so happy tonight, Mr F?' asked Dylan.

Joel glanced toward the shark-attack survivor whose opening pages of his memoir had captivated him completely. 'Happy? Hmm, I'm breathing, I'm living the dream, I'm spending the evening with you fascinating lot.' He held up his hands and glanced around. 'And I had a great day, surfing, walking, and rescuing the odd damsel in distress.'

He couldn't resist.

He glanced her way, and her cheeks flamed red.

'Yeah?' asked Dylan. 'Like, did you help an old lady cross the road?'

'Nah, helped a young lady escape the clutches of an evil monster made of wood and metal.'

'I'm confused,' said Mr Donovan. 'What exactly are you talking about?'

'It was touch and go for a while, but I managed to set her free and avoid injury myself. We were lucky. I think the damsel only suffered a few minor bruises, but I can't be sure because she wouldn't show me.'

'Sounds intriguing,' said Olivia, which surprised him, because he thought she would stay quiet and wait for the topic to be finished, even though no one knew he was talking about her. 'I'm sure the damsel was very grateful for your help, but I'm guessing she may not appreciate her predicament being discussed in a public forum.'

'Maybe not. But,' Joel said, raising his finger and walking across the front of the room, 'it's yet another example of how to draw a reader in. Dylan wanted to know what happened, Mr D was confused, and so as readers, they would want to keep reading to find out what happened.'

'What did happen, exactly?' asked Mr Donovan.

'Ah, I'll have to leave that to your imaginations so we can get onto the main topic of tonight. But firstly, on to those opening pages...'

He talked about the pages he'd read, what did and didn't work, and some samples were shared and discussed. As he helped the students find the core emotional hook of their opening pages, he was filled with a sense of gratitude. 'You know, guys, whether these books get published, read by many, or read by a few, you've done good. Even just to start something.' He walked between some of the desks and sat on the edge of an empty one. 'It's a real privilege reading your stories. And each is as important as the other. I can't wait to see the finished results, so make sure you keep me posted in our Facebook group or via email.'

'Mr F, if I get published and have a book launch, will you launch it with me and be like a guest speaker or something?' Dylan asked.

Joel smiled. 'You bet. We could have cardboard cut-out sharks, whadd'ya reckon?'

Dylan laughed. 'Totally. Sounds awesome.'

For a young dude who had almost been killed, he was amazed by his resilience and acceptance of what had happened. He'd spoken to Dylan a bit via text about his experience and his book, and knew that making a joke like that wouldn't be in bad taste. The guy made them himself all the time, he said hardly a day went by when he didn't take an opportunity to make a pun about sharks or bites. Joel had told him that despite the serious nature of his story, if he could add his sense of humour to the book it would endear him even more to readers and make his story more enjoyable to read.

He'd met many interesting people throughout his adventures, but by teaching these courses with small groups, he was meeting many more. Discovering new people and their stories was becoming an adventure in itself, one he'd never really focused on before. It had always been about the physical experience, the adrenaline, the rush... but now, and as time seemed to pass more quickly than it used to, he was beginning to understand how the human mind, and heart, held many stories of its own and many adventures yet to discover.

But still, he would always crave that rush. And would always give in. And once it was done, he'd look for the next.

'Sorry about before,' Joel said after the students filtered out and Olivia was hanging about. It occurred to him afterwards he probably sounded like a chauvinistic pig, calling her a damsel in distress.

She waved her hand. 'No big deal. You helped me out of a tricky situation, so I'm glad. And you were right, it was a good example about establishing reader interest.' She shrugged.

'Still, sorry if I offended you. Sometimes I don't think.' He switched off the lights. 'I reckon after a while you would have got yourself out anyway. I just sped up the process.'

'Who knows. I was just glad to be able to get out and get on with my day.'

'I bet. Thanks for calling me and trusting me to help you. If it were me stuck in that window, I'd probably be too stubborn to call anyone for help.'

'Probably,' she agreed with a grin.

He walked outside with her. 'Such a nice night, so clear and mild.'

'It is.' Olivia looked around. 'Today, I stopped for a moment. Like completely stopped, just to see what it felt like. You ever done that?'

Joel shrugged. 'I don't meditate if that's what you mean, but after a hike I'll stop and sit for a bit, take in the view, my surroundings. But I guess I'm always thinking of something or observing something.'

'Me too, usually.' Olivia stalled outside her car, glanced around, then looked at him. She had a different look in her eyes, like they were seeking something. 'Got time for a walk?'

Joel raised his eyebrows. Him, got time? She was the one who never seemed to have any. 'Always,' he replied. 'Anywhere in particular, or shall we see where the wind takes us?'

Olivia held out her hand. 'I don't feel any wind, so how about... Lookout Point?'

He nodded. 'Let's go.'

They walked across Miracle Park, usually coloured with children and people and sunlight, tonight subdued with darkness and moonlight guiding their way along the grass.

'My grandma walked up here one night to meet William, that man from her past I told you about, around seventy years ago.'

'Oh?' He turned his head to look at her for a moment as they walked.

'Yeah, she snuck out, climbed out the window, that's why I tried it today, for your information.'

Joel chuckled. 'A-ha, now I get it. Are you going to tell her about your adventure?'

'Of course, she will find it amusing. She tripped and fell after climbing out hers, so I blame my genes for today's situation.' She smiled, and a light breeze lifted her hair behind her shoulders.

'When in doubt, blame genetics.'

'Exactly.' They walked across the street and started up the hill towards the lookout. 'Speaking of genetics, looks like we both didn't really know our real fathers. There wasn't much in your book about him.'

'That's right. He wasn't around, don't even know where he is now. Mum hooked up with a couple of new men until my stepdad came on the scene and, well, you know the rest.' He shrugged. No matter how often he talked about it with someone, he always felt this strange sense of rawness, or was it emptiness, gnawing away inside. He hadn't had a good male role model, so he just kind of became his own. Became the person he wanted to be. But the one person he wanted for his mum to have in her life, a caring and devoted partner, he had yet to become for anyone. Didn't know how. Had never tried. Not that he hadn't had opportunities, but he'd never felt inclined to hang around long enough to find out. If he kept moving, avoided deeper, more meaningful relationships, he wouldn't risk hurting anyone, or himself.

'My mum is so much happier now she's found a new guy. Can't keep them apart,' Olivia said. 'But I do remember when I was young she was often stressed out, and it was only as I got a bit older I realised she was lonely. I'm happy for her now.'

'And what about you... any recent relationships?'

Olivia appeared to tense a little, wrapped her arms around her waist. 'It is getting a little cool now,' she said.

He nodded.

'Um, no,' she said. 'I've met a few here and there, but to be honest I haven't had a serious relationship since before Mia. And I don't mean her dad, he was just a...' She lowered her face and shook her head.

'A one-night stand?'

'I guess so. But that in itself was a one-off, I don't normally do that sort of thing. Don't ever, actually. Just the once.'

Not only had he helped open her window, but somehow she was opening her heart a little to him, and he wondered how and why she felt comfortable doing that with him.

'I understand,' he said. 'If it makes you feel any better, I haven't had a serious relationship at all.'

'Never?' She turned and looked at him.

'Never.' One-night stands, he'd had plenty of those, and a few great girlfriends, but nothing had ever lasted more than one or two months, three at the most.

'Is that because you've always been on the move?'

'Partly,' he replied. 'But when I was in sales I wasn't on the move, and even then I hadn't had one. I dunno, maybe no one liked me enough!' He laughed, but deep down he knew that wasn't the case. Some had wanted more from him, but he hadn't been able to be the man they were looking for, so he'd often let women go before they got to that stage so as to spare them any deeper hurt.

'I seriously doubt that,' she said. 'You're a charmer.'

'I am?' he asked. 'Well, I'll take that as a compliment, but the truth is, I just found it easier to keep things simple. In life, and in love.'

'So I discovered in your book. And your promise to your mum, to keep moving forward and not stay stuck in one spot.'

'Yep. And like I said in tonight's class, our past, though it doesn't define us, it does help create who we are and what we choose to do in life. If you look back, you can usually see a link between early events and future ones.'

'Are we all doomed then, do you think?' They reached the top of the hill. 'To forever live out our lives at the mercy of our childhood wounds?'

He shook his head as they neared the lookout platform. 'The wounds, they are one chapter, not the whole book. We can always start writing a new chapter. Or even a new book.'

They stopped. He leaned a hand on the railing, at the same time she did. He glanced at her hand only an inch away from his, a simple, thin silver ring on her middle finger.

'I like your perspective. I never thought about things like that till you came along. I'm glad I'm having some new experiences, so thank you for that.' Her cheeks rounding out her smile had a glow to them under the moonlight.

'It's my pleasure, Olivia. I'm having some new experiences of my own, thanks to *your* new experiences.' He smiled and resisted the urge to touch her hand.

'I'll try to keep it going once you're gone,' she said. 'I'll try not to fall back into old, safe ways.'

'Well, keep me posted,' he said. And he really hoped she would. He didn't always keep in touch with every new friend he made on his travels, but some he felt compelled to, and she was one of them. 'You don't need me to continue your new adventures. You can do them perfectly well on your own.'

She nodded. 'I guess we've both learned to do things for ourselves in life, do things our own way. Just in different ways.'

'Yes. You and me are more alike than we think, Miss Chevalier.'

'Except you move, I stay.'

And I run, you hide, he thought. 'Perfect opposites,' he remarked.

She nodded, then tilted her head. 'Have you ever climbed out a window, Mr Foster?'

'Heaps of times. But never been stuck. Have also jumped over fences, manoeuvred through barbed wire, climbed rooftops, and hidden underneath a house. But they are other stories.'

'Show-off,' she said, lifting her hand and lightly slapping his bicep with the back of her hand. When her hand lowered, it brushed against his on the railing, and her gaze followed it, as did his. His skin tingled a little at her soft skin, and he wanted to feel it again, but held his hand steady.

She glanced back up at him. 'My grandma's hands were on

here, like this,' she said. 'Although I think the railing may have been replaced at some stage, but still. Standing here at night, with William, all those years ago. Isn't it weird how the past becomes the past. Like, at what point does yesterday become old enough to be "the past"? Each day merges into another, and all of a sudden the yesterdays are the years that have gone by, and today is some magical new thing that feels so permanent yet so fleeting.'

Joel got out his phone, tapped in the words she had said, then texted it to her, her phone buzzing a moment later. 'Put that in your book,' he said. 'Those words. They're the things that people like to read, not just the action and suspense of an intense situation, but those wonderings and musings about life that people can relate to.'

'Huh,' she said. 'I never would have thought to write that. I've been focused so much on getting the facts right, all the details and timelines.'

'Those things are the structure, the framework, but what makes a real-life story magical to read are those nuances of thought, those words that jump off the page because they somehow connect with a reader's own thoughts, emotions, and mortality. Brings a book to life.'

'Wow, Joel, that was the best bit of insight you've given all night.'

He tapped in his own words so he could add them to one of his classes. 'It's usually when we don't try too hard that the right words come along. Life is the same, the best things happen unexpectedly.'

'So true,' she said softly as she looked out across the ocean. 'Well, here's an unexpected invitation.' She turned herself to face him. 'Would you like to join us for pancakes this Sunday? Before our book-worthy moment, which you are yet to enlighten me about?'

He couldn't remember the last time he'd had pancakes, and now his stomach was grumbling. 'You and Mia? I'd love to. As long as you follow through on my challenge.'

'The caterpillar shape? Of course, and if you're lucky and Mia doesn't beat you to it, you can eat the caterpillar.' She took her hand from the railing and crossed her arms. 'But you have to take your plate to the dishwasher and help clean up.'

'I always do,' he replied. 'What time shall I be there?'

'Hmm, around eight thirty?'

'Deal. That will give us enough time to eat and clean and get to your surprise on time.'

'Can't you give me a hint?' she pleaded, her hands in prayer position.

He loved watching her squirm. 'Uh-uh. The best things happen unexpectedly, remember?'

'But the day itself will be expected, I just don't know what I'm expecting,' she said.

To be honest, he didn't know either. And he wasn't talking about the book-worthy moment, but the fact that the more time he spent with her, the more surprises he got, and the less he knew how to handle his unexpected attraction to her.

CHAPTER EIGHTEEN

After their regular Friday lunch date in which Joel had convinced Olivia to eat French fries with tomato sauce (she had never tried it before in her life), he was now about to try her Sunday pancakes and meet her little girl.

This made him nervous for two reasons. Firstly, it felt more intimate, being in her house. She was a student, and a friend, but she was also occupying his mind far more often than seemed normal for a student and a friend. Secondly, he wasn't used to being around kids. He didn't know if he was any good with them. What if the girl trod on his foot or punched him in the gut or something? Kids did things like that to new people, didn't they? At least, he did, when he was a kid.

He knocked his fist on the timber door, and the curtain beside the door flicked to the side. A brown-haired girl peeked through. 'He's here!' her muffled voice said.

He prepared a smile on his face and the door opened. He glanced down. 'Hi, you must be Olivia,' he said, holding out his hand.

She giggled. 'No, that's my mum's name!'

'Oh, is it?' He scratched his head.

'Yes. I'm Mia,' she said. She lifted her hand and he tensed his gut for a moment in case the sweetness was an act and she was really a little rascal. But she held on to his hand gently and he gave it a small shake. 'And you're Joel Foster. My mum told me. She also told me I have to let you eat the caterpillar.'

Maybe she would punch him or tread on his foot for that instead.

He chuckled. 'I'd be happy to share it with you, if you like.'

'Can I eat its head?'

'Of course.'

'Okay. We can share.'

'Mia, let him in!' Olivia's voice called out.

The girl stepped back and skipped off, and he walked through, closing the door behind him. He approached her in the kitchen. 'Hi.'

'Hi, sorry, come on in. Can't leave my pancakes at this crucial moment.' She was wearing a soft-looking cream-coloured top, and a soft smile, and he guessed her skin would be even softer.

'Let me have a look.' He sidled up next to the stove and observed. 'Wait, is that a–'

'Leg!' she exclaimed. 'It's a leg, not a...'

'A...' He waved his hands around in circles.

'A different body part that isn't a leg,' she said.

Mia was at the fridge, withdrawing the jam. 'Do caterpillars have legs?' she asked.

Olivia shrugged. 'I'm sure they do. Don't they? If they didn't they would be slugs or something.'

'Eww, I don't want to eat slugs. Even pancake ones.' Mia held her stomach and pretended to puke.

Yep, she had gut-punching and foot-treading potential.

'Mia, manners please, we have a guest.'

'Sorry,' she said. 'Would you eat slugs, Joel Foster?' Mia placed the jam on the small round table and looked up at Joel.

'I would, Mia Chevalier. *Especially* pancake ones.' He grinned. Then he hoped that Olivia's daughter did indeed share the same surname as her mother, but he'd assumed so, since her father had been a one-night stand.

Mia laughed, then sat at the table. 'Boys like yucky things.'

When Olivia was turned to face the stove, he glanced at Mia and placed his hand on his stomach, then pretended to puke, silently. She laughed again. 'I think, most of the time, boys pretend to like yucky things so they look tough,' he said.

'Ah, is that right?' asked Olivia. 'The secret is out.'

''Fraid so,' he said. 'But that caterpillar is looking pretty good.'

Olivia lifted the 'legs' off the frying pan and arranged them on the plate with the circles forming the caterpillar's body.

Joel pointed to the caterpillar's butt. 'Is that a–'

'Tail!' she said. 'It's a tail.' She adjusted the small protrusion.

'Do caterpillars have tails?' asked Mia.

'This one does,' Olivia replied.

Joel smiled; this was a new experience for him. He didn't have brothers and sisters and so had not been exposed to nieces and nephews, and a few of his friends had kids but as he was always on the move he only visited them occasionally, when he was passing through various towns.

'Okay, let's eat up while they're warm.' Olivia placed the plate of circle pancakes in the centre of the table and the caterpillar creation in front of one of the chairs. 'Your breakfast is served,' she said, gesturing for him to sit.

'Thank you, madam,' he said. 'I'm very impressed with this caterpillar, even if it does have a rather large–'

'Tail! And legs.' She took her seat. Then she got straight back up again. 'Oh, coffee?'

'No thanks,' he replied. 'Just had one. The juice is fine.' He opened the cap off the bottle that was also in the centre of the table. 'Juice, Mia?'

'Yes please. And don't forget I'm eating the head.'

'Mia!'

'What? He said I could, Mum. Ask him.'

She glanced his way. 'The head is all hers. I'll have the body and the legs and tail.' He winked, then decapitated the poor caterpillar and handed it to Mia.

'I'm going to put huuuuge eyes on it.' She plonked two blobs of jam on the caterpillar's head.

'I'm going to put huge eyes on its body,' Joel said, spooning some jam onto his.

'Ha-ha! It's an alien. Like that butterfly, Mum. Except a caterpillar one.'

Olivia nodded. 'Looks that way.'

'Can Joel Foster come for breakfast pancakes every Sunday?' the girl asked.

Olivia shifted in her seat and opened her mouth but no sound came out.

'Ah, but Sunday pancakes are for mothers and daughters. I'm just a visitor today.'

And now there was another reason not to let his growing attraction to Olivia lead to anything. A child was involved, and that made it even more difficult. Kids needed stability and certainty. He'd never had that as a child, and he would never wish to be the cause of any disappointment. And she was cute, and sweet, and he could tell Olivia had done a great job. Today was a one-off, and it would be best if his interactions with Mia were kept to a minimum while he spent time in Tarrin's Bay with her mother.

'And what a nice day it is!' Olivia said with a little too much enthusiasm, glancing towards the kitchen window. 'I can't wait to see what surprises are in store.' She eyed him with nervous curiosity.

'All in good time,' he replied.

'Did you know that time can get away from you?' asked Mia, and he had lost count of how many questions she'd asked since he'd arrived. That was the other thing he'd forgotten about children – they were tiny question machines, he'd recalled a friend of his saying.

'I believe it can,' he said. 'That's why we have to make the most of every day. And what are you going to do today, Miss Mia?'

'I'm going to Nanna's, and, oh! Mum, I forgot to tell you!' She turned to face Olivia. 'I'm finally going to write you a letter.'

Olivia's eyes widened. 'Oh, yes, I'd forgotten about that too. That will be nice, I look forward to reading it.' She spread jam on a pancake and took a small bite. He wanted to tell her that she had a small smudge of jam at the corner of her lip but decided to wait a while.

'My great-grandma, Mrs May, likes letters,' Mia said. 'She's dying.'

Joel tensed slightly. He'd also forgotten how honest and direct children could be. 'I'm sorry to hear about that. I hear she's a great woman.'

Mia nodded. 'We visit her a lot. Nanna told me we are going to see her today. But Mum can't come, because she'll be out with you.'

'That's right. She can visit her another day.'

Mia nodded again, then stood. 'I'm full!' She went to walk off.

'Um, Mia?' Olivia gestured to her plate.

'Oops.' Mia picked it up and took it to the dishwasher. 'That was a delicious caterpillar head.'

'Glad to hear it,' he said. 'The rest of it was pretty yum too.' He smiled at her as she walked off to the living room.

'Sorry for the onslaught of questions and stuff.' Olivia poured herself some juice.

Joel shook his head. 'Nothing to apologise for. She's great. Takes after her mum.' He smiled.

Olivia smiled back. 'Can I get you anything else, some toast, or eggs, or…'

'No thanks, all good here.' He patted his stomach. 'And probably best if we don't eat a large meal before today.'

Olivia looked at him with eyes wide and fearful.

God he loved this.

'It's okay, it'll be fun. I promise.'

She took a breath and stood. 'I hope I don't regret this.'

'Do you regret it yet?' Joel asked, as Olivia stood in the airfield, an unsteady breeze flicking her hair around her face and in her eyes as she stared at the light plane.

Her stomach felt as unsteady as the breeze. 'Not while I'm standing here on solid ground, I'm not. I'm quite happy to stay right here and let you go up on my behalf. I won't regret that.' Her words came out shaky and high-pitched.

'C'mon, think about the future. When your grandkids are asking you about your life's adventures, what are you going to tell them, that you stood on the ground and looked at planes from a distance? Wow.'

'Yes. I could tell them that. Not everyone steps foot inside an airfield.'

'Exactly, so what a great opportunity you have right here right now.'

'Yep, I'll keep standing here and absorbing all the sensory

detail so I can relay it to my grandkids in future.' She gave a single nod.

She'd rather go on a roller-coaster than this. At least they were attached to things that were stuck to the ground.

'I'll be going up with you. It seats four.'

'Tell me you're not the one flying it?'

'No, there will be a fully qualified pilot at the controls. I'll be there purely for my own entertainment.'

'Entertainment? Watching me freak out and possibly throw up is entertainment?' A muscle twitched in one of her legs.

'Now that you say it...'

She flicked his arm.

'Am I going to be subjected to minor pain and injuries every time I'm with you, Olivia Chevalier?'

'Yes.' She flicked him again.

'Good thing I have a high pain tolerance.' He wore a smug grin. 'Nah, the entertainment is the view. You wait and see. So cool to be up there looking over the land, feeling high and free. It's been a while for me, actually. Looking forward to it.'

'Joel.' Olivia turned to face him, one last attempt to plead her case. 'People die in light plane crashes all the time. I've seen it on the news. I don't want to be tonight's headline.'

'Honestly, don't worry, they are actually quite rare. And there's usually some specific reason. But I can assure you, the plane I have arranged has been checked and tested and the pilot has never crashed in his life. Besides, the news doesn't like to show things like... "Another light plane flew today and didn't crash".'

'Very funny.'

'I thought so.'

She shifted to her other foot. 'How long will it take?'

He shrugged. 'Depends how much fun we have. We could be up there all afternoon.'

She glared at him.

'Or not. Probably not too long, it's just a joy flight.'

'People get joy out of it?'

'Uh-huh.'

'I can't imagine why.' She crossed her arms.

'Anyway, we better not let time get away from us,' he said. 'Mia is a smart girl. And she'll want to hear all about this.' His hand met her elbow and she reluctantly let him guide her towards the plane.

With each step her heart raced, and she wanted to turn in the opposite direction. But she thought of her grandma walking towards Lookout Point that night and how fleeting life was. It would all be over soon. It was just another day in the journey of her life, and tomorrow she would be back at the bookstore doing what she did best and surrounded by what she loved most. She would also have something to add to the memory jar, if there was any room left in it after Marcus had been filling it with God knows what.

All comforting thoughts of books disappeared from her mind when she lowered her head and climbed inside the small plane. *Oh good God.* 'Why does it need so many controls?' she asked.

'Hi there, Miss Chevalier,' the pilot said. 'I'm Gary.'

'Hi. I think.' Joel climbed in after her and helped her get secured in her seat, and showed her how to use the earphones. 'Holy moly,' she said.

'You think it feels scary now, wait till we go upside down!' Joel said.

'Whaaat?' Her stomach lurched at the thought.

'Kidding, kidding,' he said. 'We'll be jumping out in parachutes instead.'

Heart pounding, stomach lurching. No joy so far.

'I can make it go upside down if you want,' said the pilot.

'No!' Olivia reached her hand out to the pilot. 'You do that and I'm reporting you for... for... for...'

'For being naughty?' suggested Joel.

'Yes. That.'

'You are safe with me, Miss Chevalier.'

The pilot discussed a few things about what would happen, safety concerns, etc., and then did some things with the controls. There was a rumble and a buzz as the engine kicked into gear, and a vibration like with the motorbike, but different.

Oh well, here we go...

She closed her eyes. But then she felt trapped with no idea what was happening, so she opened them again. But then she could see the airfield as the plane moved around and warmed up, and knew soon they would be above it, so she closed them again.

'Make sure your eyes are open in the air, Olivia,' said Joel. 'You'll get more out of it.'

'More what? More terror?'

'More joy,' he said, nudging her in the side with his elbow. 'I'm right here with you. Don't be afraid.'

People only ever said that when there was something to be afraid about.

She gulped and opened her eyes, and as the plane positioned itself on a short runway, she breathed rapidly.

And then it all happened faster than she expected. Within moments the sensation of being off the ground took her breath away for a moment, and she gripped her seat. 'Oh God.'

'Woohoo,' said Joel. 'Love that feeling.'

'I don't.'

Higher and higher they rose, and up and down went her stomach.

She dared to look out the side window. 'Huh, where are we

going? Is that water? We shouldn't go over water.' Her nerves trembled.

'Just flying along the coast,' said the pilot, she'd forgotten his name. She'd forgotten her own name. 'Great views down this way. See?' He gestured up ahead and as the plane ascended further, she squinted in the hope it would lessen the stomach lurching. It didn't.

Oh, whoa. The plane tilted sideways. Her fingers gripped the seat tight. 'No upside down, remember!'

'No, Miss, just sideways so we can trace along the coast.'

She watched the ground below move, even though it wasn't and she was the one moving... the small houses and trees and streets. It looked a little like a Monopoly board. Curved lines separated the towns from the beach and ocean, and she forced herself to take a slower, deeper breath and take in the view. It was pretty, no doubt about that, but she was still tense and shaky.

'Awesome, eh?' Joel said.

She managed a small nod.

'Makes you realise we are just a small part of this world, really.'

How could he chat casually about life and the universe while we were who knows how many feet above ground?

'Indeed,' said the pilot.

The blue of the ocean was deeper in certain parts, and tiny white tips and peaks rippled across the surface. They tilted again and she tensed her muscles to hold steady. They flew further and she saw Lookout Point in the distance and managed a smile. Home. Her past, her present, and her future. It was bizarre to see it from this vantage point. Then the grand rock formation of Tarrin came into view and she could even see the bright outline of the children's playground on the beach near the holiday cabins.

Before she could take in more of the familiar landmarks, the plane began to turn around, and she breathed slowly to calm herself. They continued back along the way they had come, following the coastline and watching the world below. She wondered if anyone was looking up at them, perhaps a child saying 'Look, a plane!' as Mia had often done when younger. The world looked so peaceful from up here, and Joel was right, they were just small parts of the world really. It made her worries seem small when she was looking down on her hometown, like those thoughts were tiny little specks that didn't really matter. Despite her nerves being on high alert up here, she could see why some people loved it. Apart from the physical thrill, it was a way to get some perspective.

When the plane touched down in the airfield, Olivia released a long exhalation with a sigh.

'Wasn't that awesome?' Joel exclaimed as he got out of the plane after her, and her legs wobbled. 'You loved it didn't you, after the initial nerves.' He nudged her side with his arm. 'Didn't you, huh, huh?'

His prompting teased a small smile from her lips. 'I was still scared!'

'But...'

'But it *was* pretty cool, after a while.'

'See? Knew you'd enjoy it.'

'I don't know about the word "enjoy", it was more like... interesting, and different.' She walked with him away from the plane after thanking the pilot.

'Ah whatever, you loved it.' He grinned and slid his arm around her waist and gave it a squeeze so briefly she wondered if it actually happened.

She looked at him in silence and then looked away. He did the same.

'Thanks for taking me,' she said, as they approached his car.

'Even if I'm a complete scaredy cat, I do appreciate all this effort.'

'No effort at all, I love this stuff. And I have some spare time, so it's good to spend it doing fun things with a fun person.'

'You think I'm fun?' she said when she got into the passenger seat and he in the driver's seat. No one had called her fun before. She was nice and friendly and interesting and intelligent and caring, but... fun?

'Absolutely. Since I met you, for one thing, you've expanded your gastronomic... repertoire? Is that how you'd say it? Anyway, you've also attempted to climb out a window for the hell of it, you've created amazing pancake shapes, you've been writing a book, and you send rather amusing text messages. I'd say that's a lot of fun.'

And none of those things, apart from the book, she'd done before meeting this guy. Somehow he was bringing fun out of her she didn't know she had.

He drove and turned the volume down on the radio as they chatted.

'I'm so glad it's over,' she said, about the plane flight. 'But you're right, Mia will love to hear about it. She'll probably want to go in one herself.'

'She's really lucky to have you, you know,' he said. 'I mean that. I know her father isn't around, but she has a parent who does the job of both better than some couples do together.'

Her heart softened at his words. 'I just do what I do, she's my daughter. I love her. Looking after her has been my life.' A shimmer of emotion sparked within and she bit her bottom lip. Whenever she spoke about Mia in this way, and especially as she neared the ten-year mark, it triggered strong feelings and memories and the realisation of what she'd accomplished on her own.

'You're a special lady, Olivia.' Joel spoke softly as he looked at the road straight ahead while driving. 'You deserve the best in life.'

'Well, thank you. It's nice of you to say.' She turned her gaze slightly to watch him from the corner of her eye. His hand was steady on the steering wheel as they drove down the highway, his eyes were someplace else. 'You miss her, don't you. Your mum.'

He gave a single nod.

'You've done well too. On your own. You deserve the best also.'

'Thanks.'

'And as a mother myself, I know she would have been proud of you, what you've gone through and now what you're doing, helping others tell their stories.'

He nodded again.

'I know you feel you have to keep moving, for her, but do you ever feel like you'd like to find a place to call home?'

What was she doing? Was she trying to assess whether there was any potential between them? Some way-out hope that maybe someone like him would want to stay here with someone like her? *Crazy*. She wished she hadn't spoken her thoughts out loud, but then he said something surprising.

'I don't think home is a place.' He indicated and changed lanes. 'I think, somehow, I've been searching for the *feeling* of home, all my life. It's like there's this constant unrest in my soul, like it doesn't know what home feels like, and so it keeps on searching.'

'Wow.' Olivia absorbed his words. 'You should have put that in your book.'

He chuckled. 'The sequel, perhaps?'

'Will there be one?'

He shrugged. 'That is yet to be determined. I just hope I

don't have to go through anything too dangerous to make it a worthwhile project.'

'Not all stories have to be about physical adventures, remember?'

'True.'

They drove in silence for a while, nineties music playing on the radio, and when all sound abated as he pulled into her driveway and switched off the engine, Olivia was sure her heartbeat was audible. Something had shifted between them today. Or had it happened last Tuesday at the lookout? Maybe it had been gradual and she was only sensing it now, but there was a closeness with him she hadn't felt with a man in a long time. A different closeness. A mutual understanding, and respect. He was looking for home. She'd been hidden away at home for too long. And somewhere in the middle they had crossed paths, or collided, more like it.

'Would you like to come in?' she asked, as she unlocked her front door. 'I may even have a wider variety of food than pancakes, if you're hungry.' She smiled.

Joel's foot teetered on the edge of her top step. His mouth opened and closed. 'Thanks, but I better go and let you get back to your writing. I mean, if that's what you're going to be doing.'

A pang of disappointment pinched from the inside. 'Yes. I mean, at some stage today. But I do have some extra time to chill out.'

'That's good,' he said. 'I, ah, need to go do some laundry, of all things. Gotta love being on the road and not having a washing machine.' He chuckled and scratched his head, and his adorable forehead furrows creased even more.

'Sure,' she said. 'Well, thanks again. It was definitely a book-worthy moment.' She smiled.

'Pleasure's all mine.' His foot met solidly with the top step and he leaned forward. His lips met with her cheek for one brief, but memorable, kiss. 'Enjoy your afternoon,' he added.

'You too.' She stood there and waited until he stepped off the porch, in case he changed his mind, or in case his lips came back to her face but decided to meet with her lips instead. But they wouldn't. Because they both knew he'd be outta here in a few weeks, and that one-night stands and flings weren't her thing, and that any kind of more-than-friends affection was bound to end in awkwardness, especially with her being in his writing class.

She waved him off and her heart fluttered gently, at the tender cheek kiss, which was more action than she'd had in a long time, and also at the missed opportunity that although left her desire unmet, was probably for the best.

***

Joel drove off as quickly as possible before he changed his mind. He hoped he didn't seem rude, declining her offer. But he didn't trust himself. He was a spontaneous, impulsive person, and he didn't want to mess her around in any way. Had she not been a single parent, perhaps he would have stayed. Even if she weren't, she deserved better than a moment of animal attraction, be it just a passionate kiss or something more. There would be someone more suited to her and her lifestyle at some stage, someone different to him. And he just had to restrain himself until he left town.

But he couldn't erase the thoughts encroaching on his mind, especially after she had mentioned the possibility of a sequel to his book. To his life story.

Underneath his good intentions to remain 'just friends' and avoid any drama for her or for him, there was the truth.

He wanted her in his sequel, even if only for one chapter.

CHAPTER NINETEEN

It was best that he left. He probably had other things to do anyway, and despite his nice words about her, that feeling of closeness she felt may be one-sided anyway.

She stood aimlessly in the middle of the kitchen for what seemed like forever, her body and mind not knowing what to do next. She went over the events of the day in her mind, each time leading back to this moment. This moment when she had wanted him to come in, wanted to bask in that feeling of closeness, expand on it, somehow. But it was probably more adrenaline than anything, messing with her sense of reality.

Book. The book. Right. I'll do that.

She left the kitchen and went to her bedroom, sat at the small desk, and opened her laptop. *Coffee. I need coffee.*

She went back into the kitchen.

No, my body doesn't need caffeine, it needs calming down. Tea. Chamomile tea.

She made a cup, grabbed a cookie, and went back to her desk.

She rearranged some notes and scenes, fixed some errors, then her finger hovered on her phone's recorder. She'd listened to last Thursday's session where her grandma had revealed what happened after that night she'd met up with William at Lookout Point. But she wanted to hear it again, wanted to enjoy the nostalgia of times gone by; times and events that eventually shaped her future, because had May ended up with William, Diana and then Olivia would have never been born. But part of her wondered what if she had ended up with William? How different would her grandma's life have been? How many things in life would be different if people made different choices? The thought was both enticing and scary. She couldn't imagine not having had Mia now, but if anyone had told her back then that she was going to have a New Year's Eve one-night stand with someone she barely knew, she wouldn't have believed it.

She pressed on the dated recording and leaned back in her chair, hands behind her head.

May's Memories of Secret Meetings

A new letter arrived the next day, he must have dropped it in the letterbox early in the morning, risking being seen. But he did have to walk past our house, or the Chevalier's house, on his way to and from work.

I sat on my bed with bated breath and read...

My Majestic May,

May I call you My May? That is a lot of Mays! But our kiss, our first delicious kiss, tells me we are bonded like two halves of the same soul, two halves of the same heart, and now I am complete.

I hope I will see you in the general store soon. Though how I will stop myself from gathering you up in my arms is beyond me. Or should I? Should we declare our affection for each other in public right now, even though it feels like a tornado of passion ripping through town rather than the gentle breeze of a proper courtship, as I know your family would prefer, if they were to have any kind of acceptance of me in your life.

And I know you live with Jacques. He is by all means a better suitor for you, which is why I am so incredibly astounded that you chose to see me, to talk with me, to kiss me. I thought it would just be a fantasy, being with you. But you have made my fantasy my reality, and I couldn't be happier.

I hope you can meet me tonight, again, same place, same time, or even a bit later if that is easier. I will just wait there a while, watch the ocean ebbing and flowing and dreaming of the adventures I will have. We will have. If you still want them.

Each day will now be more magical, May, more majestic. Because of you.

W xo

I held the letter to my heart and sighed. The book I was reading held no interest for me now, my own life was becoming more fascinating. And he was right, about Jacques, I had overheard his mother talking with his father about his need to be married off and start providing for himself and a family of his own. But his father had said that his son had no passion for the tailor's shop and didn't know if it could be sustained once he retired.

I had become good at eavesdropping. I was good at looking busy, and pretending to not hear anything. And my guess was that the Chevaliers were not used to having to keep quiet in their own house and so they did not often notice that I was around, busying myself or helping out with housework where I could, dusting and dusting, listening and listening... It was a surprise that William didn't call me Cheeky May, but then again, that didn't begin with M. I wondered if he would run out of adjectives, or if he would re-use the same ones. And I wondered how many more letters he would write, or if they would reduce in number if I was able to see him regularly at night. I wondered a lot of things. And my heart longed to stop wondering and start doing, start experiencing, and it was that urge that helped me out the window that night and up to Lookout Point yet again.

'You're here!' he exclaimed as I walked up to meet him, the wind whipping his hair about his face, and mine doing the same.

'I am!'

He took my face in his hands and kissed me immediately. 'Did you trip over this time on your way out?'

I laughed. 'I did not. I looked where I was going this time.'

'I am glad. Because soon you will start looking like you've had even more adventures, and people may get suspicious.'

'But I am having an adventure. And I want more.'

'Oh, yes, that is music to my ears.' He held me close and tight to his chest. 'I would love to go up north, discover new parts of this amazing land. I want to watch sunsets from a hundred different beaches, and sleep under a thousand million stars, and... jump from trains.'

'Jump from trains?'

He chuckled. 'I don't know if I will, it just seems like a lot of fun.' He grinned.

'It sounds so wonderful,' I said, listening to the comforting thump of his heart beneath his warm chest.

We sat on the grass near the lookout for a while, his arms around me from behind, as we discussed all manner of things. We discussed whether to indeed let people know we were together, but there was something about our secret meetings that made things more exciting, and we decided to keep it secret for now. It was part of the adventure, our adventure. And I wanted to prolong it for as long as possible.

'Oh!' he said. 'Tomorrow night, if you can meet me again, I will have a surprise for you.'

I straightened up and turned to face him. 'A surprise? Whatever could it be?'

He shook his head and trailed his thumb across my bottom lip. 'You will have to wait and see.'

I smiled and leaned close to him, and my lips softened into his. And as the stars sparkled and the ocean hummed, our lips danced and my heart beat to its new rhythm.

Olivia closed her eyes, and could practically hear the ocean humming and see the stars sparkling. Even though this story was about her grandmother, it wasn't awkward, she still felt its magic; she knew what it was like to be a young woman in love. Her own first love at age eighteen had swept her off her feet for a good while, before dumping her back on the ground a few months later. But oh, that rush of young love, there was nothing like it.

By the time she'd worked for a couple of hours on her book, she was yawning. The adrenaline had worn off and she was tired, and would need to start getting things organised for school tomorrow, and for the week ahead.

A car sounded outside. She stood and stretched, then went

into the living room. The door opened and Mia burst in, a piece of paper in her hand. 'Hi, Mum! I had the most funnest day. And I wrote you a letter, here.' She shoved it into her hands.

'Wow, thank you!' Olivia bent down to kiss her daughter. Diana and Peter entered the house. 'Thanks, Mum,' she said. 'And you too, Peter.'

'She was a delight,' Peter said.

'And what was that surprise this intriguing young writer-slash-adventurer had for you?' her mother asked.

Olivia grinned. 'I went in a plane. Like, a small one. On a joy flight.'

'Great stuff,' said Peter. 'I did that once.'

'My daughter. In a plane?' said Diana. 'I don't believe it. Really?'

'Uh-huh.' She got out her phone and showed some photos that Joel had taken and texted to her.

'Can I do it too, Mum?' asked Mia.

Ha, she knew it. 'Maybe one day, sweetie. It's a little scary.'

'But I don't mind, I think I could do it.'

'I'm sure you could. Anyway, shall I read this letter of yours?'

'Yes. But maybe in private. Shouldn't special letters be read in private? Like Mrs May says?'

'Just what have you and my mother been discussing in your little book research meetings, dear?' Diana asked.

She had only told her mother the basics, but as more information came to light about William, she didn't want her to feel awkward about hearing her own mother's young love story when it had nothing to do with her father. 'You'll just have to read the book when it's done, Mum,' she said.

'Guess so. At least she seems happier, more settled lately.'

Mrs May had stopped complaining about the differences between her new room and her old semi-independent living space. So she was either more used to the arrangements, or simply resigned to the fact that this was where she would live out her final days and didn't want to waste time or energy opposing it. 'She was good today?' Olivia asked.

'Yes,' said Diana. 'Eating a bit more too. That mild temperature she had before seems to have gone, so that's good. But they said that sometimes at that age an infection can creep in quickly before their body has a chance to mount a response and a fever. So we have to make sure we're extra hygienic each time we visit.'

Olivia nodded. She already went overboard on the hand sanitiser at the nursing home entrance. And she made sure Mia washed her hands thoroughly after school each day.

'Anyway, we are off for a pre-dinner jog, so we'll see you later.' Diana raised her eyebrows.

'Okay. Thanks, Mum.' She pecked her on the cheek and Diana bent down to hug and kiss Mia. Peter did the same.

'Quick, go,' Mia said, pushing them towards the door. 'Mum needs to read her letter!'

'Mia! That's a bit rude,' Olivia scolded. 'Say thanks, please. For looking after you today.' Mia was getting so assertive lately, she didn't know where that had come from all of a sudden.

'Thanks for looking after me.'

'It's my pleasure, honey bunny.' Diana kissed her three times on the cheek, and Mia giggled.

When they had left, Mia pushed Olivia towards her bedroom. 'You can read it in private, and then come out when you're finished. I'll wait on the couch.'

'Yes, Mum.'

'Mum? Ha-ha, you're silly.'

Olivia poked out her tongue at her daughter as she entered her room, and Mia poked hers back. 'Okay, I will read the letter in private and be back out soon.'

She flopped on the bed, glad to finally relax. She unfolded the paper and smiled at Mia's handwriting, which was improving week by week, despite some spelling mistakes.

Dear Mum,

Here is your letter. I hope you like it. I like it, even though I haven't written it yet! But you're my mum, so I know it will be a good letter.

I've known you a very long time. All my life. It's been so long. I like being with you every day, especially when we do fun things like make pancakes and go to the park and to the movies and shopping.

I like that we have our very own bookstore, it is like living in a magic world.

I don't even mind that I don't have a father living with us. Maybe you are my mum and my dad all at once! But I hope you don't grow a beard.

Do you think I will have a father living with us one day? That could be weird. But if you wanted him to I don't mind. And he is allowed to have a beard. But I hope he doesn't snore.

Or maybe I will have two mothers, like Maddy at school does. I wouldn't mind if that's what you wanted instead.

I like seeing you happy. You've been very happy. Except when we're both sad about Mrs May dying.

I'm happy too.

I like that you are my mum.

Thanks for being my mum.

I love you Mum.

Lots of love, Mia. xoxoxoxo

Olivia's bottom lip quivered and warm tears welled in her eyes. A cross between a giggle and a cry emerged. This made everything worthwhile. Yes she was branching out of her comfort zone and trying new things for herself as of late, but she would not let anything get in the way of the good relationship she'd established with her daughter. She only had one shot at this, at motherhood, and so far, she knew she was doing a damn good job.

'Mia?' she called out. 'Come in here, sweetie.'

The door opened.

Olivia gestured for her daughter to join her on the bed. 'That was the most beautiful, bestest letter I've ever read,' she said, as Mia snuggled into her side.

'Really?'

'Yes, really.' She kissed her forehead. 'And one day, there might be a father, or there might not be. I'm not sure. But only if he is an amazing person who loves us both and is ready to be part of our lives. Either way, you and I will always have our own special bond.'

'Okay.'

'And guess what?'

'What?'

She gave her a squeeze. 'I like that I'm your mum too.'

CHAPTER TWENTY

This was it; a new week, new beginning, new chapter, and a new instalment of Mrs May's love story. Olivia kept busy all day at the store, picked Mia up and shared a dinner at Café Lagoon, then drove to the nursing home. Mia was going to draw a picture of Olivia in a plane flying over Tarrin's Bay, and Olivia was anxious to hear what happened next, if her grandma was up to telling her more.

'How are you feeling?' she asked.

'Old,' she replied with a dry chuckle.

'Ah, you're only as old as you think, Grandma.' Olivia kissed her cheek.

'Exactly. And I think I'm old,' she said. 'But nothing can be done about that now, age just creeps up on you like one of those pesky villains in films. You think you're safe, and then all of a sudden – you're wondering what happened and wishing you had more time.'

'Oh, Grandma, you've had such a long life. I hope I get to live as long as you.'

'With these fantastic genes, you probably will. Or even longer.' She smiled and winked.

They spoke briefly about how Mia was doing at school, and how Olivia had gone on a plane flight with Joel, to which her grandma clasped her hands together as well as she could, with one being weaker than the other, saying, 'oh dear girl, I am so proud of you.'

Olivia helped her drink some water then pressed the recorder button, as she seemed to be in a much better mental state today than last time. Hopefully she would get much more of the story this time. 'Tell me more about your love affair with William. Did you keep meeting him each night at the lookout? What was that surprise he said he had for you?'

Mrs May's mouth opened in a delighted gasp. 'Oh! I had forgotten about his surprise. I thought I knew most things about him, but the next night he showed me something new and it only made me fall in love with him more.'

Olivia adjusted the cushion behind her in the chair, and like turning the first page of a new book, she welcomed the bubbly sensation of curiosity that fizzed up inside at the promise of new discoveries...

May's Memories of Secret Talents

I noticed at dinner times that I was often seated next to Jacques. Mrs Chevalier would usher me to my chair as though it had my name on it, and it was always beside him. It was nice. I liked his company. But since things had started with William, I had eyes for no other.

'You seem especially rosy today, May,' said my mother, who was now able to sit with us instead of eating her dinner from her bed or the sofa.

'I do?' I touched my cheeks. 'The weather is warming up a little, I suppose.'

'Must be all that sleep you've been getting, going to bed early. Or perhaps having more company these days.' I noticed how she glanced towards Jacques at that moment.

How correct she was, but she was looking at the wrong person.

'Perhaps,' I said.

'May, how is that novel you've been reading?' Jacques asked.

'Oh, yes. Ah, it's quite good I suppose.' The truth was, I hadn't read any the last couple of nights. Hadn't needed to. My life was becoming more interesting.

Though I had grown quite comfortable around the Chevaliers, conversation that evening was strained. There was an undercurrent of forced connection, and although I liked Jacques, I didn't like feeling forced or required to interact a certain way. And it only made me want to run... run to where I felt natural and free, and that I did, when I retired to my room and crept out the window yet again.

'May,' William said, devouring me with his arms, sprinkling kisses on my face as I met him at the lookout. 'Let's go down to the harbour, for your surprise.'

'What's in there?' I asked, pointing to the satchel.

He smiled. 'You'll see.'

We sat on a park bench near the harbour, sheltered behind a stone wall that minimised the night breeze, and any observers.

He pulled out a large notepad from his satchel. And then some charcoal. 'I want to draw your portrait.'

My eyes went wide. 'Draw? I didn't know you could draw!'

'I mostly do it at home for my own amusement, but the other day, I was drawing at the store when it was quiet and a customer liked what they saw – asked me to draw their portrait *for a nice sum of money!' He gripped my forearm. 'Oh, May, if one person wants my services, then perhaps more will. This could be the perfect career for me, and one that wouldn't require me to stay put in a town going nowhere.' His words were laced with passion and oozed enthusiasm.*

'Wow,' I said. 'Well, hurry up, mister, show me what you're made of!' I crossed one leg over the other and held my knees with clasped hands, straightening my spine and putting an accomplished smile on my face. 'How long do I have to stay still for?'

'Until I do this.' He took my cheeks with his hands and encouraged my lips to his. It was heaven; pure, magical heaven. My body softened at his hold and I surrendered, until he pulled away and got his paper ready. 'Okay, Miss May, let's do this.'

I kept giggling and trying to peek. He kept holding the drawing up momentarily to his chest and saying, 'Uh-uh, patience, Miss May, patience.'

But he was quick. Really quick. And as I discovered when he finally showed me his creation, his drawings were both accurate and organic, with a confronting rawness and intensity that made them come alive on the paper. It wasn't a rigid, perfect, presentable portrait, but a unique and bold representation of the true nature of a person's face. Somehow, he had captured parts of my face and expression I hadn't ever taken notice of and yet I recognised as uniquely me.

'I'm... I'm amazed,' I said. 'Words don't do it justice.'

'And a drawing does not do your beauty justice,' he replied. Then he chuckled. 'That was so very pathetic, wasn't it? Like something they'd say in a romantic film full of clichés and unrealistic ideals.'

'I like pathetic. Your version of it at least. And I like

romantic films and unrealistic ideals, thank you very much.' I crossed my arms but smiled.

'What we have here, between us, seems so real yet also unrealistic, does it not? As though it does not fit into this small world here and requires some far-off magical land of equivalent beauty and intensity.'

I wondered where such places existed. Tarrin's Bay was charming and beautiful, but there was a sense of sameness to it. I loved it, and yet I also had an urge to explore somewhere new.

I accepted the drawing from William and smiled. 'This... whatever this is, is so very real to me.' And I leaned forward and kissed him, in a way that showed him exactly how real this romance was.

'Oh, Grandma, do you still have the portrait?' Olivia was literally on the edge of her seat.

'Oh golly, I haven't seen that thing for years. I kept it as a memento of him, but after the years passed, it became less important and it must have been put away somewhere. Jacques saw it once and asked about it. I told him I'd had my portrait drawn by a wanderer, a travelling artist. Which was the truth, really.'

'I would love to see it. Anyway, I can have a better look through those boxes of your old things you gave Mum and me, sometime.'

'Of course, dear. But no need to show me if you do, I have it ingrained up here.' She tapped her head. 'The only thing we can take with us to wherever it is I'm going. Our memories.'

Olivia gave a resigned nod. Talking to her grandma and hearing her stories was so enlivening, it made her forget time was running out, that soon she would not be able to tell any more stories. And all that would be left for Olivia would be her memories, of her grandma, of May.

'Do you need to rest now? Shall we leave you to it?' Olivia asked.

'But don't you want to know what happens in the next chapter, my dear?'

Olivia turned to check Mia, who was happily humming, her EarPods in, her hand holding a pencil and drawing as though she had all the time in the world. 'Of course I do, but only if you're up to it.'

'Oh, I will probably never be up for anything much except rambling on about my life, so I might as well make the most of it.' She patted Olivia's hand. 'Besides, the next two weeks were some of the best days of my life. But I won't go into details, all you need to know is what happened that night I saw my very first shooting star.'

'Oh, wow, I've never seen one of those.'

'I do not believe they occur by accident, darling Olivia. Should you ever see one, they are there for a reason.

'Did you see it from Lookout Point?'

A soft smile teased Mrs May's lips. 'Yes. So beautiful but so fleeting. And the catalyst for what William did next.'

May's Memories of Shooting Stars

The letters continued over the next couple of weeks, but not as often as our meetings, which had become even more beautiful than the letters.

He didn't limit himself to writing his words; he would also speak them. Whatever popped into his mind, or his heart. Sometimes we would simply stay at Lookout Point, other times we would go for walks, down to the beach, along the harbour, and along the coastal track between Lookout Point and the Tarrin rock formation. Time flew, but it also seemed to freeze, it was a strange, beautiful thing.

One night, while walking along the beach, the sand cool beneath our toes, the sky clear and the ocean calm, a quick flash shot through the sky. 'Look!' He pointed. We stopped.

'Oh my,' I said. 'Is that...'

'Yes,' he said. 'A shooting star.'

I glanced at his face as he stared in awe. 'Wow.'

'Indeed.' He chuckled, then turned to face me, enveloping me in his arms. 'And just what I was looking for.'

I looked up into his diamond eyes. 'You were looking for a shooting star?'

'No. A sign. And I got it.' He grinned.

'A sign? For what?'

He took my hand and we resumed walking. 'That I would know I'm doing the right thing.' He swung my arm back and forth, and it was as though I could feel his energy buzzing through me. We stopped again, and he faced me. 'I'm going to leave Tarrin's Bay,' he said, and my jaw dropped. I knew he wanted to explore the world, but I didn't think it would be so soon.

'Leave, what, now?'

'Oh yes, my darling May. Well, in one week. I've been saving up, and I will bring my art supplies to make money from doing travelling portraits.'

'But...'

'And I want you to come with me. Come with me, May.'

His eyes were unblinking, looking straight into my heart. It started beating fast.

'But... in one week? I... I...' Conflicting thoughts swished through my mind, back and forth. 'I don't think I can just leave, I mean, I have my mother, and I should be helping her as Father looks for a new house we can afford to live in, and the Chevaliers have been so good to us, and I have my sewing clients, I have curtains I need to make in a week or two for the Pattersons' home redecorating, and...'

And I couldn't just leave.

'That's all just... stuff,' he said. 'What we have is real, powerful, one of a kind.'

'I agree, but maybe we should keep things the way they are for now, while everything is good.'

'I love all of this,' he said. 'But my feet are itching to move forward. To discover new places, walk on new ground, instead of repeating the same thing, day in day out.' He caressed my cheek with his palm. 'I would love nothing more than to have an adventure with you.'

My eyes closed for a moment, savouring the soft firmness of his hand and the warmth of his skin. This. This was so good. Us. Together. I wanted nothing more than for that too.

I opened my eyes. But wouldn't that be selfish? And what would I do, how could I make my own way? I didn't own much, after the fire, so I would only need a small supply of clothing and essentials, and my sewing kit if I were to find some simple work along the way.

'We can fish, we can go fruit picking, we can find our way,' he said. 'Live off the land, see where it takes us.'

'And then what?' I asked. 'We couldn't go on like that forever.'

'We could stop and start. Settle for a while somewhere nice, move on when it feels right. Let our intuition guide us. Maybe we would find someplace else we loved and stay put, who knows. All I know is that right now, I can't stay.'

'And if I didn't come with you?' Would he really leave without me, leave what we had? I stepped away from him.

'Oh, May. But I know your heart. I know where it longs to be.'

With you, I thought. With you.

'And that is all that matters.'

'But my family.'

'You can always come back and visit. We wouldn't be disappearing without a trace.'

But I knew they would not let me leave if I were to tell them my plans. If I went, it would have to be in secret.

'My aunt and uncle know I plan to travel. They are happy for me to go. I even have my uncle's old automobile I helped him restore. I'm all set. Maybe it's easier for me to leave, I have fewer responsibilities than you. But you're a grown woman now, May. This is your time to live the life you want.'

It sounded so good. Perhaps I could bring a couple of books and do readings for people as a form of travelling entertainment? Or children's books... I could do storytelling sessions in different towns. Ideas roamed my mind at the possibilities.

'I... I need time to think,' I said.

'Of course.' He kissed my forehead. 'I don't want to rush you. I just know what I want, and I want it with you.'

We met up again the next three nights, and each goodbye kiss, although wonderful, was filled with uncertainty. On Wednesday night, he kissed me with such intensity and promise I thought I might forget my own name. It was like the kiss was either our last one, or the first one, and he wanted to imbue it with everything he felt, everything we had shared, in one perfect moment.

The next day, I received a letter...

My Memorable May,

It is time. I know you still haven't decided, but it is time. I will be leaving on Saturday at noon. Meet me at Lookout Point then, and bring whatever you will need. I have money, enough to last a while until I do some more drawings.

I am so excited. It will be amazing and fabulous. Life is for living and I plan to live it, and you are the only person I want by my side.

If you don't show up, I will assume you have decided to stay. And though I'll be heartbroken, I will understand. But all I can do is trust that your heart knows the way, and I will meet it. I will welcome you with open arms into my embrace, my life, and our future.

So I will not meet you tonight, or tomorrow night, I will only see you then.

With all my love, and the promise of an adventure you will never forget,

William.

'Grandma, are you okay?' Olivia handed Mrs May a cup of water as she covered her mouth with a coughing fit.

She went to sip but then the cough resumed.

'I'm okay, I just…' She coughed. 'All this talking, my throat's a bit strained.'

Olivia left the cup beside her and patted her back. 'Should I get a nurse?'

As if they heard her question, Sam, one of the nurses came in. 'Waking me up from my nap, I hear,' she said. She checked her grandma's handkerchief, her temperature, and then her pulse and blood pressure. 'Hmm, nothing too much to be concerned with here. Talking too much, I'm guessing.' She winked.

'Yes, yes,' she managed, the coughing dying down. 'But I'll be all right.'

Mia had unplugged her EarPhones and looked concerned. 'It's okay, Mrs May is fine,' Olivia said. She stood. 'Come on, we must let our favourite lady get her beauty sleep.'

'Sweetheart, after ninety years, let me tell you, there is no such thing as beauty sleep.'

Olivia chuckled.

'I've tried it, and I still got old.'

The nurse was right, there was nothing much to be concerned with. But the talking was fatiguing her and straining her throat.

'Thanks for sharing more of your story,' Olivia said. 'When you're up to it, I'll come back for the rest.' She was dying to know what happened that Saturday at noon. Did she meet him and tell him she couldn't go, and they had a teary farewell? Did she simply not turn up, or did she go with him for a short while and then returned to Tarrin's Bay? Olivia had no idea.

Mrs May nodded, her eyes drooping. 'Anytime, dear. Anytime. But first, my non-beauty sleep.' She smiled.

Olivia captured the memory of her grandma's smile in her mind, just in case. Every time she walked out of this room, she didn't know if that would be the last time she ever saw her alive.

CHAPTER TWENTY-ONE

J oel had had a busy and fulfilling week, with his two classes, some exercise and outdoor exploration, a conference call with his publishing team, his Friday lunch with Olivia that turned into an afternoon of work on his laptop after she went back to work, followed by a couple of drinks at the pub. But he was glad it was Saturday afternoon; he had been looking forward to this day for a while.

He parked a little further up the street from her house. He was early, which was on purpose as then she wouldn't be looking out the window waiting for him. He scrawled on the piece of paper: *Welcome to your treasure hunt.*

Clue number 1: There is a silver car just down from your house. There is a man in it. Get in the car. PS you can trust him, his name is Joel. Clue number 2 will be waiting for you there.

He peered around the tree to her front porch, then quickly and quietly went up and placed the note on the doormat. He knocked on the door then dashed off and back to his car. He laughed, like a little kid doing knock and runs.

A few minutes passed, so he assumed she wasn't ready. Then her trying-not-to-smile face came into view as she walked around the corner tree and approached his car. She knocked on the window and he rolled it down. 'Yes?'

'Apparently I'm supposed to get in this car with some strange man. Would that be you?'

'It would.' He popped open the lock and gave the door a shove.

She opened it and got in. 'My, what a gentleman you are, opening the door for me from the inside.' She placed her handbag on the floor.

'It's a treasure hunt, not an old-fashioned date.'

'So I see.' She flapped the paper about. 'So, where is clue number two?'

He lifted the corner of his mouth into a smug grin. 'It's written on my torso.' He eyed his top, as though she would have to lift it up. Okay, so it was a bit of an immature flirty guy thing, but he wanted to see her reaction. It would probably be all, 'Oh, Joel, if you think I am going to lift up your shirt and just–'

'Well, strip off then,' she said. 'I don't have all day.'

What? He couldn't help his mouth from dropping open a tad.

'Oh for heaven's sake.' She reached forward and grabbed his shirt, and before he could object she lifted it up. 'Where's the clue? I don't see anything.'

'I lied,' he said. 'I just wanted to see what you would do.'

She removed her hands and leaned back. 'Just wanted to show off your impressive torso, huh? And perhaps your ego too?'

'Oh, so you do think it's impressive then?' he joked. 'Nah, seriously, I didn't think you would do that. If I'd known, maybe I *would* have written the clue on my torso. Oh well.' He shrugged.

She shook her head. 'Men,' she mumbled.

'What was that?'

'Nothing. Where's this clue?'

He pointed to the top of the dashboard. She picked up the piece of paper and read it out loud: 'Take the first CD from the glovebox and place it in the CD player. Your driver is awaiting your instructions on where to drive to.' She opened the glovebox. 'How will I know where I'm supposed to go?'

'Just listen,' he said.

She put the CD with no label on and waited...

Music started and her face showed no signs of recognition. As he expected. It was an old, daggy song. The lyrics began and she angled her ear towards the sound. 'What kind of song is this?' He kept quiet as the chorus came on. When the main lyrics repeated, she said, 'Moving forward... energy... okay, clearly we have to drive. I get that, but...' She listened more carefully. 'You're my energy? You keep me moving...' She scrunched up her face, it was utterly adorable. 'Do you want me to drive or something? Like, I'm the energy that keeps you moving?'

He chuckled and shook his head.

'My power... my fuel... my... oh! Fuel? We need fuel, petrol? But that doesn't tell me where we are actually going.'

'Then let's go get fuel and see what happens from there.' He started the engine.

'Can we turn the song off now, it's pretty bad,' she said.

He switched it off. 'I know, right? All part of my unique chauffeur service.' He winked, then drove off down the street.

He hoped the clue was still there and that some stranger hadn't plucked it from the petrol bowser and let it blow away in the wind. When they arrived at the station just before the highway, he waited behind the car at bowser number one.

'Why don't you go to that one over there?' She pointed. 'It's available.'

'Nah, I'll wait for this one, thanks.' He drummed his fingertips on the steering wheel.

'You're weird,' she mumbled.

'I know. Don't ya love it?'

She showed a small smile and shook her head. 'I guess I have to go with the flow for this treasure hunt and see what you have in store for me.'

'Exactly.'

The car drove off and he moved forward and turned off the engine. He handed her some cash. 'Could you pop forty in there for me? Thanks.' He used his other hand to pat her cheek three times.

'Now you want me to get your petrol? You were right, a unique chauffeur service indeed.' She got out and opened the petrol tank lid, which he'd popped open with the latch, and as she watched the numbers ticking over he smiled, wondering how long it would take her to notice it.

Any second now...

She glanced around, back at the numbers, then peered closer.

His smile widened.

She reached out her spare hand and held the edge of the paper flapping in the wind, which he had sticky-taped onto the side of the bowser.

She glanced back at the numbers and then to the tank, withdrew the pump and replaced it, and the lid, and plucked the piece of paper off. A moment later, she looked at him through the window with a curious glance. He rolled the window down.

'Go inside and ask for the bonus chocolate bar?' she said. 'What?'

He nodded. 'Yes. Do as the clue says.'

He felt like he was doing secret government work, or was on one of those shows where you had to solve riddles and clues, except he was the one who knew all the answers. He'd already paid the guy behind the counter for the chocolate and told him to expect a woman asking for the bonus bar. He knew she would feel awkward doing it, which is another reason he was loving this.

He watched her walk in, noticing the subtle yet definite curve of her hips in her jeans, and then glanced away, towards another woman walking in whose hip curves were hidden by an oversized loose dress that resembled a tablecloth.

The guy took the money and handed something over, and he chuckled to himself. She came back out, looking at the bar that was wrapped in a piece of paper.

She got back in the car and said, 'Okay, so this clue tells me to head in the direction opposite to south. Hmm, let me think on that one.' She tapped her chin. 'I might have to google the answer.' She looked back at the paper. 'And we have to take the eighth exit, then turn right until my driver coughs, at which point we take another right.' She placed the paper down on the seat. 'What if you cough accidentally between now and then?'

'I guess we'll get lost.'

'Then you better not cough unless you are in a life-threatening choking situation.' She ripped open the chocolate bar. 'I take it I can eat this on the way?'

'Of course,' he replied. When he'd first met her, there was no way she would just open a chocolate bar like that, she would have asked him first. Or waited for him to offer it to her. But he liked how she was taking initiative with things now. He hoped she would continue her new-found confidence and assertiveness after he left town. If he could have any impact on this woman's life, he wanted it to be positive. He didn't want to leave any scars, unlike some of the others he'd met and gotten to know. But she was different. She was so easy to be with, to talk to... She was becoming a great friend, and despite the fact that warmth spread through his body whenever he was around her, he knew it would be best to keep this as a friendship only.

'Oh yum, I needed this.'

'I knew you would.'

'So you even went to the trouble to get that guy behind the counter in on the act?' He nodded and she smiled. 'I feel very special.'

'You are.' He reached out his hand. 'Can I at least get a small piece of chocolate myself?'

She pulled it away from him. 'What about the risk of accidental coughing or choking?'

'I'll eat it carefully, I promise.'

She broke off a small piece. 'Well, you did pay for it after all.'

'You're so generous.'

'All part of my unique passenger service,' she mumbled while eating.

He drove north on the highway and put on some regular music. Though it wasn't all that regular, it was meaningful to him. He hummed along.

'Oh,' Olivia said, when the second song came on. 'Your book! These are the songs in the chapter titles.'

He smiled, and more warmth spread throughout him. 'You noticed.'

'What a great idea, to make a playlist based on your book.' She chewed on a bit more chocolate. 'Hey, maybe I could do that for *Memories of May*.' She got out her phone. 'Just going to write a reminder to ask my grandma what songs have meaning for her. Thanks, Joel!'

'No need to thank me, it's your mind that's ticking away with ideas.'

'Oh God, yes. It's like, the more I write, the more I think of, and the longer this book seems to be becoming.'

'Been there, done that.'

'Show-off,' she said.

He chuckled. 'Did you think when we met a few weeks ago that you would be calling me a show-off, getting rescued from a window, riding a motorbike, and going on a treasure hunt with me?'

She laughed, then quickly covered her mouth. 'Oops, my chocolate almost went on an adventure of its own. Sorry.' She took a tissue from her pocket and wiped at the corners of her mouth. 'And no, I didn't think that at all. I would have thought that you were talking about someone else, not me.'

'So you're a new woman, then.'

She was quiet for a moment, then turned to face him, though he kept his focus on the road. He could feel her looking at him, feel the softening of her demeanour, and some unseen force compelling him to look back. He was glad he had the excuse of needing to keep his eyes on the road.

'I think I'm just me, rediscovered,' she said softly. 'Or at least on a journey of rediscovery.'

'Well,' he said. 'I *like* Olivia Rediscovered.' He paused. 'Which also has eight syllables, I must add.'

'Perfect then,' she said. 'But I just realised I've forgotten to count the exits.'

'Uh-oh,' he said. 'If only your driver knew where he was going. Maybe we should turn around and start again so you can count.'

'C'mon, help a girl out. How many more exits left?'

'I'm only telling you because you were so generous to give me that chocolate,' he said. 'We have five left.'

'And then we turn right and then you'll have your coughing fit, and not a moment sooner than needed.'

He pretended to have difficulty holding back a cough, and chuckled.

For the rest of the way, when he tried to speak she shushed him, and counted the exits on her fingers. 'I'm not speaking to you till after we get there,' she said sternly.

They took the exit, and he was glad they weren't speaking because their conversations often got out of hand and he could potentially miss the turn himself. When it got near, but not quite there, he coughed. A small throat-clearing cough.

'Wait, was that it? Or was that a genuine one?'

'Just teasing. But...' He took a big breath and let out a big cough.

'Okay, okay, turn! Right!' She pointed. 'I see a street.'

He obliged and drove into the street that was parallel with the coastline.

'Oh wow, it's a beautiful view up here,' she said. 'How have I never been here before?'

He shrugged, and drove slowly.

'Hang on, now what? I have no more clues.' She sat up tall and peered around. 'Where do we go? Do we continue on and... Look, there are people on those things!' She pointed up ahead. 'What are they called again?' She circled her hand around.

'Paragliders.'

'Paragliders, yes. Should we stop and watch them for a bit?'

He shook his head with a laugh. 'Sure. In fact, how about we join them? It could be another good book-worthy moment for you.'

'Oh no, let's just do what you have planned, I don't need any more.'

'Okay, we'll just do what I have planned.' He drove into the parking area near the grassed area overlooking the cliff top.

'So we *are* going to watch them first?'

'Yes. But we've also arrived at our destination.'

'What else is there to do around here?'

'Paragliding.'

'But we're not doing that, right? I mean, I'd have to hold on to one of those things with nothing below me and that would require some serious mental preparation.'

'Start preparing then.'

She stared, unblinking. 'You're messing with me, right? Taking an opportunity while it's here, and we're really just going to watch them. Yeah?'

'Nope.'

'Crap.' She remained still.

'So, let's exit the vehicle, shall we?'

'Uh-uh. No way.'

'Yes way. Come on, sunshine. Time to fly.'

'A plane was one thing, but this. It's different.'

'I know. It'll be so cool.' He got out and around to her side of the car, opened the door. He held out his hand. 'You'll be flying with one of the instructors the whole time, you won't be on your own.'

'Ummm...' Her legs jiggled up and down and she held her hands tight between her knees.

He coaxed her from the car, and placed his hand gently against her lower back.

'I won't have to steer or anything?'

'Nope, just hold on and enjoy.'

She made a nervous sound. There was that word again. *Enjoy.*

'Hey, guys,' said a woman as they approached the grassed area. 'Joel, is it?' she asked.

He nodded, and shook her hand. 'I've done this before but we have a paragliding virgin here.' He gestured to her and her belly fluttered.

She gulped, but the gulp didn't gulp properly and she had to gulp a few more times.

'And you must be Olivia. I'm Vicki.' The woman held out her hand and she shook it reluctantly, worried that she may take her hand and not let go until she was attached to one of the paragliders with no option of saying no.

'Yes, that's me. But I had no idea until now that I was going to be doing this. And I'm really, really nervous. And I wish I could get back in that car but I agreed to this ridiculous list of challenges and now–'

'Ridiculous?' Joel asked.

'Okay, not ridiculous, sorry, just *challenging* challenges.'

'That is why they are called challenges,' he replied, and they walked a bit closer to one of the paragliders where someone was getting strapped in.

'Let's watch this one take off, then we can go through what's involved and get you all ready to go,' Vicki said in an overexcited high-pitched tone.

'Watching. Watching sounds good. We could just do that, I've never seen paragliding up close before, it would still be a great book-worthy moment, Joel.' She turned to him.

'Life is not meant to be watched; it is meant to be experienced.' He stood behind her and held on to her elbows in a supportive way.

'I'll drink to that,' said Vicki. She pointed to the person holding the paraglider. 'See how they are fully supported? The air resistance will hold you up, so you won't feel like you're just hanging on. Once the air beneath you lifts you higher, you'll feel quite light. It's an amazing rush. But at the same time, peaceful.'

Olivia nodded, and nodded, and nodded. Though she wanted to nod sideways and say, 'Nope, I'm not doing this.'

But peaceful, she could do. She imprinted the word in her

mind as a way to distract from the word 'rush' which had never featured in her vocabulary of favourite words.

Maybe I could try those affirmation things April talks about. Or that Zac talks about and passed onto April. Yes, this is definitely an affirmation-worthy situation.

She tried to think up words to string together, like she'd been doing for her book.

I am peaceful and calm.

Umm... that's a load of crap.

Okay, okay: I am excited to be trying a fun new activity.

She watched the person walk closer to the edge.

Fun? I don't know if it will be fun. Excited? I'm not excited. What's the point of an affirmation if they're not even true?

'Just take some deep breaths while you watch, and think happy thoughts,' said Vicki.

Olivia breathed in deeply a few times.

'Not that much, you don't want to hyperventilate.' Joel moved his hands to her shoulders and gave them a light massage. 'Relax your shoulders, breathe in... and out.'

She slowed her breathing as much as she could, the weight of his hands comforting on her shoulders.

Peaceful, and caaalm... she said in her mind with each exhalation. *When I'm in the air, I am peaceful and calm...* Okay, that was a bit better. She could just be peaceful and calm in the air and scared out of her mind on the ground. *In the air, I am peaceful and calm.*

The paraglider did a little run up to the cliff and then leapt forward, the glider going down a little first and then lifting up, light as a bird.

In the air, I am peaceful and calm.

'Woohoo!' someone called out, but she didn't notice who.

In the air, I am peaceful and calm.

After watching for a while, Vicki led her to the side where a paraglider in the air was about to land. She watched them near, stepped back a bit and further to the side, and the person's feet touched the ground running, then slowing to a walk.

'I'll probably fall over,' Olivia said.

'I'll be right with you,' said Vicki. 'I promise you won't fall. I've done hundreds of tandem flights.'

Olivia nodded again. Though she imagined she'd be so glad to touch ground again that she wouldn't care if she fell when she got there. She'd probably want to fall to the ground and hug it if she could.

After the instructor explained everything and got Olivia ready in the harness, at least physically, she knew there was no turning back. She gripped the sides of the harness, and Vicki said, 'Okay, on the count of three, just as we practiced. Ready?'

'I think.' Olivia's head spun and her legs wobbled. The wind swept around them as though getting ready itself, and she felt the pull of the glider wanting to lift.

'Here we go. One...'

In the air, I am peaceful and calm.

'Two...'

In the air, I am peaceful and calm.

'Three!'

In the air, I am... 'Whooaa!' Her legs moved quickly and the air took the place of the ground. 'Aghhhh!'

'And we're off!' Vicki said.

Olivia wanted to put her foot on something steady and firm, but there was nothing but empty space. *Oh my God, Oh my God,* became her new affirmation.

When her brain had realised what was happening and no longer fought for something beneath her feet, she could now process the view in front of her.

Oh my God. Wow.

Her heart pounded, her belly churned, but she felt like a bird.

Endless blue sky, the odd fluffy cloud, and most of all, the rippling ocean beneath took the breath from her lungs.

If Vicki wasn't with her she would probably be having a panic attack, but with the support, she allowed herself to absorb the view and tried to welcome the 'rush' and the 'peace' at the same time.

The sensations evened out and she coasted along, gliding and flying and soaring into the sky and this new experience that she wouldn't have taken part in were it not for a certain man walking into her bookstore on what would have been just any other day.

Her gaze moved to the left as another paraglider came into view. As it lifted higher into the sky, she saw it was Joel, on his own, a wide smile on his face.

She didn't know how long they flew for, but it became rhythmic and soothing, very different than she thought it would be. Or maybe her affirmation worked.

In the air, I am peaceful and calm.

And she realised in that moment she actually was.

The next morning, Olivia gave Mia permission to remove the mattress from her bed and place it next to the couch. Her daughter kept climbing on the couch and leaping off, landing tummy first on the mattress. 'I want to do paragliding,' she said.

Olivia peered through the living room from the kitchen. 'You have to wait till you're older.'

'But Mrs May says you have to do things before you become older.'

'Yes, but not everything. And some things you have to wait until you're a grown-up.'

'Like paragliding.'

'Yes. And motorbikes.'

'And tattoos?'

'Oh yes, definitely tattoos.'

'And making babies?'

Olivia missed the frypan with the pancake batter, and a blob landed on the kitchen counter. 'Definitely making babies. You have to be very ready for that.'

'Were you ready?'

Olivia placed a blob of batter into the frying pan this time. She hadn't planned it, but... 'Once I knew you were coming, yes, I was. I was your mum even before you were born.'

'Even though you hadn't seen me yet?'

'Of course. I could feel you in my belly.' She flipped the pancakes then looked at her daughter who had just leapt onto the mattress again. 'And my heart.' She removed the pancakes and turned the stove off for a moment, then went to the living room. She climbed on the couch and raised her arms.

'Mum, what are you doing?' Mia was still lying on the mattress.

'I'm going to leap off...' she swung her arms, 'and... squash you!'

'Noo!' Mia rolled sideways until she was off the mattress, just as Olivia did a small but enthusiastic leap and fell onto the mattress with a soft thud. Her real paragliding land had been more dignified.

Mia laughed, mostly when Olivia tried to get up but pretended to fall back down, and Olivia went back to the kitchen. She turned the stove back on and stirred the remainder of the pancake batter.

When she put a spoonful in the frying pan, she shaped it

into something, and smiled. She took a photo of the letter 'J' and texted it to Joel along with a message:

Pancake tribute for you, thanks for yesterday.

Then she added:

And for the many days before that.

She didn't know how many days, or moments they would have left, but as soon as she hit send it was like her heart had leapt off into the sky on its own paraglider. She doubted it would have a dignified landing.

If it ever landed at all.

CHAPTER TWENTY-TWO

O livia sat at her bedroom desk, manuscript open on her computer, listening to Mrs May's memories on the phone recorder the next night. She pressed pause for a moment and switched back to her text messages, re-reading the ones she'd shared with Joel yesterday in response to her pancake 'J'. He hadn't been in a position to make pancakes so he made a letter 'O' with his mouth and sent a selfie.

She shook her head at how easy things were these days. If her grandma had had the technology of text messaging, her life may have taken another path. That Saturday all those years ago would have turned out completely differently with the help of a single text message...

May's Memories of the Unexpected

How do you say goodbye to people without letting them know you're saying goodbye? I asked myself this last night at dinner, but myself did not have an answer. So after our meal, I gave Mrs Chevalier a hug to thank her for the delicious food and for having us stay with them. And then I used that opportunity to hug my father for working so hard, and my mother for supporting our family despite her ill health. My gaze caught Jacques', and I wanted to say goodbye, give him a hug, but it would have been too strange a thing to do, so I simply gave him a friendly nod.

So there I was on Saturday morning, my nerves on edge, my heart racing, my soul alive with purpose, preparing to leave town with William.

I placed the goodbye letter on my bed. It explained to my parents that I loved them and was grateful for everything but needed to go and experience something new, take a chance, discover where I wanted my life to lead.

I opened my window, carefully dropped my bag out onto the ground, then climbed through. I closed the window and turned around to walk off, when I froze. There, at the edge of the garden that spanned the back of the house, was Jacques, staring off into the distance. I walked quietly so as to not disturb him, but as my pace quickened I heard his voice...

'May, where are you off to?'

I spun around. 'Jacques. Hello.' I brushed hair awkwardly from my face. 'Just ah, going for a walk.'

'That's a heavy-looking bag to carry, would you like me to accompany you?'

'No,' I said a little too loudly. 'I mean, thank you kindly, but I can manage.'

He eyed the bag.

'I'm taking some items to my friend.' It wasn't a total lie, but I was also taking myself to this friend and he was more than just a friend.

'Very well,' he said. 'Enjoy your walk.'

I smiled and went to turn away, but he looked sad. 'Jacques,' I said. 'Thank you, for your hospitality. I mean, thank you, for putting up with us living here, being in your space, your home. I'm sure it's been a bit of a disruption.'

'Not at all, May,' he said. 'It is a delight to have you present in our home.'

His words felt genuine, and guilt surfaced in my heart.

'And thank you also for your company and friendship,' I added. 'I do enjoy our conversations so very much.' It was true. I would miss discussing literature and poetry with him. But instead I would be discussing letters and love and adventures with William, and most importantly – living them.

'I enjoy them too. Perhaps we can enjoy them some more over a picnic lunch in the garden sometime.'

The guilt rippled down my spine. 'Oh. Yes. Certainly. Sometime.' I gestured towards the direction I planned to go in. 'I better get going. Bye, Jacques.'

He eyed me with a narrow, lowered brow. 'See you later.'

I gave a brief nod and scurried off before I got carried away and before too much time passed. I needed to get there soon, as Mrs Chevalier had been in a talkative mood this morning and it had been difficult to get back to my room to be alone so I could leave.

He would be okay, Jacques. He would find a nice lady to court and be with. He was a good man and deserved happiness.

I walked along and my heart raced even more. It was happening. I was really doing this. I couldn't contain my smile, it stretched and widened on my face as the sea breeze tickled my cheeks and the sun warmed my skin. I planned to walk up to the Tarrin formation first, see it one last time, and then follow the track down along the beach and up over the headland towards Lookout Point.

When I reached it, I allowed myself to stop and take a deep breath at its majestic beauty. At the beauty of nature, both the seen and the unseen. This physical structure was an example of how natural forces could create something so perfect, and it was the same for the bond between William and I. Natural forces, compelling us to be together, creating something beautiful and perfect, in its own unique way. I scanned the horizon, the expanse of sky and sea, its rich-blue opulence inviting me to admire it. I thanked the powers that be for this beautiful place, for surviving the house fire, and for the help of friends in a time of crisis. Most of all I gave thanks for what was to come, and for the opportunity to enjoy a new path towards an exciting future.

When I felt ready, I turned to walk down to the beach. My feet stopped suddenly. 'Jacques.' My heart stopped. 'What are you doing here?'

He walked closer and stood in front of me. 'I thought it was such a nice day I might go for a walk myself.' He put his hands in his pockets and glanced around. 'A nice view up here, isn't it?'

I nodded. 'Indeed. Anyway I must get going.'

He walked closer, then up to the top of the headland just beyond Tarrin, where the rocks joined the ones forming the clifftop and cascaded down to the rocky ground and ocean below. 'Stop and admire the view with me for a while, May,' he said. He gestured with his hand for me to join him. 'I've been so busy lately that I haven't taken much time to do such things.'

I nibbled my bottom lip. 'I do apologise, but my friend is expecting some, ah, items and I don't want to be late.'

'Look,' he said, pointing to a ship in the distance. 'I've never even stopped to notice them before, the cargo ships.' He stepped onto a large rock and leaned his hand on one higher to

steady himself. 'Some people live such a different life, don't they? A life on the sea, I don't know if I could do it. But it is intriguing.' He formed a shelter above his eyes with his hand and peered further into the distance. 'I wonder what sort of people are on that ship, how their families feel as their loved one sails away for weeks at a time.' He turned to face me. 'Family is so important, isn't it, May.'

I nodded. 'Oh yes.' I glanced down the beach. 'Friendships too.'

'Of course.' He tapped his foot on the rock.

'Anyway, enjoy your walk, Jacques.' I gave a little wave and turned away before I couldn't.

'Wait, May?' he said, then he made a gasp. I spun around just in time to see Jacques lose his balance and slip off the rock, sliding down, his hands grabbing the rocks as he fell, but continuing to slip.

'Oh my goodness! Jacques!' I raced towards him. 'Jacques!' I got on my knees and leaned over the edge, trying to grasp his hand but he slipped further down. The look in his eyes in that brief moment seared my soul. He thought he was going to die. Our eyes lost connection as he tumbled further down, and I screamed, my hands reaching over the edge but unable to do anything. I contemplated climbing over and trying to edge my way down carefully, but it was too dangerous, and then I'd be no good to him. My mouth gaped and my body shook as I watched in horror at his body sliding, tumbling, until he came to a stop on the rocky surface below, close to the ocean.

'Jacques!' I called. 'Can you hear me?'

He wasn't moving, his leg was at an odd angle, and one of his shoulders seemed pushed up higher than it should be. Water lapped around him and I begged for him to stay put, for the ocean not to claim him.

'Help!' I called out, looking around me. 'Help!' I found my

footing and stood, shaking, looking for the nearest person. There were a few people further along on the beach, and someone walking their dog in the direction I had come from earlier. I glanced back over the edge at his body, lying lifelessly, not sure if he was alive or dead. Then I sucked in a sharp, painful breath, and ran as fast as I could to get help.

Olivia paused the recording, her heart beating fast. She thought of how many times she'd visited the Tarrin formation, not knowing the details of what unfolded there all those years ago. How scared her grandma must have been, how scared her *grandfather* must have been in that moment. And wondering what had gone through William's mind when May had failed to turn up at Lookout Point. When Mrs May had gotten to that point in her recollection, she'd needed a drink of water and a breather. Olivia said she could come back the next day, but her grandmother had said she just had a few more words to say first...

By the time Jacques had been rescued and taken to hospital, I remembered. 'William!' I said to myself in despair, my hand on my chest. My chin trembled and tears spilled from my eyes, not only from the drama that had unfolded, but from the knowledge that he was probably gone. I had no way of contacting him. Unless word had gotten out about Jacques' accident and he presumed I had been needed, he would have assumed I had decided not to go with him. 'Oh, William!' I cried.

When Jacques had been stabilised and taken to surgery for his broken leg, after being told he was expected to make a full recovery, I left the family at the hospital. I made the trip back to

Tarrin and retrieved my bag that had been left there; thankfully no one had stolen it. I rushed along the track towards Lookout Point. If by some miracle he was still waiting there for me, I wouldn't go with him. I would simply tell him what had happened and ask him to wait for me, to wait for a better time. But when I searched the small crowd of people wandering around the lookout, there was no William. My heart collapsed and I trudged all the way up to the lookout despite the realisation that I had missed my chance. I held on to the railing where our hands had touched and looked out at the vast sea and sky. Where was he now? I don't know how long I stayed there, but it was long enough for me to understand that fate had dealt me a different path. It was no accident that Jacques had fallen, it was meant to happen, to make me stay. My life was here in Tarrin's Bay, and I would make the most of it and my blessings.

I opened my bag and got out some paper and a pencil. On it, I wrote: 'I came. I was late, but I came. There was an accident and I couldn't make it on time. If you find this, come find me so we can talk.'

I took a ribbon from my dress and tied the paper around a discreet end of the railing, at the bottom so that it wouldn't be obvious to visitors but could be found by someone looking for something. I knew it wouldn't stay there long, but I had to try. If he returned today he would have a chance of seeing it. But as I tightened the ribbon, something inside told me he was already well on his journey to wherever he was going.

I returned the next day to be sure. The ribbon was still there, and the paper, wilted a little and frayed, looked like it had not been opened and read.

I left it there anyway, and a couple of days later it was gone, the ribbon still hanging loosely from the railing. I untied it and threw it over the cliff.

Who knew where that ribbon would end up, and who knew

where William would end up. He would always wander, and I would always stay. And that was the way it was meant to be.

Olivia pressed stop and sat still for a long time. She wondered if it was better for her grandma having had the experience despite losing it, or if it would have been better, and easier, if she'd never fallen in love with him at all.

CHAPTER TWENTY-THREE

Joel shivered as he got out of the water. Despite wearing a wetsuit, the air and ocean were cold and unforgiving. He walked back up to the caravan with his surfboard and got showered and changed into warm clothes. Every few minutes he'd pause and think of her, wondering why she had been so distant this past week. There was one week left of the course, so maybe she was simply focused on getting towards the end of her book while her grandma was still alive. Or maybe things were more serious with her grandma and her mind was elsewhere.

As for his mind, it was often on her. Without control, it would flit to her without warning, and he would have to force himself back to the present moment.

He sat on the fold-out bed and opened the text messages on his phone.

> Good morning, how is everything?

Then he added:

You're not too nervous about camping next weekend, are you?

What he really wanted to say was: *Why did you really cancel our lunch last Friday? And why did you rush off after class on Tuesday? And does your mind wander to me as mine does to you?*

Half an hour later he got a reply:

All okay. So busy. Trying not to be nervous about camping.

He stared at it for a moment. Fair enough. She was just busy and probably tired. But it didn't seem like her usual self.

He hesitated about what to say next, or whether to say anything at all, but he remembered it was Sunday.

Have you made pancakes yet?

Nope, just got out of bed.

Are you up for a new #PancakeChallenge?

She didn't reply right away.

Um, sure. What shape am I supposed to make today?

Joel thought for a moment. How many more shapes could one make from pancake batter? He thought he would give her some options for variety, so he texted:

A body part.

He grinned, then added:

> And get your mind out of the gutter ;)

He hoped his light-heartedness would help her return to her usual self. His phone pinged:

> Sometimes random body parts find their way into my innocent pancake shapes anyway. #GiantButterflyPenis

Joel erupted into laughter. She was back. If only for a moment, and via text, she was still... there.

> Ha-ha. I look forward to seeing what random or on-purpose body part you create.

> Watch this space...

He amused himself for a while imagining various body parts as pancake shapes. But he guessed she would so something innocent like a foot or a nose.

When the photo came through, his eyebrows rose.

Covered in luscious red-coloured jam was a pair of perfect bow-shaped pancake lips. He smiled.

> Well done. What were they like?

The typing bubbles appeared, then disappeared, as though she was thinking of how to respond, even though it was a simple question. But he was learning that with Olivia, things weren't turning out as simple as they seemed.

Olivia's finger hesitated over the texting screen. She typed in the words, just to see how it would feel, just to imagine what it would be like if she were in a position to be able to say those words to someone. To have someone she could flirt with in that way: *I'd rather know what your lips are like.*

She giggled at the sentence that looked so foreign on her phone screen.

She could never say that. Her finger shook a little and she went to press backspace, but the message became a bubble and her phone made a whooshing sound.

'What?' She stared at the words. 'What?' Her heart raced and her finger tried to erase what she'd done. 'Oh no, oh no!' She had accidentally pressed send instead of backspace, and now her message was flying through cyberspace to her recipient.

'What's wrong, Mummy?' Mia asked, looking up from the dining table.

'Um, nothing. It's okay, Mummy's just...' *Oh God, what have I done?* 'I made a small mistake sending a message, nothing to worry about.' She escaped into her bedroom.

Nothing to worry about? She paced the room and even googled 'how to erase a sent text message' but sadly it looked like her mistake was inerasable and right now Joel would be reading her message and thinking that she was trying to seduce him.

Get a grip, Olivia, she told herself. *It was just a little flirty message, nothing major. It wasn't like it was anything erotic.*

She stared at the screen. Below the message it said that it had been 'read', but there were no bubbles indicating he was replying.

Argh! Her body clenched and she stamped up and down on the spot in frustration and embarrassment, heat filling her body.

Okay, okay, think! How to rectify the situation? Maybe she could pretend April was here and had typed in her reply as a joke. No, she couldn't lie, even a small white one. Olivia pressed the screen.

Sorry, just being silly. Trying 'something different', I guess. I wasn't being serious.

Oh, but she was.

Her heart almost stopped when words appeared below hers:

Oh. And here I was getting my hopes up.

Oh. Oh indeed. Was he being serious or just being *silly* too?

You are disappointed?

No, but I did get rather excited thinking you were flirting with me ;)

Lol. In that case I can make up a new pretend flirt? #FlirtChallenge

Go ahead.

Okay, this wasn't so bad. She could do pretend flirting. Even though she had meant what she'd accidentally texted before.

And now that she was given the green light to flirt, she couldn't think of what to say.

After a while of silence, Joel texted:

Am I that hard to flirt with?

#UnderPressure

She had no idea why she was using hashtags but they just seemed to come out.

Extra challenge. You must flirt only in hashtags.

She laughed. Okay, here goes:

#YoureNicerThanMyPancakes.

Oh God, it was pathetic.

#ThankYouThat'sVeryNiceOfYou

Joel's hashtag had un-hashtagged at the point of the apostrophe, so she said:

#IAppreciateYourGoodGrammarButHashtags-
DontLikeApostrophes

He replied with a hashtag and a laughing emoticon together.

#DidYouJustHashtagLaughAtMe?

#Yes

The corners of Olivia's lips turned upwards in a smile as their flirting triggered feelings she wasn't sure how to handle. She texted him back with a hashtag and a kiss emoticon.

#DidYouJustHashtagKissMe?

#yes

#YoureSoCute

She couldn't contain her smile. Especially when he sent another text with a hashtag and two kiss emoticons.

#DidYouJustHashtagKissMeTwice?

#Yes

And then her heart hashtag-fluttered at what he added next:

#AndThatWasntPretend

CHAPTER TWENTY-FOUR

J oel was glad tonight was his last class. Because he didn't know how much longer he could stand in front of that class and not walk straight up to Olivia and grab her, wrap her in his arms, and #HashtagKissHerForReal. After tonight, though, he would only be in town another week or so before travelling further south. But the more he thought about her, the more he wanted to stay put, and that scared the life out of him.

'As you can see,' he said, pointing out some examples of memoir excerpts on the screen, 'the ending can be just as important as the beginning. Don't skimp on it. Don't rush it. And don't leave readers hanging. It's okay to create a taste of there being more to come, but you need a resolution. The reader wants to know how everything turned out, at least for now, even though life goes on.'

And his ending had really only been a beginning, as they often were. To him, the ending of a good memoir, his especially, was more of a transition point. A time of reassessment, and consolidating all that had been learned and experienced prior to that moment, so that the next phase of life could be established and begun. No stopping, always moving forward.

'What if you don't yet know how it ends?' asked Mr Donovan.

'Good question. And the answer is simple: write about how you don't know how it will end. Write about where you are at now, and what brought you to that moment. If there is a story or journey that led you to where you currently are, then that is your book. And the ending is simply a summary of where you now are compared to where you were. A memoir needs a before and after. People want to read about a transformation of some kind... if there isn't one, there is no story.'

Some of his students nodded.

'And in many cases, I guess that transformation only continues,' Zac said.

'Indeed,' Joel replied. 'It's an ongoing process, especially in your case. But there are always points along the way that mark various levels of growth and transformation, and those are the beginnings and endings of the many smaller stories that make up the overall journey of your life.'

Zac took some notes. And Joel glanced at Olivia, whose head was down as she wrote notes too. He loved the way her hair fell over her shoulders, and he wanted to stand behind her and gently gather it in his hands and lift it back behind her shoulders and...

Stop.

He had to say that to himself sometimes. Like he'd had to say that to himself during his time in the wilderness, when his mind had become doubtful and desperate. He'd had to create a transition point then, to put an end to the downward spiral of negative thoughts and the possibility he wouldn't make it out alive. Only then could he continue his mantra of 'one more breath'. But now, his 'stop' was to stop an upward spiral, one of heightening attraction and curiosity to know and discover more and more about this woman in much closer ways than he had before. He did not want there to be an ending with her, and in order for that to happen, he could not create a beginning. Yes they'd begun a friendship, a unique and special one, but anything more and it would inevitably lead to an ending, and he wouldn't do that to her, or to himself.

'To end tonight, I want to share with you a video compilation of my journey, and I want to encourage you, if you fancy yourself a bit of a movie maker, to create a video of your own using pictures or video clips that are part of your story, words from your memoir, and music. Do it before finishing your book if you like, to inspire you and remind you of the bigger picture. It can also be a great thing to show at your book launch.'

Joel pressed play, sat, and took a breath. No matter how many times he'd seen these pictures, and heard the music, it always triggered deep emotions in him. He wouldn't let that show to the class, but later tonight, he would probably have a beer and acknowledge again to himself how far he had come.

Some of the photos that were featured in his book appeared on screen, along with some others from his childhood, his teenage years, and his many adventures and life experiences. Then there were the ones taken of him after being rescued, in hospital, and during his recovery when he'd had to rebuild his torn muscle and work to get it back to or at least close to the other leg's strength, to make sure he could walk easily throughout the rest of his life without needing a cane down the track. The idea of that spurred him on during his rehabilitation. No way was he allowing that to be an option.

The video faded to black, and he stood. Dylan clapped and stood. Maribella dabbed at her eyes with a tissue, and Olivia rested a hand under her chin, her eyes looking deeply affected and that only made him want to wrap her in his arms even more. Joel put out his hand as though to signal that there was no need for clapping, but that only seemed to spur the class on, and then everyone was standing and clapping.

'Joel Foster, what a marvellous experience your course has been, thank you,' Mr Donovan said. 'I think it will take me quite a while to write all of my book, but I wouldn't know where to start or how to go about it if it wasn't for your help.'

Joel's sense of accomplishment after a challenge or adventure rose inside. Teaching these classes was a different kind of challenge, but just as rewarding, he was discovering.

'I agree,' said Maribella. 'I have a way to go, but I have a plan now, a structure. I'm so excited to create my book.'

'And I'm almost finished,' said Dylan. 'Can't wait for you to read it, bro.'

'Can't wait either,' Joel said. 'Thanks, guys, really, it's been an absolute pleasure teaching you. And I look forward to our graduation dinner on Thursday night.'

'Do we have to wear black capes and do we get fancy rolled-up diplomas secured with red wax seals?' asked Mr Donovan.

'Not at all. Unless you really want to,' Joel replied.

'Not particularly, black is not my colour,' Mr Donovan said with a wink.

He had booked Bayside for a buffet dinner for both his Tuesday and Wednesday classes as a casual celebration for the group, and a way for students to network a bit more and make friends without the time pressure of sticking to a class time. It would also be nice to see Olivia again, and hopefully, this week, she would not cancel their Friday lunch so they could enjoy one last meal together before her camping trip, and before he left the following week.

He shook hands, exchanged a few hugs, and the students left the hall with smiles on their faces. Joel exhaled a breath of relief. When he'd first had the idea for teaching courses, he wasn't sure if he would be any good at it, just like when he'd had the idea for the book and he didn't know how he'd be able to write it with his less-than-perfect attention span and past dyslexia. But he was always up for a challenge, and that's what kept him enjoying his life.

'Will I be seeing you on Friday for lunch, Olivia?' he asked, as she exited the building.

'Miss our last Friday lunch? Never.' She smiled. 'I'll be there.'

He smiled back. 'Glad to hear it. And you can even have your boring chicken salad if you really want.'

'Oh, *can* I now? You mean you're giving me a choice this time?'

'We always have choices,' he said, but he wasn't sure what subject he was referring to. He was lucky in that he did have choices, options, and opportunities. He wasn't stuck behind a desk or job he hated from Monday to Friday; he had variety. And he had choices when it came to his personal life. He'd just always chosen the easiest option. 'I'm glad you chose to do this course.'

She gave a nod. 'I'm glad you coerced me into it.'

'Coerced? I'm starting to think I'm a bit of an arse, telling you what to eat, coercing you into my course, making you do these book-worthy challenges...' He laughed.

'You are an arse.' She shrugged as if it was obvious. 'A *nice* arse.'

'I have a nice arse?'

'No, I mean you're a nice arse! Don't go putting words in my mouth.' Her cheeks brightened.

'Now I'm forcing words into your mouth. I really am a right ol' arse.'

'Can we stop saying arse now and can I say something else?'

'Of course, but extra points if your sentence has arse in it.' He chuckled.

'Smart-arse,' she said. Then stepped closer. 'Seriously, I just want to say thanks for everything. I'm glad I did the course. I'm glad I... met you. And I'm glad you've helped me break through my discomfort zone a little.' Her body swayed cutely, as though she was younger than her thirty-something years.

He was glad of all those things too. Maybe even *gladder* than her. Despite her relatively simply and predictable life, he had never met anyone quite like her, and she stood out to him, even though it seemed she had always tried to blend in. 'A little?' he said. 'I'd say it was a lot. And there's still the camping trip to go. Do you have all the clothing and supplies I recommended?'

'Yes,' she said. 'And I'm relying on you to bring the tent and camping stuff, otherwise I'll have nowhere to sleep and I'll be cold and I will just go home.'

'Ah, you can't back out of your last book-worthy moment. Camping is the grand finale. Once you're there, you stay until it's time to go home.'

'I know, I know,' she mumbled. 'And you're sure I'll get enough phone reception where I'll be? I do need to be on call for either Mia or my grandma at all times.'

'You bet. I've picked a great spot for you. You might even enjoy yourself.'

'I'll be glad when it's all over and done with,' she said with a nervous smile.

He shifted his weight to one foot and placed his hands in his pockets. Over and done with. Soon he would be over and done with things here. Why did that make *him* feel discomfort? 'I'll miss our lunches and crazy experiences,' he blurted without thinking.

She stood still on the sidewalk outside the hall, her eyes looking into his. 'Strangely enough, I think I will too.' She smiled. 'What I mean is, it's like I can't imagine going back to the way things were before you arrived. Like I've stepped into a new world and the only direction is north.'

'Then keep following that compass,' he said.

'I will. Figuratively speaking, since I don't have a compass. Oh, will I need a compass when I go camping?'

Joel chuckled. 'You can use a compass app on your phone. But no, you won't need one unless you plan to trek for hours or days like I've done in the past.'

'No thank you.'

'And I hope you're not bringing your laptop, no work allowed while camping.'

'Nope. But I can bring a book to read, right? That's kind of work because of my job, but it's mostly fun.'

He smiled. 'Is reading as fun as the things you've done over the past few weeks?'

'Reading is always fun,' she said, crossing her arms. 'Those things I did were a different kind of... dare I say it... fun. Ouch.'

'So you did enjoy yourself!'

'Mostly after the experience.'

He gave her arm a squeeze. 'You're more fun than you give yourself credit for, Miss Chevalier.'

'You bring it out in me.'

'You bring out the bringing out of it in you in me.'

Laughter burst from her mouth, and then from his. 'I was going to say I'll miss our texting too, but... maybe we can sort of keep in touch. If you want.' She did that swaying thing again.

It would be easier to keep in touch once he was on the road, no temptation to drive right over and see her immediately. It was safer. 'Sure. We're friends, and we'll keep in touch. And you're the most fun texter I've ever known. And you brought out more texting in me than I ever thought possible.'

'You brought out the bringing out of it in you in me.'

They laughed again, and then she was closer than he'd

expected, her arms slipping around his back. 'Thank you,' she said again, resting her head against his chest as they hugged.

He allowed his chest to soften, his lungs to exhale, to welcome her body next to his right there and then. He captured the moment like he had many others when he thought they could be his last. *One more breath*, he thought to himself, before he allowed himself to release from her embrace.

CHAPTER TWENTY-FIVE

After Olivia had come home from work on Friday and finished packing for her camping trip, dropped Mia off at her mother's for the weekend, and double-checked with Marcus that all was in order to run the store while she was gone, she drove to the nursing home. She wanted some time alone with her grandma before she left, to check she was okay, and to see if she had anything more to add to the story about William and Jacques. It had seemed a bittersweet ending... the end of her romance with William, but the beginning of a slow and steady love with Jacques.

'How is everything?' Olivia asked the nurse who was beside the bed.

'My favourite patient is doing well,' she replied.

'She calls everyone her favourite,' Mrs May responded.

'Because everyone is,' she replied.

Mrs May scoffed. 'I'm sure that annoying nuisance two rooms down from me is not your favourite.'

'Shh,' the nurse said, covering her lips with her finger. 'I'll leave you both to it.' She left the room and Olivia sat on the chair.

'Oh, these days are all blending into each other,' Mrs May said. 'What day is it?'

'Friday,' said Olivia. 'I'm going camping tomorrow, can you believe it?'

'Hardly. But you'll have to tell me all about it next week.'

'I will,' she said. But discomfort twinged inside because there was never any certainty of tomorrows or next weeks or next months. 'The book is coming along nicely,' she added. 'Can't wait till it's finished, I'm thinking probably another month or so.'

'Fabulous, dear. I'm so proud of you.' She gave her granddaughter's hand a weak squeeze.

'And I was wondering, with all the letters William sent you, did you ever give him one in return?' Olivia asked.

'Oh yes,' she replied. 'Did I not say that last time?'

Olivia shook her head and leaned forward, but not before pressing record on her phone.

'Three or four weeks after Jacques' fall, when he was recuperating at home, I wrote William a letter.'

'But how did you get it to him?'

'I didn't, my dear. But I needed to write it nonetheless. The idea for the letter came about when I realised something...'

May's Memories of One Last Letter

I had finished reading Jacques a book of poetry as he lay reclined, his plastered leg raised, and closed the book with a pop.

'That is not the way one should close such a special book,' he said.

'Oh?' I asked. 'Well I am terribly sorry. May I open it and close it again for you?' I smiled, demurely of course, but with a

hint of cheekiness. William had brought that out in me, and despite what had happened, some of his essence remained with me. I opened the book, then asked, 'How should such a book be closed?'

'Slowly. With a light, reverent touch.' He modelled the correct way by closing his palms together.

I raised my eyebrows to the challenge, then closed the book slowly, in a light, reverent way. It made only a small sound, not a pop, not a thud, not a snap. But a sound I could not think of a word to describe it with. There was no other sound like it, it was the sound of beauty being recognised, of perfection, of completeness. And I never closed another book with a pop again. Books were magic that could be carried from room to room, from house to house, from town to town, from person to person. They deserved respect and tenderness.

During Jacques' recovery, we became closer. Friends, but with a hint of something more being possible. I didn't expect that, didn't even know if I wanted that. But it grew, ever so slowly, unlike the whirlwind that was William who spun into and out of my life. I knew, when I closed that book lightly, that something was different. The ache I had for William had dissolved. And if I had gone with him, I wouldn't be having this sweet, somehow comforting experience with Jacques. It wasn't the intense romance that I'd had with William, but it felt nice, and I looked forward to reading to Jacques each day and giving him company throughout his boredom and pain.

I never knew if I believed in fate, but I started to believe that Jacques' fall was no accident, and that it happened to ensure that I would stay. So I decided to honour that and stick through it, make it work, build a life with Jacques. After all, I had been attracted to him at first, ever since we exchanged smiles through the window of his father's tailor's shop.

But first, I needed to let William go. I didn't know if I

would ever see him again, if he would return one day, or I'd bump into him somewhere down the track, but I couldn't hold out hope. So I had to cut ties. And I did this the only way I knew how, by how it all began. With a simple letter...

Dear Wandering, Wild, Wonderful William,

I know you won't read this, but I need to write it. You gave me the gift of so many beautiful letters, and I want to return the favour, if only with one.

It's been a few weeks since that day I was supposed to meet you at Lookout Point. Every day I have missed you, every day I think of you. I find you in the rush of a sudden breeze as it lifts my hair from my shoulders, and in the moonlight filtering through trees, and in the sun as it warms my face.

Even in your absence you're present.

I sometimes wonder what would have become of us. But fate dealt a different journey for me that day, and therefore, for you too. So I can only hope that you are well, safe, and enjoying a grand adventure.

I found out that your aunt and uncle are selling the general store and moving north. I was sad when I heard that, because I like them, and because I guess you won't be back in town in order to visit them one day. But again, perhaps that is meant to be. I want you to live the best life you can, do all those things you talked about and dreamt of. I plan to devote my life to books, and the magic they bring to people's lives. And every time I start reading a new one, I will remember you, and the magic you brought to my life.

You were like a sunset, bursting into my life in full colour then fading into the darkness... a transient, bittersweet piece of heaven.

You were my shooting star. And like the one we saw in the sky that night you asked me to go away with you, I'll never forget you. And I hope you'll never forget me. I hope our time together will always be as magic and memorable for you as it is for me.

Love,

Memorable May.

I kissed the letter and held it up to the sky at Lookout Point one night, moonlight shining through the thin parchment. Then I tossed it over the edge and it floated in the breeze, danced about, and fell slowly, lightly, reverently, into the ocean below. I had symbolically closed our book. Like William, the letter would wander, float, let the tide take it wherever was right. And in that moment I let go of all sadness, all longing, all 'what-ifs', and said goodbye. I dreamt of him that night, but on waking the memories were hard to grasp. So I remembered him the way I wanted to remember him... his chaotic mop of hair falling over his eyes, and that glimmer of excitement in his diamond eyes that told me he would make the most of his life, no matter what happened. I knew, even though he may have missed me for a while, that he would be happy. And he may even find himself a new love. And I was okay with that. I just wanted him to be happy and follow his dreams.

When I returned home I put a wide smile on my face,

walked through the door of the Chevalier's house, straight into Jacques' room, and kissed him right on the lips.

'What was that for?' he asked.

'It's time we moved things along,' I said.

And we did. From that night on, we developed our relationship into a beautiful, close friendship-based love that brought with it many happy memories, and eventually a daughter, granddaughter, and great-granddaughter. Four generations of strong Chevalier women, and a lifetime of living my dream of running a bookstore. I was blessed. I am blessed. And I don't regret a single thing.

Olivia leaned over the bed and hugged her frail grandmother. 'I am blessed too. To hear your story, and to have you in my life.' A tear stained her grandma's gown. 'I'm so proud of what you built, both your family and your business. Your legacy will never be forgotten.' She cherished the sensation of her grandma's rising and falling chest, knowing that one day soon, it would stop. She cherished the warmth of her skin, knowing one day soon, it would cool. And she cherished her voice, knowing one day soon, that she would speak no more.

'Did you ever stop wondering what happened to William?'

'I loved your grandfather dearly. But I also loved William at one stage, and part of me always wondered what could have happened, what may have been possible. But I think books became my William. My escape into an intense version of reality, based on fantasy. Anything that resembled what we had shared, or that held exciting adventures and possibilities, I read. I devoured them. I wanted to be surrounded by books, and that was what helped me for so many years to create and sustain Mrs May's Bookstore. It was my haven, my world, but in a way it was also a tribute to William and what he did for me.' Olivia leaned back to hand Mrs May a drink of water. She took a sip and handed the cup back. 'I may not have ended up with him, but by being with him, he brought something out in me, helped carve the sculpture of myself into something deeper and more intricate, helped me become more of... myself. And this helped me not only in my career, but my marriage. I stopped being afraid to be fully myself, and I even ended up giving Jacques quite a few gaping wide grins too!' Olivia smiled as her grandma did. 'What it all comes down to is without William, I don't know if my life would be what it is today. He was only a small chapter of my story, but he helped create the whole book.'

Tears blurred Olivia's vision. 'Grandma, do you want me to see if I can find out what happened to him? With the internet, I'm sure there's a way.'

She shook her head. 'No, no, dear. I do not want to know. And if there's a heaven somewhere in this world then I'm sure I'll find out soon enough. I want the story to end the way it ended. I'm okay with how everything turned out.'

'If you're sure.'

She nodded. 'Just like in books, there is an ending, but also the promise of a new beginning. We don't need to know all the details of what happens after that final page, but can be content knowing that the characters, the people, are on the right path and living the life they are supposed to.'

'You're absolutely right.' Olivia was glad her phone was still recording; she wanted to include those words in the book.

'Now go and make some memories on that camping trip of yours, young lady.'

Olivia smiled. 'I'll do my best.' She kissed her grandma's forehead and stood. 'Bye, Grandma.'

'Bye, sweetheart.'

And once again, she walked out, trying to prepare herself for the possibility of that being their last moment together.

CHAPTER TWENTY-SIX

'Tent?'

'Check.'

'Sleeping bag?'

'Check.'

'Blanket?'

'I thought you were bringing that,' Joel said, even though he had a woollen one in his car.

'I don't have outdoorsy ones, I thought you were packing that,' she replied, her face taut and her body tense.

He smiled. 'Relax, I have it.'

'Oh. Good. Right... okay, I have my esky with food supplies, and my phone with cordless charger backup, and, oh! Hang on, forgot to pack reading material.'

He chuckled as she scurried back into her bedroom and came out holding three books.

'Three? You're only going for one night.'

'I know, but I don't know which one I'll feel like reading when I get there, and I'll also have plenty of time on my hands, I may even get through two books, or three if I'm really bored.'

'Don't forget it's good to sometimes just be. To stare out at nature and contemplate life, or to walk and get into a nice rhythm. You don't have to keep busy like you always are.'

'I know, I just like to be prepared.'

Fair enough. He was always prepared for anything. His car was always stocked with supplies and equipment and whatever he may need if he decided to spontaneously live off the land for a week or so.

'Got a spare pair of socks? In case one gets wet?'

'Yep.' She nodded. 'But how would one get wet, I'm not planning on taking off my shoes until I'm just about in my sleeping bag.'

'You never know. You could feel a bug or slimy creature of some kind squirming inside your shoe and be compelled to yank it off and then step in some mud. It happens.' He shrugged.

'Oh, you! Stop!' She whacked him on the arm. 'Don't even put that thought in my head.'

'Just being an arse again.'

'Yep.' She flung her bag over her shoulder and picked up the esky. 'Right, good to go, I think.'

'Okay, time for your last book-worthy adventure, Olivia Rediscovered.' He held open the door for her. 'At least, last for now. I hope to hear of many more adventures down the track. Keep me posted.'

'Sure thing. But let's get through this one first, shall we?'

'Shall you,' he corrected. 'You're the one that wanted to do this on your own.'

'I didn't exactly have a flurry of volunteers to join me,' she said. 'Camping, in June. Great time of year.'

'You've got some extra-warm clothing, and the cold weather is good for the metabolism.'

'Are you saying I need to boost my metabolism?' She narrowed her eyes.

'Not at all. Just sayin'. It's an interesting fact.' He shrugged.

'In fact, did you know that immersing yourself in really cold water is actually good for the immune system? There's a spring where we're going, and even a small waterfall. Fancy an outdoor shower or bath?'

'No way in hell.'

He laughed. 'The shower water in the facilities building may not be the hottest either, but it'll do. And hopefully you don't catch one of those fungal foot infections.' He chuckled.

Olivia scrunched up her nose, then sighed. 'It's only one night, and I won't be working up much of a sweat. I probably won't need a shower till I get home.'

'Let's go.' He let her in the car and drove south onto the highway, Olivia's fingers twisting together on her lap the whole way.

They arrived at the camping grounds and checked in through the gates, and he drove to the parking area near the facilities building. He showed her inside to give her peace of mind that yes, there was a toilet, and yes, there was a shower, and though it wasn't five-star luxury, it would suffice for the duration of her stay.

They carried the supplies and equipment up a walking track, through a clearing where a few tents were set up with some younger kids running around with their parents, beanies on their heads, and then up another track and to a semi-cleared area that had smaller spots for tents that enabled privacy among the trees. 'What a great view you have here.' He gestured to the side of the spring where water trickled down gently over the rocks. 'You may even get this area to yourself. But look, you can still see the family area down below if you look through these trees.' He showed her.

'Okay, this isn't so bad. Nice spot. Secluded, but not isolated. Fresh water, so I won't dehydrate if I run out of my bottled water. Okay, I can do this.'

'Of course you can. And I'm only a phone call away.'

'Phone. I must check.' She got it out and nodded. 'Good, reception.'

'Told you. We're not that far into the sticks out here.' Joel placed the stuff on the dirt. 'I'll help you set up.'

But he did most of it, while she watched and did a few things he asked. 'Pitching a tent is a good skill to learn,' he said.

'It's not a skill I've needed yet in my life.'

'Still, a good thing to know. So pay attention.'

'Yes, sir.'

After a while the tent was up, and Olivia crawled inside to check it out and put the sleeping bag, foam mat, and blankets inside. She arranged all her belongings then exited the tent and stood, hands on hips. 'Now what?'

'Now you enjoy.'

'Hmm.' She glanced around.

'Bored yet?'

'A bit. You can go now, if you like.'

'Fine.' He pretended to be offended.

'Sorry, that sounded a bit harsh. I mean, you've probably got other plans and stuff, so I'll be okay. Thanks for helping me set up. I'll see you tomorrow when you pick me up as planned.'

'My pleasure.' He checked his watch. 'Lunchtime. You've got enough food?'

'Heaps. Enough for a week, I think.' She chuckled.

He double-checked the tension on the tent and that the tent stakes were deep enough into the ground.

'You hungry?' she asked.

'Me? Always.'

'Stay a while if you like. I have sandwiches.'

He smiled. 'I could be coerced into staying for sandwiches.'

'Now I'm being the arse, coercing you.'

'A huge arse.'

'I have a huge arse?'

He grinned. 'Knew you'd say that. But no, of course you don't. And even if you did, what does it matter?'

She shook her head. 'How do we get onto these bizarre topics?'

'We just do. It's our thing.'

'Let's sit our huge arses down over here, eat some sandwiches and admire the view.' She gestured to a large rock overlooking the view to the spring and waterfall, and opened the esky.

He accepted her offering of a cheese, ham and lettuce sandwich and munched happily as they sat, mostly in silence. It was peaceful, comfortable, relaxing.

He had no desire to leave.

She didn't want him to leave. So she kept offering him food until she could figure out what to do with those feelings. She made a quick trip to the bathroom, returning to find him lying on his back, hands clasped behind his head, smiling up at the sky.

'Having fun?' she asked.

'Sure am.'

'And don't you have plans today?'

He shook his head.

Damn. Now what?

'So, if I was to go for a walk, and not get lost, where would I go?'

He stood. 'I'll show you. Or I can give you the general directions and leave you to it, you're probably sick of me by now.'

'No, you show me. I don't want to get lost. You can stay a bit longer.'

Just how long would a bit longer be?

'Okay,' he said. 'I wouldn't want you to get lost. And we do have to work off those sandwiches.'

'True. Okay, let's go.' She zipped up the tent and grabbed her backpack with water, snacks, a spare jumper, and her phone.

She followed his steps up a trail and over the rocky ground, until they reached a higher point where the bushes became denser. He held branches out of the way as they walked through, then stopped. 'You know, it's taking all my willpower not to let these branches snap back and grab them just before they whack you in the face, like my friends and I used to do with each other on bushwalks.' He chuckled.

'Gee thanks, nice to know.'

'Of course, I *wouldn't* do that, I'm just being a sarcastic arse.'

'I know you are. And it's taking all my willpower not to grab a stray branch and whack you in the arse with it.'

'Who needs willpower? Go for it.'

'I might. When you least expect it.'

'While hiking, I'm always prepared for anything,' Joel said.

'Even spontaneous arse-whackings?'

'Even spontaneous arse-whackings.'

She grinned as she looked around, watched his broad back swivel side to side slightly as he moved through the trees, muscled shoulders rising to move the branches out of the way. How did she even get here? She barely recognised the person she had become, or was it that before she had become diluted in the sameness of her life, and now the real her was surfacing, crystallising?

They walked on, and got into a comfortable rhythm. She could see why he liked it, the repetition and being surrounded by nature was starting to put her at ease, and her legs had more stamina than she knew.

They stopped at a clearing, which looked over the expanse of bushland in the valley below, as they sipped water. 'Wow,' she said. 'To think I've never even seen all this before. There is so much... *world* out there, and this is only a small part.'

'So true. I've seen a lot, but there is still so much more I'd love to see.'

'I feel like I've been living under a rock.'

He looked at her. 'Not at all. You've just had a different life journey. One could say that when it comes to responsibility and being the sole carer of a child for over nine years, I've been living under a rock. I wouldn't know how to do that. How did you do that?'

'You just do. You have to. My circumstances changed and I changed with them.'

'I may have survived a lot physically, but you've survived a lot emotionally.'

'So have you. Your past. And the mental challenge you needed to get through your physical challenge.'

'Life is an adventure in itself, isn't it.'

'Sure is. And my grandma has taught me a lot recently about that. It's been so great to learn more about her past and her perspective on things.'

'How's she doing?'

Olivia shrugged. 'Good, but they only keep saying that because... why beat the drum of the reality of the situation? We all know she doesn't have long.'

He touched her arm.

'People die, people leave, and life goes on. Nothing more to it.' She shrugged in resignation, though her heart quivered.

'But in between all of that, some people live, some people stay, and life is lived.'

'Sometimes,' she said.

They resumed walking, but back the way they came, in silence for a while.

'Do you think you'll ever settle somewhere?' she asked him, then regretted it. It sounded like she was asking 'do you think you would ever settle down and be with someone like me?' What did settle down mean anyway? She'd been settled for years, she didn't know if she wanted 'settled' anymore, she wanted stability and consistency for Mia, yes, but if she was taken out of the equation, what did she really want for herself?

Excitement. Passion. To feel alive and to feel loved and to feel important.

The answers came to her instantly though she tried to ignore them.

Joel shrugged. 'I don't know. I don't know if I've ever had a reason *to* settle, or to stay put for a long time.'

Sometimes you need to make a reason, she wanted to say.

'I guess I'm so used to taking things one moment at a time.'

She nodded. 'And I'm so used to planning ahead and making sure everything is in order, sometimes I forget about the moment.'

He nodded. 'Nothing wrong with that, parenthood requires that, and that's what has helped you raise Mia to be the happy young woman she is.' They walked on, and the spring came into view beyond the trees. 'But right now, Mia is in good hands and you're here, in nature, in the moment. So what would you like to do to enjoy this moment, and the next, and the next?'

Olivia stopped and looked around. The sky was muting a little. Had they really walked for so long? 'I'd like to watch the sunset,' she said.

Joel smiled. 'Good idea.' He pointed down the hill toward the waterfall. 'Let's go sit over there near the water.'

They took residence on a rock and drank some more water. 'Cheers,' he said, clinking his bottle with hers.

'Cheers. To...' she said.

'To... camping.'

'To camping.' She laughed. 'Never thought I'd say that. And to... sunsets.'

'To sunsets. And to friendship.'

The word sounded different coming from his lips. 'To... friendship.'

They drank, and watched, as the bluey-grey became pinky-orange filtering through the trees. She could smell a barbeque cooking down in the family area below, though she couldn't see them from here. She really did have her own little secluded piece of paradise here, if only for one night.

The sunset darkened and the almost full moon began to glow. 'What about the next moment?' she asked Joel.

Joel took a deep breath, sighed an exhalation, and looked around. He honed in on the spring a few metres away. 'Something I haven't done for years.'

'What's that?'

'A bit of immune-system boosting.' He stood suddenly and lifted off his jumper and started unbuttoning his shirt with a shiver.

'Huh?' Olivia's mouth hung open. 'Um, what are you doing?' Though she knew full well what he was doing, unless he was doing another of those tricks where he pretended and then said 'just kidding'.

The shirt came off, and his back muscles rippled as he bent down and untied his boots, removed his socks, then turned to face her with a grin. 'Don't look so shocked,' he said. 'But the pants are coming off too, so I'm giving you fair warning in case you want to look away, or join me.'

'Join you? Are you crazy?'

'Probably. But we can either sit here and keep talking about living in the moment and making the most of life, or we can live in the moment and make the most of life. I'm choosing the latter.'

'Clearly! Umm.' Olivia stood, glancing around to see if anyone could see. There was no one around. 'But skinny-dipping?'

His zipper unzipped with an almighty zip sound. *Oh dear.*

'Okay, maybe I'll leave my underwear on, since I'm in your presence, but if you weren't then yeah, I'd totally skinny-dip. It's a liberating rush!'

'Sounds more like a freezing, uncomfortable experience to me.'

'Don't knock it till you've tried it.' The pants came off.

Olivia turned her gaze to the side, but not before she'd seen the bulk of his thighs and something warmed her up inside in spite of the cool weather.

He hurried to the water and waded in. 'Woo!' He turned around. 'Whoa, I feel so alive right now!'

'And I'm perfectly alive standing right here.' She crossed her arms.

'Come on in, for just a minute!'

'But then I'll be all wet and cold and...'

'And you brought spare clothes, right?'

'Yes, but...'

'Then no excuses, I officially present you with an almost-skinny-dipping challenge.'

'You can't do that, I've had enough challenges.'

'*And* I'm adding hashtags. That means you have to.'

'You can't add hashtags to something you've said, don't be ridiculous.'

'I just did.'

'The cold water is messing with your head.'

'I know, isn't it great! Come on, when will you get this opportunity again? Think about the future when your grandkids are asking you about your exciting adventures. They'll never believe their beloved grandmother went almost-skinny-dipping.' He splashed the water around and let out another 'woo!'

Even if she did, she didn't know if she was more scared of getting in the cold water or of him seeing her in her underwear. She could get in and make a fool of herself, or she could stand there while he made a fool of himself, or she could go back to the tent and read. Reading sounded good, but as she turned away to go to the tent, his delightful laughter and splashing made her turn back to watch him again. A smile grew on her face. He was having a ball, apparently. He looked like he'd even stopped caring if she came in or not.

Should I?

She could go in for a few seconds and get right back out again and say 'there, I've done it'.

'You know you want to.' He caught her gaze with a tempting stare, his eyes pinning her.

Oh dear God.

She lifted her jacket off her shoulders slowly.

'Woohoo! I knew it.'

'But don't look!' she called out. 'Turn away until I say so.'

'Okay, okay.' He turned his back to her.

She double-checked no one else was watching then quickly slipped out of her jacket, her top, her shoes and her jeans, leaving them in a pile on the dirt. At least she was wearing decent black underwear, and not white that could go see-through. She shivered from both cold and trepidation and quickly went to the water's edge, testing it with her toe. 'It's so cold!'

'Quick, get in, it'll feel better once you're in,' Joel said.

She clenched her jaw and tensed her muscles and stepped in. 'There aren't any weird creatures underneath, are there?'

'No, this water is pretty clear. You're safe.'

She went in deeper as water enveloped her skin and goosebumps sprung up all over. 'Eek!'

'Can I turn around?'

'Okay, I'm in.'

Joel turned and grinned widely. 'Ha-ha! You did it, you really did it.' He waded closer to her.

Olivia moved her arms around in circles across the surface of the water, her teeth chattering. 'Am I turning blue?'

'I'll resuscitate you if you do, don't worry.'

And then she thought of his lips again and how she'd embarrassed herself by sending that accidental text that day.

'You don't even seem to be cold anymore,' she said.

'It grows on you. And the adrenaline has kicked in to keep me warm.'

They splashed and swam and laughed, and the sky darkened further.

'I'm still bloody freezing!' She moved around, trying to keep her muscles warm.

'But you feel alive, right?'

'Very.'

'See, another book-worthy moment, and it wasn't even planned. Dare I say I am good for you, Miss Olivia?' He flashed a smug grin.

'You're both good for me and bad for me,' she replied. 'You're like chocolate.'

He burst out laughing, and she laughed in response. She splashed him, he splashed her, and she forgot that she was only in her underwear in an extremely cold body of water in the middle of winter. They were well and truly living in the moment. And as she knew, even though chocolate was not the best food to have a lot of, she would always, *always* want it anyway.

***

They rushed up to their clothes and Olivia raced to the tent to get a towel, drying herself off quickly. 'I need to change my underwear, go away!' She went into the tent.

'Can't I get a towel too?'

'I only have the one,' she called from the tent, then a moment later, tossed it out to him. 'Catch!'

When she emerged, she was fully dressed and he was zipping up his pants, his torso still shirtless.

'That's the quickest I've ever known a woman to get ready,' he said.

'I'm not about to go put on any make-up or do my hair. Though my head is freezing now! Hair dryer wasn't on my list of essentials to bring.'

'Here.' He tossed her the towel and she wrapped her hair in it.

He replaced his shirt and jumper.

'I'm getting back in the tent, I'm still cold.'

'What about me?'

'You can keep boosting your immune system.' She smirked, then said, 'Well, come on. There's plenty of room in here.' She sat and slid her legs into the sleeping bag and wrapped herself in the blanket. He sat next to her and she opened the blanket for him, and a sense of vulnerability came over her. It was close, intimate, and she wasn't used to it.

He sidled up next to her, the blanket around them both. 'We'll warm up soon enough,' he said. 'Body heat and all that.'

'My body is cold so you won't be getting any benefit from it.' She realised after she said that what else it could have meant.

'But mine will warm you, and then yours will warm mine, and we'll just keep heating up and we might even spontaneously combust.'

She nudged him. 'That water really did mess with your head.'

'Do you feel glad now you've done it? Added another experience to your list. Your life?'

She pondered his question. It was a pretty silly thing to do, and it didn't really serve any purpose except to get a quick thrill and perhaps tell someone about it to show off, but it made her smile. And she figured anything that could make her smile was something to be glad about. 'I am. Even though I don't have any desire to do it again, I am.'

He smiled, and though the tent was dark, moonlight filtered through the tent fabric and the mesh created tiny spots of light that sprinkled across the blanket.

'I'm glad you're glad,' he said.

'I'm glad you're glad I'm glad.' She grinned.

'Here we go again.' He chuckled, then an arm slid around her back. 'It's that whole arse conversation again, but with a different word.'

She allowed his arm to warm her, to feel... nice, against her back. 'How do we do this?' she asked. 'Talk so well?'

'We just do. I guess some people can simply... click, like that.'

Conflicting feelings swam within. Was she confusing a close friendship for something more, simply because it had been so long for her since she'd had an experience with a man? Maybe this was what a strong, platonic, male-female friendship felt like. And even if it was more, it wouldn't stay more, because he would leave.

When her thoughts settled, she turned to find his eyes on her. 'What are you thinking?' she asked.

'I'm wondering why you haven't kicked me out yet. I dropped you off hours ago, and yet I'm still here.'

'So you are.' Her chest tightened and her breath warmed. 'Maybe I did need some company after all,' was all she could think of to say.

'I like your company,' he said, and she noticed their voices were turning more to whispers.

'I like yours.'

He was so close, so relaxed, and in such an enclosed space, she couldn't think straight. But her body, and her heart, didn't want him to go. She turned her face to look at his again, and his eyes watched hers. She didn't know where her confidence came from, but words found their way out of her mouth and into the air in front of him... 'I want to do something different again.'

'What sort of something?'

'Something I've never initiated before.'

His eyes widened a little and specks of moonlight reflected off them.

An audible intake of breath followed, and then she leaned closer and pressed her lips lightly against his. Their softness was unexpected, delicious, comforting, and exhilarating. She wanted more. She pressed a little more firmly. He pressed back. She accepted his bottom lip between hers and a sigh escaped him. *Oh God, that sound.* It only invited more.

She brought her hands to his firm, sculpted shoulders, slid them around and up the back of his neck. His hands went to her waist, holding her close against him.

'Mmm,' she mumbled through their kisses, unable to hold in her pleasure.

They pulled back for a second, long enough for their gazes to connect and his hand to trail down the side of her face, spreading tingles across her skin. Their lips met again, their tongues, their moans, merging and feeding off each other.

The cold melted away and only warmth remained as they lay gently down on the floor of the tent, his legs sliding inside the sleeping bag next to hers, the blanket on top. The more they kissed, the more their hands wandered, and she lifted off his top. Hers followed, the warmth of their skin heated each other, and the outside world fell away.

Her senses both heightened yet relaxed with him, Olivia's hands moved to the top of his jeans. He grasped her hands gently and broke their kiss. 'Olivia,' he breathed. 'I can't do this to you, you deserve better. You deserve someone who's going to hang around.'

'It's okay,' she breathed back, returning her lips to his.

He pulled away again. 'I want to, I *really* want to. But you're so, you're so... different. Special. You deserve a future, not a one-night stand.'

With his shallow breaths, she could tell it was taking all his willpower to hold back.

'Right now, all I want is this moment. This experience,' she said, entwining her fingers with his. 'Joel, it's been so long for me. I don't want to wait anymore.'

He caressed her cheek again. 'You deserve the best.'

She held both sides of his face with her palms. 'I like you. I trust you. If it's going to be with anyone, I want it to be with you. Even if only once.' She pressed her lips against his, and though hesitant at first, he followed.

'It's okay, really,' she said in between kisses. Then his kiss intensified, they removed each other's clothes, and he held the blanket close around her body.

'Are you cold?' he asked, sprinkling tiny kisses all over her face.

'Not anymore.' She smiled and pushed her body close against his, revelling in his heat and firmness. Then memories of ten years ago forced their way into her mind. 'Oh, wait. I don't take anything. I don't have anything.' *Crap*. She'd been prepared for everything, except this.

Joel pulled back a little. 'I really hope I've got one in my wallet,' he said, rummaging behind for his jeans. 'If not, I'll have to make a mad, naked dash to the car!' He chuckled, and she waited with her breath high in her chest.

He opened his wallet. 'Bingo.' A wide smile graced his face. 'But only one.'

She kissed him again with a smile on her lips as her hand slid down his torso. 'Then we'd better make it count.'

Olivia slept fitfully, occasionally opening her eyes to see that Joel was still right beside her, breathing loudly, and his body still warm against hers. Bliss. She would smile and return to sleep, wake again, and marvel at how she had gotten to this point where she was sharing a tent with a gorgeous man next to her. Memories of the night kept replaying in her mind, like a movie she wanted to enjoy over and over again... how it was so different to the experience with Mia's dad, and the others she'd been in relationships with before him... the way his body had felt... right with hers, not awkward or different or mismatched, just right. He had taken things really slowly with her, even though part of her wanted everything to speed up... years of waiting building up and urging to be satisfied. But he kept bringing her back to the present moment ... a light caress down her spine, a kiss behind her ear, he'd even kissed all the way down her legs to her toes – something so simple yet divine that she'd never before experienced. Then, one by one, he'd kissed her fingers, opening her hand to expose her palm and kissing its centre, and as for the rest of her body... *ahhh*, she sighed and closed her eyes again, nestling in close to his body behind her, his arm over hers from behind.

The sound of the phone beeping was foreign to where she was. It took her a moment to register and reach behind into her bag to get it. She opened the text message from her mother: *Grandma's not well, possible pneumonia. They're doing tests, but not looking good. Going there now with Mia and Peter.*

Olivia sat bolt upright and shivered. She pulled on her top and rummaged around for her jeans.

Joel rolled over and moaned, but as she stood to get dressed his eyes opened. 'Running off so soon?' he mumbled, sleep in his voice.

'My grandmother's really sick,' she said. 'I have to go see her.'

Joel sat up. 'Oh no. Okay, let me drive you. We can be out of here in no time.'

'But the tent, we have to pack it up, and pack stuff away, and–'

Joel stood and held her arms, looking into her eyes. 'I can take you right there now,' he said. 'Don't worry, I'll deal with the camping stuff.'

Olivia glanced around. 'You're right, it won't take long. Let's just chuck everything in the car and then you don't have to worry about coming back.'

'Onto it,' he said, dressing quickly. Then he held her again briefly. 'It'll be okay,' he said, pulling her into a warm hug. 'Breathe.'

She nodded, took a breath, then continued packing up.

They made it to the car in record time and Joel drove, and once they were on the highway he placed his hand on her thigh and gave it a reassuring rub. 'I'm here for you,' he said.

She placed her hand on top and pressed her palm into it, capturing the moment, because she knew that once she arrived at the nursing home, her brief, beautiful interlude with Joel would come to an end, and like Mrs May's William, she would think of him as a sunset, bursting into her life in full colour then fading into the darkness... a transient, bittersweet piece of heaven. Or perhaps her shooting star. Either way, he would be gone in a few days, and possibly, so would Mrs May. Olivia bit her bottom lip and tried to quell the flow of tears.

CHAPTER TWENTY-SEVEN

Olivia had been imagining her grandmother as the young, vibrant woman who fell in love with William, and then Jacques. But now, seeing her as the frail old woman lying in the bed seemed unreal, unfair, and reminded her of her own mortality.

The IV lines ran across the bed, fluids and antibiotics helping her fight the infection, but everyone knew there was little that could be done. Olivia sat by her side and simply stroked her hand, as did Diana, while Mia held on to the side of the bed, her face red and blotchy from crying. Peter was sitting in one of the chairs by the wall, and Olivia was grateful her mum had someone standing by her. Mrs May's death was inevitable and imminent, she knew it, but did it have to happen so soon? And she had even indulged in the hope that maybe she would still be around to see Olivia finish the book, so she could print it out and bring in all the pages, which she would read through and edit with highlighters and red pens.

'I'm here, Grandma,' Olivia whispered. 'We all are.'

Diana gave her one of Mrs May's favourite books of poetry, and Olivia read it to her while they sat there, not leaving her side, until Mia had to go to the bathroom and began yawning. They had a quick break for lunch, she took Mia for a walk around the grounds for fresh air, and then returned for more reading and... waiting. Doctors and nurses checked on her, but still she kept breathing, though her breaths were shallow and strained. By the time the sky outside the window darkened and Diana closed the blinds, Olivia sighed. 'I'd better take Mia home and get her some dinner and rest.'

'Can I take the day off school tomorrow, Mum?' she asked feebly.

'I think that might be a wonderful idea,' she replied. 'Let me check if Marcus can come in earlier to open up the store.'

'I can come to the store, I don't mind being at your work with you. It always feels like Mrs May is in there.'

Olivia held her daughter close to her side. 'We'll see what the morning brings, sweetie. We might just come straight back here. For now, let's go have some pizza and a nice bath and a good night's sleep.'

'Okay.' Her daughter wiped her eyes.

'Oh,' she said. 'I don't have my car. Joel dropped me off.'

'I can take you back,' Peter said.

Olivia eyed her mother, her body seeming frail itself as she watched her own mother decline. 'No, it's okay, thanks. Joel said he could come get me, since he has some things of mine to drop off anyway.' She texted him and waited outside the nursing home until he arrived.

Joel was glad to hear Olivia's grandmother was still going by the time he picked her and Mia up. He let Olivia lead the conversation and didn't try to make light of things through small talk. Instead, he shouted them pizza on the way home and though he didn't want to get in the way, Olivia invited him in to share dinner. Mia was quiet, and after dinner Olivia ran her a bath and while her daughter was in there, she sat with Joel on the couch in the living room with a cup of tea.

'Thanks for everything,' she said.

He waved his hand. 'Don't mention it.'

He felt like he should say things like 'how long do they say she has?' and 'is there anything I can do?' but it wouldn't make a difference and he knew that there was nothing he could do except be there if she wanted him there.

'When do you leave?' she asked, tucking hair behind her ear and lifting the teacup to her lips.

'Probably Wednesday, but that depends.'

'On what?'

'On if you need me around a bit longer, or... want me around a bit longer.' He placed his hand on her thigh like he'd done in the car, not in a flirty way, but a supportive way. His hand tensed when she gently lifted it off.

'Joel, I...'

His eyes sought out hers until she looked at him.

'I want to end things on a good note. Our night together was so great. It was a shame the morning was rushed with my grandma's turn, but I'm so glad we had that night together.'

Despite her removing his hand, he was relieved. For a moment he'd worried that maybe her experience hadn't been as fulfilling as his. She must have had high expectations after so many years.

'But you've got your next intake of students to teach down south, and I have my grandma and family to be with, and my book to finish, so it's easier if we part ways now. Tonight.'

His relief turned to regret. Regret he hadn't pursued her properly earlier; regret he hadn't taken a chance to try something deeper with her before it was too late. 'I understand,' he said. 'But although I'll be a few hours away for the next couple of months, I'm only teaching two nights a week. I could always drive back on weekends to see you, if you wanted me to. If you wanted to, I dunno, maybe *try* something, see how it feels?' He shrugged. This was foreign to him, he'd never had to suggest anything like this before, had always been the first to leave or take an out when the opportunity arose.

'Joel, don't.' Olivia's gaze diverted to her hands. 'After that you have your next adventure, next trip.'

'Yes, but plans can change. I can change them.' Was he... pleading?

She shook her head, looked him in the eye with a resigned smile. 'You're a wanderer. I'm not. I'd rather leave things where they are than get deeply involved and have to deal with the fallout when it doesn't work out.'

He lowered his head. Damn it, despite the short time frame, she had come to know him too well. But that didn't change the fact that something inside felt different this time, urged him to take notice and want to take a risk.

'We became great friends,' she said. 'Why change that? I love how we can talk, be silly, and just kind of... get each other, even though we're opposites. I don't want to lose that.'

'Me neither.' This time he took her hand and didn't let her remove it.

'We shared a beautiful, unforgettable night together, a book-worthy moment under the stars.' She glanced up with a smile. 'I'll never forget it. Or you.'

He wanted to kiss her. Right now. Deeply. But it would be a mistake, and her daughter was in the bath and it wouldn't be appropriate, and she would probably make him leave.

So he stood. Before he did something stupid. 'I better let you two get some rest.'

Olivia stood and lightly brushed her hand with his. 'So I guess I'll see you. Or text you. Or...'

'Yes,' he said. 'Text me. Or call me. Anytime. That's what friends do.'

'They do.' She nodded.

'Let me know what happens, with your grandma. I'll be thinking of you.'

'Thanks.' She leaned forward and her arms slid stiffly around his back. He forced himself not to soften, not to tangle his hands in her hair and pull her close like he'd done last night. He put his hands on her back and gave her a few light pats.

When they pulled away, he went to the door. 'Say bye to Mia for me.'

'I will.' She saw him out and as he drove away, he watched her standing on the porch until he was forced to watch the road.

It was time to move on.

CHAPTER TWENTY-EIGHT

When the remains of sleep fell away and reality jerked her awake, Olivia shot upright and grabbed her phone. She didn't want to look at the screen but had to. She'd set it to silent during the night so she could get enough sleep to be able to get through the day, but just as she thought, there was a message from her mum who had stayed at the nursing home during the night. She mentally prepared herself for the words, then read the text: *Your grandma is one tough cookie. She's actually improving, can you believe it?*

Olivia gasped. 'What?' She had thought she would wake to bad news.

She sent a reply to her mum who explained the latest situation. Antibiotics seemed to be kicking in and her temperature and oxygen levels were improving.

After a quick breakfast she took Mia and visited Mrs May, though she decided not to stay too long. Her grandma needed rest, and the nurse said she would call if she worsened. So Olivia did what she'd always done to keep her mind off waiting, she went to work, and Mia said she would be okay to go to school, despite being late.

The day went fast, she checked her phone every spare chance, and she even added 'first camping trip' to the memory jar, but decided to leave out the bit about the passionate sex.

They went back to the nursing home that night, and the next morning Mrs May had improved even more, though was not yet speaking. Olivia resisted texting Joel to update him; she thought if she told him of her grandma's fighting spirit it might jinx the situation and then she'd have to tell him the bad news. Which still she knew would happen, but it didn't appear to be happening right now.

Late afternoon a text from her mother came in: *She's asking for water, which is a good sign, and chocolate!*

'Ha!' Olivia laughed out loud. She knew where she got her chocolate addiction from. She couldn't wait to get there after work and speak to her again, since she'd thought she'd never get another chance.

When she arrived with Mia that night, her grandmother was semi-reclined and lifting her oxygen mask off slightly to speak. Olivia caught the end of the sentence: '...give them a piece of my mind.'

'Give who a piece of your mind?' Olivia asked, walking towards the bed with a smile and open arms.

'Long story,' Diana said.

'How are you?' Olivia kissed her grandma's warm forehead. She was still looking pasty but had more life in her than the last time she'd seen her.

'Been better,' she said, her voice raspy. She took a few deeper breaths through the mask.

Mia rubbed Mrs May's arm slightly. 'Does it hurt?' she asked quietly.

'No dear.' Mrs May glanced to her granddaughter. 'They take good care of me.'

Diana stood and stretched.

'Take a break, Mum,' Olivia said.

'Might do that. Mia? Would you like to come get a drink?'

She nodded and took Diana's hand.

Olivia sat in the chair her mother had been in, the vinyl still warm beneath her trousers.

'Camping,' Mrs May said, lifting the mask off slightly. 'Tell me.'

'Grandma, you should keep that mask on and not talk so much, it'll wear you out.'

'Already worn out,' she replied, continuing to alternate with deep breaths and speaking. 'You enjoyed it?'

A smile warmed Olivia's face, or was it the memories? 'Yes,' she nodded. 'I actually had a bit of company too.'

Mrs May's eyes widened slightly. 'That chap of yours?'

'He's not my chap, but yes, the writing teacher. He's much like I imagined William would have been, it's bizarre.'

Her grandmother smiled. 'I hope you two will...' she breathed through the mask, '...be able to give things a good old shot.'

Olivia tensed. 'No, he's on his way this week, wandering to his next adventure. He actually offered to try, to have a go at something, but I told him we are better off as friends.'

'And you're okay with that?'

She didn't know what to say.

'Darling,' she breathed, 'if a man makes an attempt to win you over, then by golly, you should give him the benefit of the doubt. Because so many of them give up, don't make any effort, and leave you wondering if romance really exists.' Her grandma leaned back and breathed deeply for a while, and Olivia hoped she wasn't overdoing it.

'But I don't want to get hurt, it's easier to leave things on a good note.'

'Honey.' Mrs May reached out her hand and Olivia took it.

'We must take risks in life, don't live in fear.' Olivia stroked her grandma's hand. 'Don't die wondering about the wanderer.'

The words went straight to her heart, her soul, and somewhere deep inside that felt like an arrow, Joel's arrow, had been shot right into the centre.

If she went on with life as it was, she would *always* wonder. Yes, perhaps if they saw each other again in a romantic way, it may not work out, and it may hurt, and things may be forever awkward between them or they might lose contact and be gone forever from each other's life, but what if... what if life surprised her? What if it went right? She would never know.

'But what do I do?' she asked. 'I pretty much told him he should leave.'

'Then un-tell him, dear.'

Could I?

Could it be as simple as a phone call, an 'I've changed my mind' plea, and he would rush over and wrap her in his arms?

'Do it, now. Don't waste time.' Her grandma's mask clouded with her breaths, and Olivia realised it was now or never. Life could be over in a flash. Her heart pounded in anticipation. 'I will, thanks, Grandma. I'll go get Mum and Mia to come back in.'

Olivia went to find them, and told her mother she had to step outside to make a call.

When she got outside of the entrance, lit by a pair of subdued lights either side of the automatic doors, she took a nervous breath and pressed call on Joel's contact.

'Hey,' he said. 'Is all okay? Is she...' His voice trailed off.

'Oh, yes, she's fine. Well, not fine, but she's actually improved and is responding to the medication. She's even talking.'

'Wow.' He let out a relieved-sounding sigh. 'Really? That's great news. When I saw your caller ID, I...'

'I know,' she said. 'And it'll happen at some point, but...'

'Not today.'

'Exactly.' She almost forgot why she was calling. 'So, ah, you plan to leave tomorrow?'

'Yes,' he said. 'And I've been thinking...'

'You have?'

'Is that such a surprise?' He chuckled.

She smiled. 'Of course. I had no idea you thought about things. How strange.' How was this becoming one of their usual silly conversations, instead of the serious one she planned to have with him?

'I think you were right,' he said. 'We are great friends. We shouldn't disrupt that. And you know me too well... I've never been able to stay still, stay put, and the idea of trying to do anything other than what I'm used to is a bit of a risk.'

Uh-oh. No. This wasn't how it was supposed to go.

She almost said 'hang on, but...' but he kept talking...

'I loved our night together, Olivia, it was so different to anything else I've experienced. And what a great memory it will be, and the fact that we can both be adult about the situation, and stay friends like this, is pretty special.'

She nodded, as though to convince herself again, though he couldn't see her.

'Olivia?'

'Yes. Yes, you're right. We're both right. Our friendship is pretty cool. We're lucky to not have any... awkwardness between us, after the weekend.'

'None at all. I've always felt comfortable with you.'

'Me too. Well, maybe not at first, but pretty soon after!'

'Once I got you out of your comfort zone.'

'Yes.'

Damn it. She had been right to leave things where they were, hadn't she? He was agreeing with her now, and she was probably saving herself a lot of heartache down the track by not giving in to this risk. It was better to stay friends, she would rather have that than for their relationship to go sour at some point. So why, when she ended the call, could she not stop tears from flowing out of her eyes and down her cheeks? Why did the thought of being only friends bring a different kind of heartache all of its own? She leaned against the outside wall of the nursing home and wiped at her tears. Why? Because she had already fallen for him, big time. She was glad she had experienced a night of pleasure, and she didn't regret going into that knowing it could be a one-off, but it didn't take away the fact that her heart ached for more. But she knew it was time to let it go, just like her grandma had tossed that letter into the ocean for William, she too had symbolically tossed aside her chance for a new possibility with a wanderer of her own.

And she wouldn't have to die wondering, because she would convince herself, day in and day out, that it wouldn't have worked. That it wouldn't work. Because it wouldn't.

And that belief would get her through until the right man came along.

CHAPTER TWENTY-NINE

The next three weeks were a flurry of writing, working, parenting, and checking on Mrs May, who was still fighting and hanging on. Olivia liked to believe it was because she was waiting to hear when Olivia had finished the book. This both spurred her on and delayed her, because it would be so rewarding to finish and share that moment with her grandmother, but it could also make her grandmother more likely to be ready to die once that moment had passed.

But the book needed to be finished, and so Olivia had worked late into each night, sometimes at quiet times at the store, and on weekends, to do the book justice. It seemed fitting that after saying goodbye to her romantic life three weeks ago, here she was on a Saturday night at home, in her pyjamas, about to type the words she thought she'd never see: *The End.*

She typed each letter consciously, thoughtfully, mindfully. And with that final letter she let out a little squeal. Then she stared at the screen.

I've done it. I've really done it.

She stood and without thinking, her arms shot up in the air, her fists in victorious clenches, and she squealed some more.

'Are you okay, Mum?' Mia called out from the bathroom.

'I'm great!' she said. Then she dashed into the bathroom where Mia was engulfed in bubbles. 'I just finished writing Mrs May's book! I wrote a book!' She held out her hand and Mia high-fived it.

'Oh wow, Mum! That is amazing. My mum is an author!' Mia jumped from the bath, bubbles and water splashing everywhere, and flung her arms around her.

Olivia laughed. 'We must celebrate tomorrow, with cake and hot chocolate, how about that?'

'Yesss!' Mia jumped.

'Careful, sweetie, it's slippery.'

Mia got out. 'I'm finished getting clean.' She grabbed a towel. 'Can we have ice cream too, like, right now?'

Olivia smiled, a gaping wide grin. 'You bet,' she said. 'You bet.'

***

The next morning they forwent their usual Sunday pancakes and had a quick breakfast, then Olivia picked up the three-hundred odd pages of manuscript she had printed out before bed last night and put them in a tote bag along with her pens and highlighters. She grinned with excitement at being able to finally show her grandma, even though she most likely wouldn't be able to read it, or be around long enough to have it read to her. She could show her a few parts of it, maybe even get her to sign the front of the manuscript. It would need lots of editing, but she could do that over the next few weeks, then hire an editor to go through it properly. She thought about texting Joel to tell him the good news, but wanted Mrs May to hear about her accomplishment first. Besides, having minimal contact with him of late was helping her focus, and get through her sadness at leaving the possibility of him behind. She'd resume their regular 'friendship' once things settled down a bit, and he knew she was busy dealing with everything right now.

She got Mia in the car and her phone beeped with a text: *Are you coming in? She's not great again. Bit of a temperature, but mostly she keeps getting palpitations and high blood pressure surges.*

Olivia's own heart palpitated. She had to get there soon. She drove carefully but efficiently, and when she arrived and went straight to her grandma's room, Diana was standing next to the bed with her hand on her mother's. A nurse was nearby.

Please still be alive!

She approached the bed and saw the subtle rise and fall of Mrs May's chest.

Oh thank God.

'Hi there,' the nurse said. 'I've just administered another dose, that should keep her blood pressure under control for a bit longer. But she's needing more and more, and there's only so much we can give before the side effects cause more problems than they're worth.'

Olivia nodded, and the nurse left.

Mia went to Diana's side and joined her in holding Mrs May's hand. Olivia stood on the other side. 'Grandma?' she said softly.

Her eyes opened slightly. 'Hello there,' she whispered weakly.

Olivia smiled and relief flooded her body. 'I know you're not feeling great, but I wanted to show you something.' She opened her tote bag and withdrew the manuscript. '*Memories of May.* All complete.'

Diana gasped. 'You've finished?'

Olivia nodded.

'My mum's an author,' said Mia proudly.

'Well, it needs editing, but it's done.' She smiled.

Mrs May's hand rose slightly, but Olivia patted it down. 'You rest. Here. I'll show you.' She held the cover page closer to her grandma's line of sight, then turned to the dedication page.

To my grandmother; the miraculous, magnificent, marvellous, magical, memorable May. Your life helped give me mine. You will always be remembered, and always loved.

Olivia read it out in case she couldn't read it properly.

Her grandma's eyes glossed over and moisture welled at the edges. Olivia held her hand and a light squeeze came from her grandma's weak muscles. 'You don't have to say anything, it's okay.' She glanced at her mother who also had tears in her eyes. Mia only smiled.

Mrs May's mouth opened and closed. Olivia lifted the mask off slightly. 'I hope,' her voice scratched, 'you didn't write The End at the end.'

Olivia chuckled. 'I did, and it was a very exciting moment.'

'Take it out,' she said slowly. 'There are no endings...' a wheeze sounded between her words, '...only beginnings.'

No, no, not yet. She still wasn't ready. Didn't know if she ever would be. It sounded like she was saying the last words she wanted to say.

'Wherever I'm going,' she managed, as Olivia leaned closer to hear her words, 'it's not an... ending. Even if... my new beginning... is simply knowing that... you are having one.'

Olivia bit her lip to hold back tears. 'I don't want to say goodbye, I don't...' Her voice shook.

Mrs May gave another light hand squeeze. 'Live without fear,' she said. 'Make... memories.' She turned her gaze slowly to face Diana and Mia. 'All of you.' She took a sharp intake of breath. 'Make memories matter.'

They all nodded, stood around her bed, and stroked her hands as she fell into a sleep, until later that afternoon, when her chest rose and fell for the last time.

CHAPTER THIRTY

Were it not for the scarves and coats people were wearing, and the crisp winter breeze floating across from the ocean, it would look like a summer's day. Blue skies with only a few wisps of clouds spanned the horizon, and as Olivia looked out from the cemetery to the ocean opposite, she hoped her grandma could see what a beautiful day it was. She hoped that wherever she did go, or was going, that somehow it *was* a new beginning for her.

There were so many people, so many who had known her or simply visited the store throughout their lives, who came to pay their respects. Olivia had never felt so proud.

She held Mia's hand tight and led her over to the coffin, which had been lowered into the ground. Mia picked up one of the lilies and so did Olivia and Diana. 'Let's do all three together,' said Diana.

On the count of three, they each tossed the flowers on top of the coffin. A huge weight released from Olivia's chest, and a surge of emotion spilled up and out. Tears fell, and she held her daughter close on one side, her mother on the other, as they embraced and shared tears and comfort. Friends came over to hug them, but that only made more tears flow, and by the time most people had started leaving the cemetery, Olivia wiped at her eyes, which seemed to be an endless reservoir of tears.

'C'mon, let's go to the high tea in honour of Mrs May, now, hey?' she said to Mia, kissing her forehead.

Her grandmother had wanted them to do something different to remember her, and so they had invited a smaller number of people to a fancy high tea just outside of town at a heritage-listed art gallery that had a small restaurant, where they could sit around tables of delicious food, surrounded by art, and share memories of an amazing woman.

They were walking across the cemetery and towards their car when Olivia noticed a man standing by a familiar-looking car. When she neared, she recognised him.

Her breath paused. Their gazes locked, and he offered a small wave, but made no attempt at walking over.

'Mum, I'm just going to thank Joel for coming, do you mind?'

Diana glanced in Joel's direction. 'Of course not.'

They separated from each other's hold and Olivia walked across the grass, her heels digging in slightly with each step.

Seeing his face was a welcome surprise, but also brought a sense of longing that ached to be fulfilled, especially as Mrs May's departure had created such a feeling of loss and emptiness inside.

'Joel,' she said. 'I didn't know you were coming. Thank you.'

'Olivia,' he said, holding out his arms. She didn't accept them at first, knowing what would happen if she did. But he stepped closer. 'Come here.'

She allowed his arms to wrap around her, and she slowly slid hers around him. And then the tears fell down her cheeks and against his suit jacket.

'I'm sorry,' he said. 'It's so hard. I know there's nothing I can do, except say that time will make it easier.'

'It's okay,' she sobbed. 'You being here is enough. Thank you.' She waited until her tears lessened then pulled away.

He wiped her cheeks with his thumb.

'You drove all this way just for today?' she asked.

He nodded.

'You must be in the middle of your course by now.'

He nodded again.

She wanted him to stay, but also wanted him to go; she didn't know which would help her more.

Let him go, a voice said inside.

So before she asked him to wrap his arms around her again she stepped back. 'Thanks for coming, I really appreciate it. Good luck with the rest of your course, and your next trip.'

'Thanks,' he said.

She offered a tired smile then turned away. Then turned back. 'Joel?' He raised his eyebrows. 'I finished writing the book.'

His solemn expression morphed into a genuine, satisfied smile. 'Congratulations. I knew you'd do it.'

She smiled back. 'I had some fantastic support and encouragement.'

She waved again and turned away, glad she had seen him one last time. She approached her mother's car with a sigh. Time to get through the high tea, then go home where no doubt more tears would fall and she could go through more of her grandmother's things, including her large book collection, which Olivia knew, had given her grandma company and support throughout her whole life. Just as running the bookstore was doing, and would continue to do, for Olivia.

A week later, while on the phone with a sales rep at the store, Olivia smiled at the florist who entered with a huge bunch of colourful flowers. She waved her over and gestured to the counter to leave the arrangement there, and mouthed a 'thank you'. She ended the call with the rep and read the card attached.

I thought you'd be inundated with flowers, so I decided to wait a week. Thinking of you. Joel.

Olivia placed a hand over her heart. A lot of flowers had come in for Mrs May, but most had died or were on their way by now, and most she had taken home or to her mother's. It was nice to have a fresh bunch.

Thank you for the flowers, she texted him.

My pleasure. How are you holding up?

Getting there.

And that night, after Mia was in bed, she returned to her computer to start editing the book. It was time. She needed to move on to the next step, and after a week of crying and trying to survive daily life when everything felt so different, so strange, without Mrs May around, she needed something else to occupy her mind.

She had read some blogs on editing and taken on board the advice. She had learned about structure through Joel's course, so felt that she had all of that right, and that everything was in the right place, so now it came down to making the words shine and the story as compelling as possible. She sipped tea, ate chocolate, and edited. The repetition was soothing. But after an hour, she yawned and stood for a stretch. She glanced at the box of some of her grandma's old books in the corner of her room. She had to decide which ones to keep, and which ones to donate, or to perhaps even put in a charity sale at the store.

She sat on the floor next to the box and sifted through. She flipped through pages, unsure which ones she should keep. A book of poetry caught her eyes; she didn't recognise the author's name, but it was in hardcover. The book had a jacket cover, and when she opened the first page, a piece of paper fell out from between the hardcover and the jacket. Olivia gently opened the thin, yellowed paper, and gasped.

It was her. A drawing of her grandmother, but as a young woman. The charcoal was smudged and faded, but not too much that she couldn't recognise her radiant eyes and rounded cheeks, her flowing hair, and good posture.

Olivia's breathing came faster as her eyes scanned the artwork. 'William,' she said. 'William's drawing.'

She laid the drawing on her desk and smoothed it out, then took a photo. She wanted to show Mia but didn't want to wake her, so she texted it to her mum, hoping she wasn't asleep too.

OMG, was her reply. *That William fellow drew her?*

Yes, Olivia replied. She hadn't yet told her mother the full story, as she'd had enough to deal with knowing her mother was dying, but she'd told her the basics – that Mrs May had fallen for a man called William and had considered going away with him, but ended up staying with Jacques. Soon, if Diana wanted, Olivia would let her listen to the recordings to hear the full story.

It's beautiful, her mother texted back.

Olivia had been trying to keep her distance from Joel so she could get on with editing and grieving, but he'd sent occasional messages to check how she was. Something compelled her to text him the photo, and he replied right away: *You may have just found your book cover image.*

Olivia smiled widely and her fingers traced the shapes of the drawing. *Yes. Yes, it would be perfect.* Though her grandmother had loved Jacques and built a life with him that had been written about in detail in the book, May and William would have a symbolic chance at being together too, if only by their connection being immortalised on the cover of the story of her life. After all, as she had said, '*He was only a small chapter of my story, but he helped create the whole book.*'

And as Olivia replied to Joel's text to thank him for the idea, she realised that she could say the exact same thing about him.

CHAPTER THIRTY-ONE

Olivia didn't know what had helped her focus so well over the past two weeks, and three weeks since the funeral, but she liked to believe her grandma was with her, helping her edit the book.

'*No, that goes there,*' she'd say, or, '*What about emphasising this bit, it was such a memorable day,*' or, '*I remember what I was wearing that day, put that in too!*'

Though Olivia's name would be on the cover as the author, to her it was a joint project.

And as she came to the last page on the final read-through, her heart beat faster in anticipation. She reread the last line, and smiled, knowing it fit perfectly. Then as her grandma had asked, she deleted the words 'The End'. In their place, she typed: *The Beginning of a New Adventure.*

She clicked save and stood, then did her victory jiggle again as she'd done when she'd first finished the book. It was late, and Mia was asleep. She'd talk to her mother about the book tomorrow, when she was planning on giving her the recordings and a copy of the manuscript to read before sending it to the editor Joel had recommended. She was going out with April for lunch tomorrow and could tell her then, and then she would start planning publication and a launch for May the following year.

But first...

She pressed Joel's number on her phone.

'Hey there, night owl,' he answered.

'Hey. Guess what?'

'You went abseiling? Parachuting? Bungee jumping?'

'Funny. No, I finished the editing, so I'm ready now to go to the editor and to get the ball rolling for publication!'

'Woohoo, fantastic!' he said.

'And of course you're going in the acknowledgements,' she added.

'Not necessary, but thank you.'

'It is necessary. You helped me so much,' she replied. 'In more ways than one.' She noticed the date on her wall calendar. 'Oh, you're probably just about ready to leave on your next adventure?'

'Yep,' he replied. 'Just about ready.'

This was it. She couldn't be sad, had to be grateful for what they'd had, however brief. 'And where to this time?'

'I'll let you know when I arrive. Maybe I'll send a postcard or something.'

'Do people still do that these days?'

'Don't know, but I can if you want.'

'I want.'

'Done.'

She smiled. It was nice to have something to look forward to, even if it was just a simple postcard. 'Thanks again, Joel. And enjoy your next adventure.'

'I will, for sure.'

CHAPTER THIRTY-TWO

O livia hugged April after lunch at Café Lagoon on Friday and they both returned to their respective stores.

'Yes, you can go now, Marcus,' she said when she entered, as her employee paced anxiously behind the counter. 'Enjoy your date, and be good.' She smiled.

'Always.' He winked.

After he left, she sat on the chair behind the counter and opened a new book to start reading. It was a new release, and she needed to stay on top of what was selling well so she could advise customers. Plus it had a damn cute guy on the cover.

A slow stream of customers filtered in throughout the afternoon, and she yawned when five o'clock neared.

She stood, deciding to close up a few minutes early.

She went into the back room to get her bag and the keys, when she heard footsteps in the store. *Oh, typical. Last minute customer who wants some obscure book that's been out of print for decades.*

She walked out prepared to say 'how can I help you' but stopped still. 'Joel.'

He scratched his head and smiled, his raised eyebrows accentuating his cute forehead furrows.

'What are you doing here?' Her stomach fluttered.

He held something up. 'I thought I'd bring the postcard to you directly.'

Oh. He was coming to say a formal goodbye. Just when she'd gotten used to the fact he would be leaving for good.

She approached him and took the card. It had a photo of Lookout Point. 'It's Tarrin's Bay. Huh?'

He smiled. 'Exactly.'

'I thought you were going on a new adventure.'

'I am.' He stepped closer. '*You're* my new adventure.' His smile widened, and he put the postcard down and took her hands in his.

Her skin tingled and confusion swept through her. 'But... we talked about this. What are you doing?'

'I want my next adventure to be with you. Here.'

She tried to remove her hands but he gripped them firmly. 'But Joel, you're a wanderer. An arrow. We're good friends who have a nice memory. Why rock the boat and risk that?'

He stared deeply into her eyes. 'I don't want to be an arrow anymore. I want to be a boomerang. *Your* boomerang. Yes, I'll still travel, and explore, but never for long, and maybe sometimes with you, and most importantly... I'll always come back.'

Oh wow. Olivia's head was spinning, conflicting thoughts and feelings clamouring for space. She let go and closed the doors to the store, and pulled down the blinds. 'I... I don't know if I can do this. I'm scared. I don't want to have you then lose you.' Her eyes sought the depths of his, trying to figure out what to believe.

'I'm the same. But I'm willing to give it a damn good shot. I've taken a lot of risks in my life, and this kind scares me the most. But what I've realised is… I've never really had a strong friendship as the basis for a relationship before. It was always short-term attraction. That's why it feels different. It's also why it feels so good. I know it's real. Whatever we have,' he moved his hands up to her shoulders, pulling her closer, 'it's something real. Something worth pursuing.'

Oh God, it so is. And that was what made it so incredibly terrifying. Her belly fluttered. 'I'm so used to being on my own. I'm not sure how to… *do* a relationship yet.'

'Same boat,' he replied with a smile. 'We can learn together. That's all part of the adventure.'

With his hands on her shoulders, his gaze on her eyes, and his words floating with the breath from his lungs that tickled her face, she was succumbing, surrendering, and wanting so much to just trust it and say yes.

'How do you know you won't change your mind in a few weeks, get itchy feet?'

He took a deep breath. 'I've always said that my adventures choose me. I follow my gut. I go where it feels right. And I could say that I'm here today because I choose you, Olivia, but I don't. I don't choose you. This, *us*, chooses me.' He patted his chest where his heart would be.

Her hands trembled and her voice shook. 'Wow,' she said. 'Wow.' Her hands found their way to his chest. 'And what about your next trip, surely you don't want to stay in Tarrin's Bay and never go anywhere else?'

'Hmm, well,' he said, eying her with an eager glimmer in his eye. 'I was hoping to have a travel companion with me. Or even two.'

'Two?'

'You and Mia.'

Olivia's eyebrows rose.

'Uh-huh,' he said. 'I was thinking something even more risky next time, like, say, a five-star hotel perhaps? Gold Coast, theme parks, something terrifying like that.'

Olivia laughed. 'You're really serious. You want to give up the travelling bachelor lifestyle and go on a highly commercialised expensive holiday with a single mother and her nine-year-old, no, make that soon-to-be ten-year-old daughter?'

'Yes. I do. Except I don't want the mother to be single.'

Olivia smiled, his face coming close to hers.

'You and me,' he whispered, his voice genuine and his eyes serious. 'Let's just give it a shot. Make some memories that go beyond May, and June, and July.' He caressed her cheek, then ran his thumb across her lips. 'Do you accept the challenge?'

Her body softened at his touch, her soul soothed by his words, his promises. Being in his presence again felt so right, so normal, so perfect. 'Does it come with hashtags?' she asked with a chuckle.

He laughed. 'Of course. I call it the...' He made a hashtag symbol by crossing his first two fingers of each hand over each other, 'Relationship Challenge.'

'And that R word doesn't scare you?'

'A little, but what scares me more is the idea of moving on without you.'

He pulled her body close to his, nestling his lips into her neck, sprinkling kisses below her ear.

'Oh God,' she said. 'I missed this.'

'Me too. I don't want to miss this again. I want you close to me, every night, every day.'

She moaned and ran her hands over the back of his neck.

'I thought I just wanted to stay friends, that it would be easier. But what was I thinking?'

'You were thinking out of fear,' she said. 'Live without fear, my grandma said. That's what I plan to do from now on.'

'Wise woman,' he replied. Then he pulled back and stared

into her eyes, and it was then she noticed that the ocean-blue shade had a sort of... *diamond* look about them, like her grandma had observed about William's. 'So, do you accept the challenge or not?'

She raised up onto her toes, kissed his lips, and said with a grin, 'Challenge accepted.'

Their lips kissed, their hands caressed, and they moved backwards into the storeroom. Olivia giggled as he moved items across her desk and sat her on top of it, wrapping her legs around his waist.

'One question before I am unable to do anything but rip your clothes off,' Olivia said. 'When did you decide you were going to come in here and win me over?'

He grinned. 'Ever since I saw you at the funeral. I couldn't bear the thought of not being a part of your life and supporting you in moments like that. But I knew you needed time to grieve, time to write, and time to process everything.'

'And the postcard... nice touch!'

'That was your idea. A great one too, I might add.' He leaned forward and kissed her lovingly. 'Plus I wanted you to have another book-worthy moment.'

'This one takes the cake,' she replied, sighing at his delicious touch and his kisses.

He ran his hands through her hair and she watched in awe as his eyes scanned her face like he was admiring a piece of art. 'You know what?'

'What?' she asked with a curious smile.

'You, my dear Olivia Chevalier with eight syllables, may just be my biggest adventure yet.'

'I never thought that by writing my grandmother's story, I would end up writing my own.'

Olivia stood at the microphone at the back of the store, reading out her speech to a small, but special gathering of people at the *Memories of May* book launch.

Marcus had started off the evening by reading out memories from the memory jar to warm up the crowd, and Mia had handed out canapés and drinks. Joel, who was standing at the front corner of the crowd with Mia, caught her eye and winked in support. She smiled then returned her gaze to the piece of paper in her hand.

'Mrs May said that there are no endings, only beginnings, and she was right. Life goes on, new memories are created and shared, and I was privileged to be part of hers.' She cleared her throat. 'This book was a long time coming, but I'm glad I persisted with it. Glad I was able to finish it and tell her it was complete before she died. She trusted me to tell her story, and I'm forever grateful for that.'

She glanced at the soft smiles of the people in the crowd, all listening intently to her speech, and was overcome with emotion. Her hands shook a little. She promised herself she wouldn't cry, that she would get through this speech and get all the words out, and she would try to keep that promise. She could shed a few tears later, but for now, the words were more important.

'I learned a lot more about my grandma while writing this book, a lot more than anyone else knew, about her personal life and experiences. And I didn't know back then how much of an impact her stories would have on my own life. I learned that we were similar in many ways. She encouraged me to step out of my comfort zone and take a few risks, and with the help of someone else who did the same, I'm glad to say those risks paid off.' This time, she glanced at Joel and winked.

'I'll never forget my grandmother. She truly was miraculous, magnificent, marvellous, magical, and memorable. A beautiful, special soul, who touched the lives of many. And now I'd like to share with you a small video I've created with some of her photos, her favourite music, and a few words from the book.'

Joel came over and helped with the projector, and the cover of *Memories of May* graced the screen as music played. Olivia looked down at the copy of the book in her hand with William's drawing on the front cover, and smiled. And as the images transitioned on the screen and everyone watched with glossy eyes, she flipped the book to the final page and read the last line to herself:

Life is merely a collection of moments, of memories. Every life matters. It is up to you to take risks, live your life fully, and follow your heart. Don't settle for a life half lived. Make amazing memories. Make memories matter.

She closed the book with a light, reverent touch, and held it to her heart. She glanced towards the velvet armchair in the corner of the store. A warm rush ran through her body as the scent of lilies arose, and she could have sworn for a moment that she saw her grandma sitting there smiling, at peace, knowing that her life had made a difference.

292

THE END OF ONE STORY, THE BEGINNING OF ANOTHER

ALSO BY JULIET MADISON

Also in The Tarrin's Bay Series

The January Wish

February or Forever

Miracle in March

April's Glow

Home for June

ACKNOWLEDGEMENTS

Thanks to the readers and reviewers who support my books and especially this series, I hope you enjoy the latest new beginning in Tarrin's Bay! Writing about a bookshop was so much fun.

To my critique partners, Alli and Diane, thanks for your help with brainstorming as I worked out the plot of this story. To Ruth, thank you for helping me with the Ducati motorbike information for one of the scenes, and for the friendship you offered me when I needed it.

Thanks to Betsy and the team at Bloodhound Books, and my editor Belinda Holmes for your editing expertise.

Thanks to both of my late grandmothers who helped inspire this story about a special grandmother, and thanks always to my family, my loved ones, and my friends for their support as I live my dream career.

ABOUT THE AUTHOR

Juliet Madison is a bestselling and award-nominated author of books with humour, heart, and serendipity. Writing both fiction and self-help, she is also an artist and colouring book illustrator, and an intuitive life coach who loves creating online courses for writers and those wanting to live an empowered life.

With her background as a naturopath and a dancer, Juliet is passionate about living a healthy and positive life. She likes to combine her love of words, art, and self-empowerment to create books that entertain and inspire readers to find the magic in everyday life.

Juliet lives on the picturesque south coast of NSW, Australia, where she spends as much time as possible dreaming up new stories, following her passions, being with her family, and as little time as possible doing housework.

You can find out more about Juliet, her books, and her courses at http://www.julietmadison.com and connect with her on social media at Facebook http://www.facebook.com/julietmadisonauthor and Instagram http://www.instagram.com/julietmadisonauthorartist

A NOTE FROM THE PUBLISHER

Thank you for reading this book. If you enjoyed it please do consider leaving a review on Amazon to help others find it too.

We hate typos. All of our books have been rigorously edited and proofread, but sometimes mistakes do slip through. If you have spotted a typo, please do let us know and we can get it amended within hours.

info@bloodhoundbooks.com

www.ingramcontent.com/pod-product-compliance
Lightning Source LLC
Chambersburg PA
CBHW061522210726

48287CB00006B/1782